DEBBIE MACOMBER

THREE BRIDES, NO GROOM

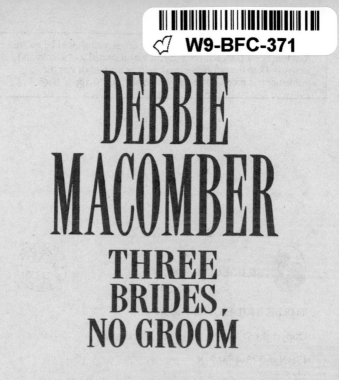

Silhouette Books

Published by Silhouette Books
America's Publisher of Contemporary Romance

SILHOUETTE BOOKS

THREE BRIDES, NO GROOM

Copyright © 1997 by Debbie Macomber

ISBN 0-373-48352-X

CONTENTS

To my mother, Connie Adler, who gave me life, love, and taught me to laugh. To Marie Macomber, who shared her wisdom and her son, and Sophie Koonce, who touched my heart.

Prologue

The fountain. Located in the center of Nelson Lord University in Seattle, it was thought to be the very heart of the private college. It was here, in the dead of night, where young lovers with pounding eager hearts rendezvoused. It was here that words of love were whispered between urgent kisses, where promises were made and, sadly, promises were broken. Its shadow had entertained laughter and joy, sorrow and tears.

The fountain had borne witness to it all.

It was to this fountain that three women came that summer afternoon, each arriving from a different direction, each burdened with memories from fifteen years past.

The first to arrive was Gretchen Wise. Miss Popularity, the class president, beautiful and smart, too. Unfortunately not smart enough to recognize the kind of man Roger Lockheart was before she accepted his engagement ring.

The second was Carol Furness, the head cheerleader, filled with energy, enthusiasm, joy and purpose. She'd built her future around a football hero, only to learn Eddie Shapiro was anything but.

And lastly Maddie Cobain, the class "bad girl," who'd played a tricky game of looking for love and, like so many before her, searched in all the wrong places. Who would have believed that math professor John Theda would steal far more than her heart?

The fountain welcomed all.

Gretchen Wise walked slowly toward the old cement fountain and smiled as the memories swirled around her the way water rushed around a rock in a swift stream.

She could almost hear the echo of laughter from those long-ago years. How happy she'd been back then: young, carefree, excited and so very much in love—with the wrong man. Fifteen years earlier she'd barely been able to appreciate her own graduation, not with her head full of wedding plans and Roger.

Roger Lockheart, the love of her life. The man of her dreams.

The rat.

She thought about him now and again, fleetingly and with a twinge of sadness. Sometimes she entertained thoughts of all the might-have-beens. Only natural, she concluded.

How handsome her old college sweetheart had been, how confident, his future on a fast track to success. He'd been scheduled to take his bar exam two weeks before their society wedding and had been guaranteed a position in his father's high-powered law firm.

The day Roger had presented her with an engagement ring had been one of the happiest in her young life. The day she'd removed it from her finger one of the saddest.

Many an afternoon had been spent soaking up the sunshine at the beautiful old fountain. Students had cooled off in the cold spray or splashed barefoot in the ankle-deep water. The fountain was as old as Nelson Lord University itself. Every brochure the college had produced in its distinguished one-hundred-year history had pictured students gathered around the fountain socializing and studying.

Sitting on the cold concrete rim now, Gretchen swung her gaze to the nearby law school. The two-story redbrick building with the wide flight of stairs leading up to the set of double doors remained much the same. The ivy had been clipped back, and the lawn on the side of the building had been replaced with a concrete patio.

Many an idle afternoon had been spent sitting at this very spot, anticipating Roger's arrival, never guessing where he'd actually been.

It had been a warm afternoon like this one when she'd first talked to Josh Morrow. Heedless of rules, Josh had ridden his Harley-Davidson motorcycle down the narrow pathway and attempted to pick her up. The man lacked nothing if not audacity. It was one of the rare times she'd seen him without some blond bimbo sitting behind him, clinging to his waist. More often than not it'd been Didi Wilson. When Roger had seen Josh flirting with Gretchen, he'd been livid. As if she'd ever given Roger reason to be jealous! Maybe she should have.

Gretchen nearly laughed out loud at the memory. Josh Morrow had enjoyed life on the edge. He drank, swore and gambled on a conservative college campus that frowned upon all three. He was said to live on beer and cigarettes. He challenged every teacher unfortunate enough to have him in class, fought the establishment and raised cain. Josh had grabbed life by the throat and courted danger, and he'd fascinated her.

Everything was different and yet nothing had changed. Carol Furness strolled across the lush green grass toward the fountain. Oh, my, had it really been fifteen years? It didn't seem possible, and in many ways it felt like yesterday.

Carol had been the envy of every girl in class. Shortly after Christmas her senior year, she'd become engaged to Eddie Shapiro. Eddie was now a football legend at Nelson Lord. A legend in Carol's mind, too, but for other reasons. Their romance was a classic: the football hero and the head cheerleader. Fifteen years ago Carol had been athletic, bright and talented. She liked to believe she still was.

No thanks to Eddie. The worm.

And yet she had much to thank Eddie for. If he

hadn't dumped her, she might never have gotten to know Clark Rusbach. The class brain, a wizard with computers, a genius. Clark was technically too cute to be classified a nerd, although Eddie had often referred to him as one. In retrospect it was easy to recognize that Eddie had been jealous of Clark.

Clark knew a lot about computers, but next to nothing about women. Carol had admired him from afar, went out of her way to be friendly in the few classes they'd shared and tried to tell him, without vexing Eddie, that she admired him.

The dividends of her kindness had been rich indeed, if only she'd been smart enough to recognize what she'd had.

Maddie Cobain wondered if anyone would recognize her as she sauntered across the Nelson Lord campus in the direction of the fountain. She'd changed. The outlandish attention-seeking bad girl of her youth was no more. The girl she'd been had died a painful death, the victim of a costly, but worthwhile, lesson.

With the fountain in sight, her steps slowed. It'd been at this fountain fifteen years earlier that she'd last seen John Theda.

The cheat.

A number of other choice descriptions filled her mind, but she pushed them aside, refusing to dwell on her former mathematics professor. He'd courted her, wooed her with words and deed—all on the sly of course, lest word escape he'd fallen for a student. John had pledged his love and asked her to be his wife. Maddie had accepted, her joy exploding. What fun it had been to pretend with John, to act as if there was nothing romantic between them.

While she might have fooled everyone else, Brent Holliday had known. Who or what had allowed her secret to escape, Maddie never learned. The preacher's son seemed to think a few well-chosen words would set her on the path of the straight and narrow, but Brent had been wrong. But then, she'd had a few difficult lessons to learn in those days. Lessons that hadn't come easy.

"Gretchen?"

At the sound of her name, Gretchen turned and was greeted by a familiar face. Someone else from her graduating class. She struggled to dredge from her memory a name to go with the face.

"It's Carol. Carol Furness."

"Carol." Gretchen couldn't believe she'd stumble on a sorority sister here at the fountain an hour before the formal festivities were scheduled to start. They hugged each other fiercely.

"I wondered if that could possibly be you," Carol said, sitting down next to Gretchen on the edge of the fountain.

"Have I changed so much?" Gretchen asked. "Lie, if you have to."

Carol responded with a good-natured laugh, her blue eyes twinkling. "Not at all. You look the same as you did the day we graduated. I would have known you anywhere. The years have been good to you."

"Ditto for you, Carol." She smiled. "I couldn't resist coming down and walking around the campus."

"Me, either," Carol admitted as her gaze scanned the grounds. "I haven't been back in all these years."

"Nor have I." But Gretchen doubted that the reasons for her absence were the same as her old sorority sister's.

"Are you attending the dinner and the dance later?"

The day of the reunion was here, and Gretchen

had yet to make up her mind. "The dinner definitely, but I don't know if I can drag my husband to the dance."

"The same with me," Carol said. "My husband's a wonderful dancer, but he refuses to believe it."

"Gretchen? Carol?" The voice belonged to the tall striking auburn-haired woman approaching.

Gretchen hadn't a clue who it was, and she looked at Carol for help. Carol just shook her head.

The redhead grinned. "Not more than two minutes ago I wondered if anyone would recognize me. I've changed, I know. It's me, Maddie Cobain."

"Maddie?" Gretchen couldn't believe it. The Maddie Cobain she remembered was nothing like the well-groomed woman who stood before her now. Maddie had been outlandish in appearance, as well as in word and deed. Stubborn and defiant, a nonconformist. Yet beneath all the bravado Maddie had a heart of gold.

Gretchen recalled that Maddie had struck up a close friendship with John Theda, a math professor. It was supposed to have been a secret, but everyone knew the two were secretly engaged. The romance had caused quite a stir about campus, but then "controversy" was Maddie's middle name.

"You look wonderful," Carol said, standing up and hugging Maddie. Gretchen did likewise, and then all three sat on the edge of the fountain, with Gretchen in the middle.

"I'm pleased someone else thought to stop off at the fountain," Maddie said.

"It brings back memories, doesn't it?" Carol murmured thoughtfully.

The three were silent for several moments, caught up in the wonder of years past, Gretchen suspected.

"I was hoping to get a chance to talk to you, Carol," Maddie said excitedly. "I bet you've had a fabulous fifteen years. I don't pay much attention to professional sports, but whenever I hear anything about football, I keep my ear open for news of Eddie."

"Eddie Shapiro?" Carol asked on a disdainful note. "The guy's a worm."

Maddie looked shocked. "You were engaged to Eddie, weren't you?"

"Yeah, at one time, but he dropped me like a hot potato once he was picked up by the pros." She folded her arms and crossed her legs. Her foot swayed so hard she created a draft. "Let's change the subject, shall we?"

"Of course," Maddie said apologetically.

A short awkward silence followed while Gretchen absorbed the information. Like Maddie, she'd assumed Carol and Eddie had married. "What about you, Maddie? Being a professor's wife certainly appears to agree with you."

Instant hot color blazed in the brunette's cheeks, and her eyes snapped with fire. "I never married John Theda. The man's a cheat."

"Weren't you two engaged?"

"Oh, yes, until John got what he wanted, and it's not what you think. I suspect it was one of the shortest engagements on record."

"What about you, Gretchen?" Carol asked, quickly changing the subject once again. "How many children do you and Roger have?"

"Roger Lockheart?" she cried. "I haven't seen that rat in years!"

Gretchen watched as her two college friends exchanged glances. It seemed they were as shocked by her news as she was by theirs.

"Well, it appears we have a lot more to discuss than we realized," Gretchen said. And to think she'd worried herself sick about this silly reunion.

She leaned back on her hands and smiled softly. "If I'm hearing you correctly, you were both engaged and then dumped."

They nodded.

"Me, too," Gretchen confessed. "So there we were—three brides and no groom. Who would've believed it?"

"You didn't marry Roger," Maddie whispered, apparently having trouble taking it all in. "But Roger was always so...so perfect."

"I used to think he was wonderful," Carol added.

"At one time I thought so, too," Gretchen muttered.

"What happened?" Carol asked. "I can barely comprehend this. From what I remember, you and Roger were less than a month away from your wedding."

"Yup."

"I'll tell you what happened with John Theda," Maddie promised. "I'd like you to know."

Carol grinned. "And I'll spill my guts about Eddie Shapiro."

Gretchen laughed. "Hell hath no fury like a woman scorned."

"You don't know the half of it," Carol said.

"I do—" Maddie smoothed her hand down her skirt "—but you'll get the whole story from me. It's time someone knew exactly what kind of person John Theda really is." She glanced at Gretchen. "You go first, then Carol and then me. I can't think of a better way to spend the afternoon."

Gretchen

Chapter 1

This was supposed to be one of the happiest days of Gretchen's life. The day was memorable all right, but it would be forever marked as a day of pain and betrayal. Emotion clawed at her throat and she battled tears. She wanted her mother, but her parents had already left the campus. They'd driven up to Seattle from San Francisco to attend her college graduation and were taking a few extra days to visit Victoria, British Columbia, before returning home and making the final arrangements for her wedding to Roger.

Only Gretchen was beginning to doubt that there would be a wedding.

She stood at the far end of the sweeping veranda of her sorority house, out of view of her friends. Most were excitedly loading up their cars with another year's accumulation of treasures. Gretchen could hear their tearful farewells, their promises to keep in touch.

Promises.

She held her stomach and raised her chin in an effort to forestall the brewing emotion. Her long blond hair cascaded down the middle of her back. Roger loved her hair long, enjoyed playing with it, brushing it, burying his face in it.

"Sweetpea?" The sound of Roger's contrite voice came from behind her.

She'd always hated his pet name for her, but no amount of protest could persuade him to come up with another.

Standing directly behind her, he cupped her shoulders and nuzzled her neck. "Let's talk about this, all right?"

"Talk?" Gretchen asked with a short abrupt laugh. As far as she was concerned they had nothing to discuss.

"You've got to know Didi doesn't mean anything to me." Now his hands were in her hair lifting the thick tresses to his face. He wove his fingers into it and brushed his lips across her crown.

Gretchen's eyes slammed shut at the sharp pain.

"It was stupid," Roger continued. "I want to throw up every time I think about how incredibly asinine I was. My only excuse is that I was drunk."

"You made love to another woman and I'm supposed to forget it ever happened because you were drunk?"

His hands returned to her shoulders and squeezed. "Didi's always had the hots for me. You said so yourself, remember? I...I wasn't thinking straight. I was with the guys, celebrating, drinking, and the next thing I knew Didi was coming on to me. She wouldn't take no for an answer. Ask anyone. She was all over me and...you know how those fraternity parties can get."

Gretchen's stomach clenched. "Don't tell me any more. I don't want to hear it."

"But I have to tell you. I need to. This is going to stand between us unless you know it all. You've got to believe me, Gretchen, I'm as sick about what happened as you are."

She said nothing, too numb to argue.

"Didi knows we're engaged, but that didn't stop

her. I told her again and again that it was you I loved, but she wouldn't listen. The next thing I knew she'd undone my zipper and stuck her hands inside my pants.''

"In front of everyone?" Gretchen cried in disbelief.

He hesitated, and when he spoke, his voice was barely audible. "We...we were in a closet."

"A closet?" Gretchen nearly choked on the word.

"She was feeling me up and, Sweetpea, I'm so very sorry, but I'm only human. I was hard and hot and then she had her mouth on me and was saying things like she bet my uptown girl never did anything like this for me and—"

"I don't want to hear any more," Gretchen said again, more forcefully this time.

"But it's true," Roger whispered. "You insisted on waiting until we were married to make love, and I've respected your wishes. But I don't think you appreciate what sexual frustration can do to a guy."

"In other words this is all my fault."

"No, no. If anyone's to blame, it should be Didi. When I woke up this morning, I was sick to my stomach, knowing what I'd done. I couldn't be sorrier. Say you'll forgive me. I'm begging you, Sweetpea. We can't let someone like Didi come between us. If you do something foolish, you'll be doing exactly what she wants. The only reason she came on to me was to hurt you."

"And you let her."

He paused. "Let's put this behind us, all right? Mom's looking forward to you spending the next few days with her. All she can talk about is the wedding plans, and that's exactly what you need to help take your mind off my unfortunate slip."

So that was how he thought of infidelity: an unfortunate slip.

"What do you say, Sweetpea?"

She pressed her fingertips to her temple. "I need time to think."

"What's there to think about? I told you everything. This isn't easy for me, you know. I just bet Didi took delight in letting you know what happened. She's a bitch, looking to ruin both our lives. You're not going to let her, are you?" The soft pleading quality was back, the desperation to make matters right, as if that were possible now.

"What did you expect would happen when you went into a closet with Didi Wilson?" she demanded, whirling to face him.

His bloodshot eyes revealed his shock at being confronted. "I...I was drunk."

"Not too drunk apparently." If he expected her to sweep his indiscretion under the proverbial carpet, she couldn't do it, wouldn't do it. Not without giving the matter a great deal of thought.

"The wedding's less than a month away," he protested.

He didn't need to tell her the date of her own wedding. "Are you saying it's too late to change plans?"

"You wouldn't! Baby, please, don't do anything stupid."

"Like you?"

He let her words soak in before saying, "Two stupid acts don't make a right."

It amazed Gretchen how desperately she wanted to forget what Didi had taken such pleasure in telling her. The other woman's timing didn't escape Gretchen's notice, either. While she was escorting her parents to the best of Seattle's tourists attractions, her fiancé had been screwing his brains out.

As if that wasn't bad enough, Didi hit her with the ugly details shortly after the graduation exercise. Instead of enjoying the sense of exhilaration and accomplishment she'd felt upon receiving her diploma, Gretchen had seen her world fall apart when Didi had cornered her on the front steps of the sorority house shortly after her parents had left for Canada and delivered her news.

"Mom's waiting," Roger pressed.

"Then she'll just have to wait. I told you I need time to sort everything out." Gretchen knew that his mother was not a patient woman. Stella Lockheart was a forceful woman who generally got what she wanted. Both Roger and his father catered to her wishes rather than risk dealing with one of her explosive outbursts.

Gretchen could tell by the way Roger's breathing pattern altered that he wasn't pleased with her decision. He'd been calm and in control, at his persuasive best. Now he was impatient and frustrated. Fine, so be it. She wasn't going to let him pressure her, nor would she be rushed because he feared a confrontation with his mother. This was *her* life and she was determined to take a long hard look at the future.

"OK, if that's what you want," Roger said shortly. "I'll tell Mom to go on ahead without you."

She nodded.

He lingered a moment longer, his gaze boring

into hers. "There isn't any reason to tell Mom about what happened, is there?"

Gretchen almost felt sorry for Roger. "Why would I want to humiliate myself even further?" she asked.

He was visibly relieved as he turned and hurried toward the parking lot. As Gretchen watched him go, the knot in the pit of her stomach tightened. Needing to do something, anything other than stand here on the veranda, she moved down the steps and began walking. She soon found herself by the fountain, and with a heavy heart, she lowered herself onto the concrete rim. The urge to bury her face in her hands and weep was nearly overwhelming, but she had too much pride to publicly display her pain.

Most of the activity around the school had lulled. Graduation was over, and the majority of students had already left the campus. Gretchen was grateful for the quiet, a rarity at the university. She needed to mull over what she'd learned, to assimilate what Didi had told her, followed by Roger's weak justifications.

Every time she tried to make sense of the cold ugly facts of his infidelity, distance herself from them, she stumbled over the pain.

Again and again, Roger had told her how much he loved her, how she would be the perfect wife for him. His insistence caused her to wonder if he was mouthing his mother's sentiments, not his own. A man who truly loved her wouldn't step into a closet with Didi Wilson. But at the same time, Roger was full of regret. Even in her pain, she could sense his own. He was genuinely sorry. She wanted, needed, to believe that.

One thing he'd said rang true. Didi had never made a secret of how attractive she found Roger. Nor had she bothered to disguise her dislike for Gretchen. It was probably her dislike that had prompted Didi to confront her. For why now, when they were both leaving the school and the likelihood of meeting each other again was slim to none?

Didi's neck had been covered with hickeys so livid that no amount of makeup could fully hide them. She'd boldly walked up to Gretchen, looked her in the eyes, smiled and then casually asked her if she knew what Roger had been doing the night before. At Gretchen's stunned silence, Didi had crudely asked if Gretchen thought she was woman enough to satisfy Roger's healthy sexual appetite.

The question insinuated that she wasn't. Never would be.

The roar of an engine shattered the peace. Gretchen glanced up to see Josh Morrow speed across the campus parking lot on his Harley, a plume of dark exhaust in his wake. He'd been cited by the campus security a dozen times, she'd heard, for driving above the speed limit, but it hadn't fazed him.

Josh was a loner, a known troublemaker, a rebel. She'd spoken to him once months earlier, and Roger had been furious with her. In the weeks since, she'd avoided Josh, but that didn't stop her from noticing him. He stood apart from everyone, watching, studying. The outsider, looking in. He hadn't sought her out again, and she was grateful. She supposed it was natural to feel a certain attraction toward Josh. She suspected a lot of the women at Nelson Lord did. Maybe it was the black leather and the motorcycle, the sense that the love of a good woman would tame him.

Now her gaze must have lingered on him a second longer than was prudent, for he eased his huge bike to a stop, placed his feet on the road to maintain his balance and stared at her. After what seemed an eternity, he revved the engine, roared over the cement curb and onto the narrow walkway, directly toward her.

Gretchen stood, her heart in her throat. The last thing she wanted was company.

Josh pulled to a stop right in front of her. Lifting the helmet from his head, he studied her for a moment and then asked with surprising gentleness, "Gretchen, what happened?"

She stiffened, shocked that he had read her so easily. "Nothing."

His smile was decidedly off center. "You should never lie, not when you do such a poor job of it."

She lowered her gaze and rubbed her palms together. "It's something I'd rather not discuss."

He stepped off the Harley and lowered the kickstand. "Fair enough."

His size was intimidating. He was at least 6' 2"– 6' 3", almost dwarfing her five foot eight. She crossed her arms over her chest, wondering at his intentions. As if he didn't have a care in the world, he leaned over the fountain, scooped up a handful of water and drenched his face.

He glanced toward her and chuckled, the sound low and teasing. "Don't worry, I won't bite."

"I'm not worried," she lied.

His soft snicker told her she hadn't convinced him. "I don't sacrifice virgins, either."

"I suggest you don't try. I'd crawl off the altar."

He laughed, but this time the sound was rich and deep. Ignoring her, he turned his face toward the sky and his features glistened as the water dripped from his face. "Where's lover boy this afternoon?" he asked.

His question caught her off guard. Apparently Josh knew about Roger and Didi. How many others did? Her face filled with a rush of hot embarrassed color.

"Who told you?" she asked, her voice low and trembling despite her effort to remain cool and calm. Between Didi and Roger's so-called friends, the news must be everywhere by now.

"Is it important?" he asked. His words were soft, quiet, as if he feared saying them would increase her pain.

"No, I guess it isn't." Some students thought of Gretchen as advantaged. While it was true her family had considerable wealth, when serving as the student-body president, she'd crossed swords with any number who willingly tossed her background in her face. But her hard work as a communicator and her fervor for honesty and justice often won them over. Until recently she preferred to think of her friends as many and her enemies as few. Now she wasn't so sure.

Josh's gaze turned narrow and assessing, which increased Gretchen's embarrassment tenfold. She inhaled a quivering breath.

"Roger's a first-class fool," Josh said at last. "He deserves to have his teeth kicked in."

While in theory Gretchen agreed with him—she wanted to see Roger suffer for what he'd done—her sensibilities didn't lean toward violence. Roger had allowed the blame to ricochet from Didi to Gretchen and then back to Didi. Gretchen wanted to scream and demand that for once in his life Roger accept responsibility for his own actions. To own up to what he'd done, instead of listing excuses meant to absolve him of any guilt.

"Gretchen!"

As if her thoughts had conjured him up, Roger was striding across the lawn toward the fountain. "What the hell are you doing here, Morrow?" he asked, arriving breathless, his chest heaving.

When Josh didn't immediately answer, Roger faced Gretchen. "Is he pestering you?"

"Of course not," she replied, angered by the question and by the insinuation.

"I told you to stay away from Gretchen," Roger snarled at Josh. As though she needed his protection, he reached out and grabbed hold of her arm.

"I suggest you let go of her," Josh said, his voice deceptively calm.

Roger ignored him. "Come on, Gretchen, let's get out of here."

She jerked her arm free of his grasp and met his look squarely. "I haven't finished thinking about you and me yet."

Anger flared in Roger's dark eyes. "What's Morrow doing here?"

"What do you care?" Josh asked, his words a challenge.

Roger glared at Josh and seemed to be weighing the odds of engaging in a fistfight, then decided against it. Wisely, she thought.

"Gretchen, I think you'd better come with me," he said, calmer this time.

"I'm not ready to leave yet." She wasn't looking to defy Roger, but she needed time to deal with a multitude of pressing questions. Decisions had to be made, the consequences of which she would have to live with for the rest of her life.

Again Roger's eyes flared with anger.

"You heard the lady," Josh inserted smoothly with that cocky grin of his.

Gretchen whirled on him. "I can do my own talking, thank you."

"Fine." Josh raised his right hand in a mocking gesture of peace.

Tight-lipped, Roger said, "Either you get the hell out of here, Morrow, or I'm calling security. Your kind isn't welcome around here. Why don't you go visit your daddy in prison, have a good look around, since that's where you're headed yourself."

Josh looked exceptionally bored, which only served to anger Roger more. But Gretchen noticed the vein in Josh's temple throb and knew Roger's words had effected Josh.

"You should have been expelled long ago," Roger hissed.

To Gretchen's mortification, her fiancé obviously had second thoughts about a fight. He doubled up his fist and took a wild swing at Josh. His punch went wide, and Josh didn't so much as blink.

"Maybe Dean Williams is looking for a valid excuse to be rid of me," he suggested casually. "What he really needs is a charge that'll stick. How about assault?" Having said that, his fist shot out and exploded against Roger's nose.

Stunned, Roger stumbled backward. His hand flew to his face, and blood oozed between his fingers. "I'm bleeding," he cried in horror. He reached into his back pocket for a handkerchief and held it against his nose. "Now you've done it, Morrow," he threatened. "You're finished at this school. I'll make damn sure of that."

"I can't tell you how worried I am." Josh reached for his helmet and climbed aboard his motorcycle. He started the engine and then, as though in afterthought, he turned and looked at Gretchen. His eyes locked with hers as he slowly extended his arm to her.

She hesitated, unsure what to do.

"Go with him and the engagement is off," Roger threatened with a nasal twang.

It was all the incentive she needed. Slipping the diamond ring off her finger, she tossed it to Roger, then leaped onto the motorcycle behind Josh.

He revved the engine, spewing exhaust at Roger, then raced off in the direction of the sun.

Chapter 2

Gretchen had never ridden on a motorcycle before. Her arms gripped Josh's waist tightly as they headed down the narrow asphalt pathway. When he changed gears, she could hear Roger shouting curses after them. Closing her eyes, she savored the look of shock and dismay on Roger's face when she'd returned his ring and leaped onto the back of the Harley with Josh. In retrospect her actions had been foolhardy, but also purely instinctual. The wind slapped her hair about her face; nevertheless she smiled. This one small act of rebellion had cheered her considerably.

They sped across the school parking lot toward the busy four-lane street that bordered the university. Gretchen didn't have a clue where Josh was taking her. At the moment she didn't care. She angled her face into the wind, letting it dry the tears from her cheeks. For the first time since Didi had confronted her, the oppressive tightness surrounding her heart lessened.

Josh eased to a stop in a restaurant parking lot several blocks from the university. He twisted in the seat to look at her, keeping the huge bike balanced between his legs.

"Where do you want me to take you?" he asked.

"Where?" she repeated, not knowing how to answer him. It would have suited her to ride off into the sunset and forget everything. Forget Didi. Forget Roger and the ugly scene by the fountain. Forget that she had less than fifty dollars cash on her and nowhere to go.

"To the airport?"

"I...Roger's mother has my ticket. I'd originally planned to spend a week with her putting the finishing touches on our wedding plans."

Josh glared at her. "You're not going to ask for the bastard's ring back, are you?"

"No." And she meant it. Despite all the time and energy that had gone into the wedding plans, she could not rationalize what he'd done. One part of her had wanted to look past his infidelity and pretend everything would eventually be all right. But the other part knew their relationship would never be the same again. If Roger was unfaithful before they were married, she could never trust him after the wedding. He was nowhere near ready to be a husband.

"Good," Josh said. "You deserve better."

"Could you take me to Mary Ann Seawright's?" she asked. Mary Ann was a friend who lived in the vicinity. Gretchen could stay there until her parents returned from British Columbia. Of course she could always contact Mrs. Lockheart about her airline ticket, but she preferred not to. She feared Roger's mother would attempt to change her mind, and Gretchen hadn't the emotional energy to lock horns with the woman. If anyone was forced to deal with her, it should be Roger himself. Gretchen preferred to sever all ties.

"Does Roger know Mary Ann?" Josh asked.

"Yes. Mary Ann goes out with Bill Beckett. The four of us often double-dated." Of course, she realized, that meant Roger would soon know exactly where she'd gone.

"Where's home?" Josh asked next.

She bit her lower lip. Home had never seemed so faraway. "San Francisco, but my parents are vacationing. They won't be back for several days." Not until then did she realize she had no means of getting home.

That cocky half grin of Josh's slid into place. "As it happens, I'm headed in that direction. You can ride along with me, if you want. I'll drop you off in Frisco and continue on my way." He paused as if to read her reaction to his offer. "Fact is, I'd welcome the company."

Gretchen wasn't sure how to answer. While it was true that he offered her a way out of a tricky situation, she didn't really know Josh Morrow. His reputation would be enough to turn her mother's hair prematurely white.

His eyes glinted with challenge, and it seemed he was waiting for her to reject his generosity.

"I appreciate it, but..." She stalled, unsure and a little afraid.

"But?"

"I don't have much cash with me. Fifty dollars

at the most, although I do have a gasoline credit card.''

''Hey, we're in fat city,'' Josh teased. ''I've got little more than a hundred bucks myself.''

She grinned. ''OK, I accept.'' She'd never done anything more impulsive in her life. She might not know Josh very well, but she trusted him. Of course, she'd also trusted Roger. But dammit, she was her own woman, and despite the bad-boy tag Josh wore like a badge of honor, she'd rather ride home with him on the back of a Harley than deal with Roger, or his family, again.

''I'm sure my father would be more than happy to reimburse you for any expenses,'' she said.

''We'll discuss that later. What will you need to take with you?''

''Not much,'' she promised, knowing he wouldn't have room for more than the essentials.

Once he checked to be sure Roger was nowhere in sight, Josh dropped her off at the sorority house with a promise to return within the hour.

Mrs. Vance, the housemother, regarded her anxiously when Gretchen walked in the front door.

''Thank goodness you're back,'' the middle-aged woman said on a hefty sigh. ''Roger Lockheart was here no more than five minutes ago looking for you. He's such a nice young man, and he's worried sick about you taking off with Josh Morrow that way. I never did trust a man on a motorcycle.''

Gretchen bit her tongue to keep from saying that she trusted Josh far more than she did Roger, but stopped herself. It wouldn't do any good to argue, and she didn't have time to waste.

"Give Roger a call, why don't you," Mrs. Vance called to Gretchen as she raced up the stairs. "I'm sure it's nothing more than a lovers' spat."

Ignoring the suggestion, Gretchen hurried to her room, where her two large suitcases rested undisturbed. She quickly sorted through what she'd packed, scooped up what she needed and stuffed it into a clean pillowcase. Then she sat on the edge of the bed, went through her purse and counted her cash. Fifty-five dollars. Fearing if she lingered much longer Roger would return, she raced down the stairs to the hall phone.

Luckily Mary Ann was home. "I need you to do something for me," Gretchen said without preamble.

Her longtime friend must have heard the urgency in her voice. "Of course. What do you need?"

"I'm leaving my suitcases with Mrs. Vance. Could you come and get them for me?"

"Uh, sure, but why in heaven's name do you need me to—"

"I don't have time to explain now," Gretchen broke in. "I've broken my engagement to Roger."

Mary Ann gasped. "Gretchen, for the love of heaven, what happened?"

"I'll phone and tell you everything once I'm home."

"Home? But how are you going to get to San Francisco?"

Gretchen heard the unmistakable roar of Josh's Harley outside. "I can't tell you now. I'll phone soon, I promise."

"But...but..."

Gretchen severed the connection. She reached for her purse and the pillowcase and discovered Mrs. Vance standing in front of the living-room window. The older woman was holding the curtain to one side and glaring, her mouth twisted in disapproval.

"I wonder what that Morrow boy is doing back here," she muttered.

"He's here for me," Gretchen announced, enjoying the pure shock value of the statement.

The housemother gasped and swiveled to stare at her. "But you—"

Gretchen interrupted her. "I'm going with him." Until that moment, she didn't realize how much she longed for her home and her family. "Goodbye, Mrs. Vance."

"Gretchen…Gretchen, I must insist—"

"I'll be fine, don't worry." She kissed the woman on the cheek, then raced out the front door and bounded down the steps. Josh handed her a second helmet, and while she placed it on her head and fastened the strap, he tucked the pillowcase in one of the leather bags draped over the side of the bike. He climbed on and she positioned herself behind him.

Before they roared away, Gretchen turned back to find Mrs. Vance standing on the porch. She waved to Gretchen, then placed her fingertips to her mouth as if she wasn't sure what she should do.

Gretchen, however, had never been more confident. Only a few hours earlier, her heart had been breaking. Now, on the back of Josh Morrow's Harley, with the wind in her face and her arms securely wrapped around his muscular torso, she was free. Truly free.

Unfortunately the feeling didn't last. Before long, questions and doubts buzzed about her head like mosquitoes over a stagnant pond. The wedding invitations had been engraved and her wedding dress ordered from an exclusive boutique. Her parents had booked the ballroom of a five-star hotel for the reception. All the money and effort, all the planning and dreaming were wasted. Her face burned with humiliation, knowing she'd be the one who'd be forced to deal with the cancellations. But what was the use in dwelling on the negative aspects of canceling the wedding? The only important thing was that she couldn't marry Roger.

After some time on the road, the deafening sound of the Harley vibrating in her ear, Gretchen shifted on the seat, both physically and mentally miserable. What had seemed daring and exciting a few hours earlier appeared exceedingly foolish now. Her back ached from holding herself upright and not leaning against Josh. Her legs felt as if they were glued into one position, and she was certain her calves would soon cramp up on her.

To top everything off, Josh Morrow apparently had the bladder of a camel.

When at last he did stop, Gretchen feared he'd need to pry her off the bike with a crowbar. She looked around and realized they were at the ocean. Huge rolling waves crashed against the shore, then lovingly stroked a frothy trail across the sand. Large gray-and-white gulls circled overhead, and the scent of the sea lingered in the moist air. The sun appeared, a brilliant orange on the horizon, ready to slip out of sight. Already dusk was settling in.

"Where are we?" Gretchen asked, easing first one leg and then the other away from the motorcycle. Josh lent her a hand, which she gratefully accepted.

"Cannon Beach, Oregon," he replied.

Vaguely Gretchen recalled crossing the Columbia River at Astoria, but that seemed hours ago. She'd kept her eyes closed most of the time, needing to think. She should be home within two days, three at the most.

With his hands braced on his hips, Josh surveyed the sky. "I don't think it'll rain." He left her and walked toward the beach. Gretchen looked longingly at the public rest room, but followed him, instead, wanting to know where he intended to spend the night. It went without saying that they wouldn't be sharing a hotel room.

Her shoes quickly filled with sand and she found keeping pace with Josh difficult.

"We'll bed down here for the night," he announced.

"Here?" she asked, looking around. All she saw was barren sand. "The beach?"

"Do you have any better ideas?"

Gretchen glanced over her shoulder at the long row of oceanfront hotels.

"For seventy-five bucks you'll get a room the size of refrigerator," Josh said, his gaze trained on the ocean.

Gretchen squared her shoulders. "Well, then, the beach it is."

He grinned as if to say he admired her adventurous spirit. "There's a shower in the public rest room, if you want to take one."

Gretchen did. She was afraid to look in a mirror, certain there must be bugs glued to her teeth. Her clothes felt plastered to her body.

She took what she needed from the saddlebag—a towel, washcloth and her cosmetic case—and headed for the rest room. It smelled of urine and ocean, but looked clean enough. The shower stall, minus the curtain, was in one corner. She stripped off her clothes and stood under the spray. Despite the lukewarm temperature, it felt luxurious.

As she turned her face into the water, the ache returned to the pit of her stomach. She leaned against the back of the open stall and cradled her middle. That morning she'd awakened thinking all was right with the world. She had her business degree and within weeks would be wed to Roger. The future had looked rosy indeed. And now within the space of a few hours, her reality had changed completely.

When the water turned from lukewarm to chilly, she reached for the towel. Once she was dressed, she felt better. It was when she combed out her long blond hair in front of the metal mirror that she made the decision. She stared at the distorted reflection, the comb halfway down the side of her head.

She had only herself to please now, not Roger. Her fingers trembled as she dug through her cosmetic bag until she found a small pair of scissors. Seizing the pale tresses, she attacked the sides with erratic, disjointed chops. She hacked and cut until the long strands of hair lay at her feet like discarded remnants of spun gold. Despite the distorted reflection, she knew she'd brutalized her once lovely hair. Breathing hard, she waited several minutes before she gathered up the courage to go back outside.

By the time she left the rest room, the sun had completely set. A full moon cast a golden glow across the beach. Josh had spread out a blanket and lit a small driftwood fire, and was now working his pocket knife against a stick, whittling it to a point. He glanced up as she approached. He said nothing about her mutilated hair.

"There's a grocery store not far from here," he said. "I got us a package of wieners and buns."

Gretchen nodded, then self-consciously sat down on the end of a log and started to shake. Exhaling harshly, she raised her fingers to her head to investigate the damage. It wouldn't have hurt to wait, she realized. In a couple of days she'd be home and a trained professional could have cut it. She could only guess how horrible she looked. Tears stung the back of her eyes.

"Give me the scissors," Josh said gently.

She still had them clenched in her fist. He took them from her and sighed as he ran his fingers through the uneven tresses, his touch strangely intimate.

Gretchen swallowed tightly. "Roger insisted I keep it long," she whispered. Cutting it had been an act of defiance, a way of casting her former fiancé from her life, but in doing so she'd only hurt herself.

Josh took his time clipping away here and there. At last he stood back to admire his handiwork. "Not bad," he said with a slow smile, "even if I do say so myself."

Gretchen reached for her compact and flipped it open. With the light from the fire and the moon, she could see that his touch had been masterful. Gretchen barely recognized herself. She now wore a short pixielike cut that flattered her cheekbones and deep blue eyes.

Her gaze returned to Josh. "You're a man of many talents. Thank you," she murmured.

Her words appeared to please him. He reached for his knife and the stick he'd been sharpening earlier. "I don't know about you, but I'm starved."

Gretchen couldn't have eaten if her life depended on it. She sat with her chin resting on her knees and studied the fire. "You go ahead. I'm not hungry."

They sat side by side, surrounded by the sound of the ocean and the crackle of the fire. Josh cooked himself a wiener and gingerly tested it with his fingers.

"Is it true what Roger said," Gretchen wondered aloud, "about your father being in prison?" She wasn't sure what had prompted the question. Probably she should never have asked.

Josh stilled. "Yes." But he didn't elaborate and she didn't question him further. Although he claimed to be hungry, he didn't eat more than one hot dog. For a long time afterward he sat cross-legged on the blanket staring into the flames as though hypnotized.

"Josh," she whispered, after a few minutes of uncomfortable silence. He didn't look at her right away. She waited until he grudgingly gave her his attention. "I'm sorry. I had no business asking you about your father."

Without acknowledging her apology, he rose to his feet and disappeared into the darkness. She watched him go, resisting the urge to go after him and apologize again. Angry with herself, she pressed her forehead against her knees and wondered how she could have been so insensitive to a man who'd been so kind and helpful.

After the tumultuous events of the day, Gretchen was convinced she'd never be able to sleep. She stretched out on the blanket, covered herself with a thick sweater and tucked her head against her bent arm. She was asleep almost immediately, only to jerk awake a moment later. This happened a time or two before the physical demands of her body won out over the emotional trauma of the day.

Gretchen wasn't sure at what point during the night Josh joined her. Her eyes fluttered open to see the fire had died down to glimmering coals. She was on her back and all she could see was the dense spattering of stars above. She rolled her head to one side and found Josh asleep on the other side of the blanket. Relieved that he was back, she rolled onto her side and tucked her sweater more closely about her shoulders.

The next thing Gretchen was aware of was the loud discordant cry of a seagull. She opened her eyes to gray light. To her surprise she felt warm and cozy, although the fire had long since died out. She soon realized the source of her comfort. Josh had placed his leather jacket over her shoulders.

He sat nearby, his hair apparently wet from a shower.

"What time is it?" she asked, lazily stretching her arms above her head and yawning.

His grinned. "Morning."

"That much I guessed." Raising herself on one elbow, she strained to see her watch.

"About five-thirty or six, I'd guess," Josh said, looking toward the rising sun.

She sat up and rubbed the sleep from her eyes, then realized she was famished. Her stomach growled loudly. "Oh, dear," she said, and flattened her hand against her abdomen.

"Looks like we'd best scrounge up something to eat," he said. He stood and extended his hand to her. It took them a while to pack up everything. While Josh loaded up the Harley, Gretchen brushed her teeth in the rest room, put on some lip gloss and combed her hair, amazed again at the transformation the haircut made in her appearance. She doubted that Roger would even recognize her now.

When they rode into town and parked the Harley at a curb, another question came to mind, one she felt Josh could answer. Needing someone to hold on to, she fit her hand into his.

"How well do you know Didi Wilson?" she asked. She'd often seen Didi with Josh. It was none of her concern. Nevertheless she needed to know.

His gaze narrowed and his steps slowed. "How much did Didi tell you about her and Roger?"

Gretchen frowned, her hand still in his. "Just that...that she was at the fraternity party with him."

Josh's fingers tightened around hers.

"I don't hate Didi," she said, although it was difficult to regard the other woman with kindness. In many ways Didi had done her a favor, but it was difficult to think of it in those terms just then.

Josh heaved a deep sigh. "Didi's pregnant."

"How can she know so soon?" Gretchen asked indignantly, and then it hit her. Hard. Square between the eyes. It hadn't been one time that Roger had been with Didi Wilson, but several. She closed her eyes and swayed with both shock and anger.

"How long have they been lovers?" she demanded. When he hesitated, she asked again, more loudly this time, steeling herself for the answer. "Tell me, Josh. I have a right to know."

"Six months, maybe more."

She grimaced and clenched her fist at her side.

The entire time she'd been engaged to Roger, he'd been physically involved with Didi. It was enough to make her ill. She recalled all those afternoons he'd been late to meet her. It got to be a big joke between them. All the nights when he'd claimed he was studying. She should have known, should have realized. What about her friends? Her face burned with the realization that others must have known and yet no one had bothered to tell her.

As if reading her thoughts, Josh said, "Roger kept it quiet. I doubt anyone else knew."

"You did," she said.

"Didi's my friend."

But she noted he didn't say how good a friend the woman was. Gretchen didn't really know Didi. They didn't run in the same circles. If she remembered correctly, Didi had dropped out of college after her freshman year, but continued to work part-time at the bookstore.

"Does Roger know about the baby?" she asked once she found her voice.

"No." Josh shook his head.

"Is Didi going to tell him?"

Again Josh paused. "I don't know. That decision is hers."

She studied him and wondered if Josh had been

Didi's lover, too. If so, she didn't want to know about it.

His grip on her hand relaxed. "Come on, you look like you could use a cup of coffee." He led her to a café on the main street and held open the door for her. Although it was still early, the place was hopping. With a majority of the tables occupied, Josh opted to sit at the counter. Once they were settled, Josh turned over the ceramic coffee mugs and handed Gretchen a menu.

The harried waitress cast them an apologetic smile as she raced by, her arms loaded down with plates. "I'll be with you folks as soon as I can."

"We're in no hurry," Josh assured her.

The woman returned a few minutes later with the coffeepot. "The other waitress called in sick at the last minute, along with the dishwasher. Mighty convenient case of the flu, if you ask me," she muttered as she filled their cups.

The cook slapped the bell and set two more plates on the shelf. The waitress glanced over her shoulder and grumbled under her breath. "I'll be back to take your order in a couple of minutes. I don't want those breakfasts to get cold."

"No problem," Gretchen said.

Josh helped himself to a couple of doughnuts

from a plate beneath a plastic dome. He handed one to Gretchen.

As the waitress moved past, Josh said to her, "Listen, if you're shorthanded, I can wash dishes."

The waitress hesitated.

"All I want in exchange is a decent breakfast for me and my friend."

"Harry," the gal called into the kitchen. "We got ourselves a volunteer. The guy claims he can wash dishes." She looked at Gretchen. "What about you, honey? Did you ever wait tables?"

Gretchen could see that Josh was about to answer for her. "Sure," she said quickly, although it was a bold-faced lie. She brushed the doughnut crumbs from her hands and slipped off the stool.

"There's an apron and a pad behind the counter."

"Great," Gretchen said. She wasn't at all sure she'd be able to pull it off, but she was willing to try. She tossed Josh a saucy grin as she tied the apron around her waist. Then he disappeared into the kitchen.

"If you'd do the coffee refills, I'd appreciate it," the waitress said, swishing past her. "Those tables need to be cleaned, too." She pointed at two that had just emptied. "By the way, my name's Marge."

"I'm Gretchen," she said, and reached for the glass coffeepot. It didn't demand a lot of skill to refill coffee cups around the room. Once she'd finished that, she found a large square tub and hauled it over to the vacated tables, then dumped the dirty dishes inside. After she wiped the surface clean and handed Marge her tip money, Gretchen turned to discover the booths had filled up with customers.

By the time the breakfast crowd had thinned out, it was midmorning. Gretchen sat down and counted her tips. She collected close to twenty bucks.

"Sure do appreciate the help," Marge said, sitting down next to her at the counter.

"Glad I could do it."

Josh appeared from the kitchen, drying his hands on a dish towel.

"I'm so hungry I could eat a cow," Gretchen said.

Marge winked at Josh, then looked toward the kitchen. "Harry, cook me up a couple of our best steaks, and don't be frying up any of those skinny breakfast ones, either. These kids deserve T-bones."

Chapter 3

Gretchen couldn't remember when she'd enjoyed a meal more, although she felt like a fraud accepting it. Her waitressing skills left much to be desired, and by the end of three hours, her feet hurt, her back ached, and she had a new appreciation of the skills required to wait tables.

It was almost noon by the time they were back on the road. Unlike the previous day, when they'd ridden hour upon hour without a break, Josh stopped every ten or fifteen miles. Gretchen had traveled down the Oregon coast any number of times and found the scenery breathtaking. But nothing compared to viewing the magnificence on a bright sunny day in June from the back of Josh's Harley. It went a long way, in fact, to assuaging the ache in her heart.

She didn't want to think about Roger or the wedding, and yet it filled every corner of her mind. She didn't mention his name, not once, during any of their stops, but she talked about everything else, without pausing for breath. Josh's patience was nothing short of chivalrous. Gretchen couldn't remember ever being so talkative. She told him story upon story of growing up in San Francisco. She endlessly bragged about her older brother and dragged out four or five pictures of her eighteen-month-old niece.

At each stop, Josh would sit on the rock-wall railing with his back to the ocean and listen as if he'd never heard anything more fascinating. Gretchen wished she'd paid more attention in psychology class so she could appreciate what was happening to her. Could analyze it and stop this infernal chattering.

Josh rarely commented, but sat and listened, nodding and smiling now and again. Their last stop to view the scenery was Rockaway Beach. While standing in the glorious sunshine, looking out over the relentless surf, Gretchen started laughing as she told a story about her niece. She'd asked Jazmine to get her a pair of shoes, and the toddler had promptly delivered every pair Gretchen owned.

As she neared the end of the tale, her laughter altered and unexpected tears flooded into her eyes. "I...I don't know why I'm doing this," she said when she found it impossible to hide what was happening.

"I know why." He stood and gently placed his hands on her shoulders. Then with a tenderness that made her want to weep even more, he pulled her close and wrapped his arms around her. "It's all right, Gretchen. Go ahead and cry. You're hurting. The man you loved isn't the person you thought he was."

Like a burst dam, Gretchen's sobs broke free. They seemed to surge upward from the deepest part of her, until it wasn't only her shoulders that shook, but her entire torso. She tried to break away from Josh, but he wouldn't allow it. He pressed her closer, murmuring words of comfort all the while.

Gretchen clung to him, burying her head against his shoulder, letting him absorb her anger and pain. The roar of the ocean slamming against the rocks seemed to echo her pain.

Once her energy was spent and her sobs turned to sniffles, she eased away, keeping her head lowered in embarrassment. Josh would have none of it. He tucked his index finger beneath her chin, raised her head and met her eyes.

"It's all right," he said.

A slight smile trembled at the corners of her mouth and she nodded.

"Oh, what the hell." The words were half whisper and half groan. As soon as he said them, he lowered his mouth to hers. The kiss was slow and deep, so deep she felt it all the way to her toes. Intense, yet incredibly tender.

After a moment Josh slid his fingers into her short hair, cupping the sides of her head as he angled his mouth over hers, urging her lips apart with the tip of his tongue. He sighed when, in a daze, she accepted his invitation and opened for him. Shyly her tongue met his, but gradually she gained confidence as the love play continued. What had begun as a slow easy exercise quickly became demanding and urgent.

Gretchen wasn't sure what would have happened if a car hadn't pulled off the highway just then. Hearing the sound of wheels grinding against the gravel, Josh broke off the contact. He studied her for a moment.

"You OK?" he asked, touching his forehead to hers while holding her face between his hands.

She nodded, not knowing how else to answer him. But she wasn't OK. She'd been weeping for one man and then kissing another. And liking it so much she didn't want to stop. She glared at the new arrivals, wishing they would leave, then realized how ridiculous she was being.

"We better get back on the road," Josh said, steering her toward the Harley.

Although she silently followed him, her mind brewed with half-formed questions. First and foremost she wanted to know what had prompted him to kiss her. She didn't want his pity, but at the same time, she'd be a fool to believe any part of that soul-stirring kiss had been because he felt sorry for her.

Once she was safely tucked behind him on the Harley, Josh started the bike and steered them back onto the road. The wind whipped against her face and Gretchen closed her eyes. Josh was dangerous—that was what she'd always heard. Now she knew why. The danger wasn't his arrogance, the way he challenged authority or defied danger. It was the effortless way he could make a woman feel desirable.

They didn't stop again for what seemed like hours. The day before, Gretchen had held herself away from Josh, her spine rigid, determined to minimize any physical contact. Not so now. Her grip about his waist was tight, for she craved the physical reassurance of his solid body.

Josh stopped in Tillamook at a red traffic signal. "You hungry?" he asked.

Gretchen realized, somewhat to her surprise, that she was. "Yeah, I guess I am." Then, knowing their finances were limited, she asked, "What can we afford?"

"Cheese."

"Cheese?" While she knew neither one of them had a lot of cash, she didn't think they were in dire straits.

"Some of the best in the country. I'll show you."

Tillamook was home to a huge dairy-products factory. She smiled and flattened her cheek against his back, grateful to have him for a friend. It felt good and right to be this close to him. Her entire four years of college, she'd barely talked to him.

By all accounts they were little more than strangers, yet she felt closer to him after these two days together than she did to some of her sorority sisters with whom she'd lived for years.

Josh turned left at the next light and then pulled into a large bustling parking lot. The building was enormous, complete with gift shop, touring areas and plenty of free samples of a surprisingly large selection of cheeses and ice cream. He purchased a box of crackers, some cheese and a bottle of red wine.

"For a picnic," he explained as they headed back to the bike. He smiled, and it was such a rare thing it caught her unawares.

"You should do that more often," she said as she fastened the strap of her helmet. At the question in his eyes, she said, "Smile."

His response was to frown, drawing his thick eyebrows together and darkening his face. Not for the first time she was struck by what an attractive man he was. She wasn't alone, either. In the cheese factory, Gretchen had noticed a number of women openly assessing him. Apparently they liked what they saw. For his part, Josh appeared oblivious to the attention his looks generated.

Seeing him now, wearing that well-practiced

scowl, Gretchen couldn't help it, she laughed out-right. It was all for show. Beneath that dark brood-ing exterior lay a man with a kind and generous heart. A man she was only beginning to know, yet already liked immensely.

"What?" he demanded.

"You. Let's get moving, pal. I'm hungry."

He grumbled something she couldn't hear under his breath and climbed on the Harley. Without hes-itation, she positioned herself behind him and au-tomatically locked her arms around his middle. It felt so right and natural to be close to Josh. Less than twenty-four hours earlier, she'd taken the most daring move of her life by trusting him to deliver her home safely. And trust him she did, more with each passing hour.

Josh found them a quiet corner on a secluded section of beach. The afternoon was glorious. The ocean breeze was blessedly cool and a thicket of tall grass rustled softly behind them.

They sat on the blanket, nibbling the cheese and crackers and sipping the wine from plastic glasses. After a while, replete, Gretchen lay on her back and gazed at the sky. She was amazed by how tranquil, how at peace, she felt. Stretching her arms above her, she smiled lazily. All she could hear were the waves pounding the shore and the frantic cries of gulls.

The wine seemed to have loosened her inhibitions—at least that was what Gretchen blamed for the path her thoughts traveled.

"Josh, can I ask you something?" she said.

An uncomfortable silence followed. Uncomfortable enough to cause her to turn her head and look at him. He was sitting with his arms braced behind him. "You don't want me to ask you the question?" Surely he'd want to know the question and *then* decide if he would answer it.

His frown was back, darker and more intimidating than ever. "Are you looking for me to apologize for kissing you?"

"No!" If he did, she'd be offended. Her response to his kiss had been relegated to the far reaches of her mind. She needed time to analyze what had prompted her heady reaction, but she wasn't up to a lengthy examination just yet.

"What then?" He crossed his arms.

Gretchen closed her eyes and angled her face toward the sun rather than look at him. "Never mind," she said, silently laughing at him. "It wasn't important."

"Ask me," he barked.

Gretchen rolled onto her stomach and trained her gaze on the ocean. "It has to do with Didi Wilson."

"What about her?"

Gretchen paused, unsure now she wanted to proceed, but the need burned within her, and she knew she wouldn't be completely at peace until she discovered the answer. Besides, with her unintentional lead up, she couldn't walk away from the subject gracefully. She inhaled and held her breath momentarily. "I realize it's none of my business…"

"Listen, if it has to do with Didi and Roger, I'd rather not—"

"No," she said, interrupting him. "Not them. This has to do with Didi and *you*." Her words were like a hatchet coming down on a chopping block.

His gaze pinned her. She exhaled sharply and blurted, "Have you…did you and Didi…you know…do that?" She couldn't make herself say the words. *Make love. Did you make love with Didi?* Her heart was laid open, exposed, revealing everything. Over the past six months, she'd frequently seen Didi riding through the campus on the back of Josh's Harley. Her arms had squeezed him while her ample bosom had been pressed against his back. Speculation regarding the two had been rampant on the campus for months.

Now of course she knew that Josh wasn't Didi's only love interest. But while the news of Didi and Roger had shattered Gretchen's world, if she learned that Josh had been Didi's lover, as well, she'd be devastated. She should have known better than to ask a question when she was afraid of the answer.

"I've changed my mind. I don't want to know," she said hurriedly, then leaped to her feet, kicked off her shoes and raced toward the surf. Her face burned with humiliation, but she had no one to blame but herself. She raced into the ocean, gasping at how cold it was. The surf surged against her thighs before she stopped running. Her pulse pounded in her temple.

"Gretchen!"

She heard Josh call, but she ignored him. The lunch that had made her feel so pleasantly replete now felt like a rock-hard lump in the pit of her stomach.

"Dammit, Gretchen, would you listen to me?" He stood at the water's edge, glaring at her.

"I shouldn't have asked," she said. "It was

none of my business. Please, I don't want to talk about it anymore." She pranced about in the shallows, trying to make him think she was having the time of her life.

"Dammit, Gretchen, stop that right now." It was the same tone of voice her father used to employ with her when she was a child and misbehaving. A tone full of authority she didn't challenge.

She stopped playing in the surf and faced him.

"Didi's my friend," he said. "Nothing more. Never has been and never will be. Understand?"

She nodded miserably.

Josh extended his hand to her in much the same way he had the day before when he'd invited her to climb onto the back of his motorcycle. "Come here before you're completely drenched."

The water was so cold her feet had gone numb. Mustering every shred of dignity she possessed she remained where she was, her chin angled high and proud. How desperately she longed to believe him!

"Don't make me come in after you."

"Would you?"

He didn't hesitate. "Yes, but trust me, you'd regret it."

The threat was as bold as the man himself. "Really?" She reached down and with feigned nonchalance dangled her fingers in the water.

The challenge was there, bold as ever. The confidence he'd exuded didn't waver as he lowered himself onto the hot sand and removed his boots one at a time. Then he stood and unfastened his belt.

"Josh." She watched, fascinated.

"I'm not getting these jeans wet. It's damn uncomfortable riding in wet pants." He peeled down the zipper and hooked his thumbs on the belt loops, prepared to remove both his jeans and his underwear.

"Okay, okay. You win." She raced out of the surf and onto the beach, heading for the blanket. She heard him chuckle and call her a coward as she passed him.

His taunts evolved into a sexy smile as he followed her back to the blanket. It had been a childish thing to do, she thought, to challenge him that way. Especially when the outcome had already been decided. Josh would win because he always won.

Soon they were back on the road again, breezing

down the highway, soaking up the sunshine and scenery.

The sun was just beginning to set by the time they reached Newport. Dozens of mammoth kites of various colors and designs battled the wind, rising and plummeting on the fickle fancy of the currents. Campfires flickered here and there along the beach, competing in color with the setting sun.

Gretchen was tired, more tired than she wanted to admit, even to herself. They hadn't traveled nearly as far as Josh had hoped they would, but then they'd gotten a late start and taken two hours out for a picnic lunch.

Josh parked the Harley and reached for her hand once they'd stored the helmets. "Let's get you a hotel room tonight."

She didn't miss the implication. While she was nestled up warm in a bed, he'd be sleeping on the beach. Alone and cold.

"Hey, I go where you go," she said.

His eyebrows shot up. "Is that an invitation to your bed?"

She blushed. "No."

"Pity." He grinned at her.

Josh teasing? Josh joking? His brief smile went

a long way toward lightening her spirits. "You're nothing but a big phony," she declared.

His gaze narrowed. "What do you mean?"

"Beneath that he-man exterior, you're a pussy-cat."

He shook his head. "I wouldn't count on it if I were you."

"But I already am."

Once again she found Josh grinning as he located a quiet spot on the beach, one protected from the elements, as well as the curious stares of others. Soon they had a fire of their own blazing away. While he unpacked their things, Gretchen smoothed an area of sand and spread the blanket over it. Silently they worked together, a team, then sat down in front of the fire.

"Why'd you want to get me a hotel room?" she asked. They had a perfectly good spot on the beach. The weather was great and she was as comfortable here as she'd be on any bed.

He didn't answer and Gretchen, puzzled, glanced at him. "You assumed I need to be pampered, right?" It irked her that he would think that, and her tone told him as much. People often assumed that, because her family was wealthy, she'd been spoiled and coddled. Certainly she'd been given opportunities not available to most people her age, but her parents had never overindulged her.

Josh shook his head. "When I first met you, I assumed you'd be another one of those spoiled rich kids, but you've proved otherwise."

Gretchen was pleased. Pleased enough to forget her inhibitions, lean over and kiss him. The action had been purely instinctive, without forethought.

Josh brought his head back in surprise. "What was that for?"

"To thank you for the compliment."

"I complimented you?"

Willing to admit her weariness now, Gretchen let her body rest against his, her head on his shoulder. After a time his arms circled her and she smiled, utterly content.

"Tell me about your family," she said lazily. If she hadn't been propped against him, she might not have felt the tension shoot through him. His back went rigid and his arms stiffened slightly. She'd done it again. Just when it seemed they were comfortable with each other she'd say or do something to upset the delicate balance. "Josh, I'm sorry, I didn't mean to pry. It's just that my own family is so very much a part of me."

He didn't respond for what seemed like an eternity, and when he did speak, his voice was gruff with emotion. "My mother died when I was sixteen." His hands stroked her upper arms as if he needed the reassurance of human contact.

Gretchen placed a hand over his. "I'm sorry," she whispered.

"It happens. My dad was never the same. It was as if he couldn't bear the agony of losing her and so he chose to self-destruct. He's serving time, as you know." He didn't elaborate and she didn't ask. Instead, she brought his hand to her mouth and gently laid her cheek against it.

"A lot of people wonder how I landed at Nelson Lord," he continued, his voice close to her ear. "My grandfather left me money in the form of a trust, the condition being that, if I wanted a college education, I attend his alma mater."

"Do you want a college education?"

His short laugh was without humor. "I'm there, aren't I?"

All evidence she'd seen to this point said otherwise. Josh constantly challenged authority. He appeared to go out of his way to cause trouble. Why, only the day before Josh had given Roger the incentive and opportunity to end his college career. It would be just like Roger to make whatever trouble he could for Josh and delight in it.

"Why'd you do it, then?" she asked, confused. "Why'd you slug Roger? He'll go out of his way to hurt you."

"Let him," Josh answered. "I can deal with it."

"But—"

"The bastard deserved it."

That much Gretchen agreed with. It had been all she could do not to cheer when she saw Roger's bloody nose. Especially after he'd attempted to sucker-punch Josh.

Before she allowed herself to think what she was doing, Gretchen broke away from Josh, shifted around and knelt in front of him. His questioning gaze met hers in the dim light afforded by the fire. Smiling, she placed a hand on either side of his face and leaned forward to kiss him.

The surge of desire she experienced when their lips met was enough to make her bold. She wrapped her arms around his neck as their mouths worked together in a frenzy of tongues, lips and unmistakable desire. Gretchen offered and Josh took, greedily.

Abruptly Josh jerked his mouth away from hers.

He sat back, panting, his shoulders heaving. "What was that for?" he demanded, sounding none too pleased.

Gretchen's eyes remained closed. "Don't ask. Just kiss me like that again."

"No."

"No?" Disappointed, Gretchen opened her eyes. "Why not?"

"Because you haven't a clue what you're doing." He stood, and she was pleased to note that he didn't look very steady. She felt decidedly off balance herself, but somehow it was a good feeling.

"Wipe that silly grin off your face," he muttered.

If she wasn't so happy she would have been downright insulted. He'd kissed her and it had been the most wonderful experience of her life. Josh didn't seem able to hold still. He circumnavigated the blanket three times. Gretchen was getting dizzy watching him.

Suddenly, it dawned on her, and it was all she could do to keep from giggling. "Joshua Morrow, I tempt you, don't I?"

He started to deny it and then appeared to think better of it. "I'm getting you that hotel room and

I don't want any arguments, understand?'' His voice was hard and unfriendly. ''You'll sleep alone, too.'' She wasn't sure if he was telling her this for her benefit or his.

Gretchen covered her mouth in an effort to contain a brewing fit of laughter.

''Dammit, stop looking at me like that,'' he demanded.

''Like what?''

''Like...that.'' He pointed his index finger at her and wiggled it as if at a complete loss for words.

Gretchen had never seen Josh unnerved, had never suspected she'd be one to shatter his cool. It told her that their kisses had affected him as much as they had her. She felt almost giddy with a sense of wonder and power.

''Come on,'' he ordered brusquely.

''Where are we going?''

''I told you. I'm getting you a motel room for the night.''

''Josh—''

''Don't argue with me.'' From the tight set of his mouth and his defensive stance, she wasn't inclined to do so.

''Oh, all right, but you're being ridiculous.''

She rolled her eyes, and feeling happier than she had all day, she gathered up her personal items and obediently followed Josh to the bike. They set off and didn't find a vacancy until their third stop. Although she was the one who registered, the man at the desk handed the room key to Josh. Josh hesitated before accepting it, for it seemed he didn't want the man to think he'd be spending the night with her. Apparently he changed his mind, because his hand closed over the key and he escorted her outside.

The room was small, the furniture cheap, but overall the place looked clean, despite the faint scent of mildew hanging in the air. Gretchen set the pillowcase holding her belongings on top of the bed.

Josh stood outside the room, his arms crossed in the defensive way that defied someone to even try to talk to him. She'd seen him assume that same stance at college a hundred times. The hard-edged look that said he didn't give a rip about anything or anyone, so you'd better keep your distance.

"This OK?" he asked.

"It's fine," she assured him.

"Good. I'll be going, then."

"You won't leave me, will you?" Gretchen blurted without pausing to think he might take her question differently than she intended. "In the morning," she qualified. "You'll still be here, won't you?" It wasn't the thought of him abandoning her that worried her as much as not seeing him again.

His features softened fractionally before he spoke. "I'd never do that. I said I'd deliver you to your family and I will."

"Promise?"

"Promise."

Out of gratitude, or perhaps relief, Gretchen walked across the room and hugged him. He returned the gesture with what seemed a good deal of reluctance. Once she was in his embrace, she closed her eyes, savoring the closeness.

"Good night," he whispered, and kissed the top of her head.

"Good night," she returned, stopping herself from asking a series of unnecessary questions, which would've only been an excuse to delay him. She didn't want to think of him out there alone on the beach, but she couldn't stop him, either.

After what seemed like an inordinate amount of time, they dropped their arms and stepped away from each other. "I'll stop off in the morning and shower here, if you don't mind," he said.

She nodded and clenched her hands, already missing him and he hadn't even left.

He hesitated a moment, then was gone.

Alone in her room, Gretchen was certain he'd wanted to tell her something. She'd recognized the look in his eyes. But whatever it was he'd decided to keep it to himself.

She showered, enjoying the glorious sensation of standing under the spray and letting it splash over her face. She slipped into her pajamas and used a sweater for extra warmth. Then, sitting on the bed, she watched reruns of *The Dick Van Dyke Show* and brushed her hair, or what there was of it. She wondered how long it would take her to get used to its being this short. Josh had worked miracles with the hack job she'd done to it. She sighed. For two days they'd spent nearly every minute together, and without him there to share these quiet moments, it felt as if a part of her was missing.

The sitcom ended and she was about to turn off the television and go to sleep when a loud knock sounded against her door.

Gretchen scrambled off the bed, wondering who

on earth could be coming to her room this late. "Who is it?" she called, making her voice sound strong and confident.

No response.

"I'm not opening this door until I know who's there."

Another moment passed before the answer came.

"Josh."

Chapter 4

"Josh!" Gretchen twisted the lock and threw open the door. Why was he here, especially after acting as if he couldn't be rid of her fast enough?

"Hi." He stood on the other side of the door, looking decidedly uncomfortable, as though he wasn't entirely sure himself why he was here.

"Come in." She stepped aside to let him pass, yet he made no move to venture farther than the doorway.

"I can't," he muttered. He rubbed his hand down his face and shook his head, as if to clear his thoughts.

"You wanted something?" Gretchen asked when he wasn't immediately forthcoming. She drew the sweater more tightly about her and was glad she'd thought to wear socks. Frowning, she thought she smelled beer on him.

He seemed to read her thoughts. "I figured it'd take a little fortification to say what needs to be said out here."

"It's that bad?"

"It's about what happened," he said.

"What happened?" She wasn't playing dumb. She honestly didn't know what he meant.

"Us, you know?"

It seemed difficult for him to say it.

"About us...kissing, you mean?"

"Yeah." He buried his fingers in his jean pockets, in what looked to be a painfully awkward position. His gaze stubbornly refused to meet hers.

Gretchen had never seen Josh look so self-conscious or tense. She waited, deciding to let him speak without further coaxing from her. The seconds ticked by, and still he remained silent.

At last Josh met her gaze and said, "Don't put any stock in those kisses, all right?" His words were stark and half-angry.

At first she didn't respond, but then couldn't keep from asking, "Why not?"

"Because," he said forcefully, "girls like you don't get involved with guys like me, understand?"

"Josh—"

He raised a hand, stopping her. "Let me speak. You've had a hellish couple of days—"

"But I haven't, not really, I—" His gaze narrowed at her intrusion and she shut up.

"You're no longer engaged to Junior Warbucks. You're separated from your family at a time when you need their love and support most. It's only natural for you to turn to me for comfort—natural but not advisable."

"You're making me sound like a child."

"All right, fine," he announced crisply. "I'll just say it. Listen, Gretchen, don't set your sights on me. I'm not your type."

She opened her mouth to argue that he was quite possibly *exactly* the type of man she could love, but he stopped her once again, yanking the rug out from under her feet.

"You're not my type, either!" he growled. "I can't say it any plainer than that, can I?"

His words smarted and she instinctively jerked

back, as if she'd taken a punch in the solar plexus
and had the wind knocked out of her. Every breath
brought her pain.

"I don't mean to hurt your feelings," he said.
"You're a sweet kid, but it's best to get this out
in the open before you end up getting hurt."

He thought of her as a kid! Worse, a sweet kid!
He made her sound like she was in pigtails, skip-
ping down the beach licking a rainbow lollipop.

"I don't want there to be any misunderstanding
between us," he continued. "I'll deliver you to
your family and that'll be the end of it. So don't
be putting any credence in that kiss. It should
never have happened—but I blame myself. Rest
assured nothing like that'll happen again."

"That was what you wanted to say?" she asked
as though exceedingly bored. She wrapped her
dignity about her as tightly as she had the sweater.

His eyes registered his surprise at her easy acceptance. "Yeah."

"Fine, then, you've said it."

He blinked once. No doubt he'd anticipated an
argument. Well, she wasn't about to give him one.
If that was the way he felt, she wasn't going to
force herself on him. After all, she had her pride,
a thin layer, which was about all she'd managed

to salvage after Roger. What little remained she was determined to guard very carefully.

"If you don't have anything more to say, I'd like to go to bed." She forced a loud yawn. She'd go to bed, all right, but she knew it'd be one hell of a long time before she slept.

Josh turned abruptly and walked away.

Gretchen shut the door, closed her eyes and pressed her forehead against the cool wood. Her heart was heavy. Really, she had no choice but to accept him at his word. But he hadn't fooled her. He was interested in her. Very interested.

Her fingers investigated her short locks of hair as she climbed into bed. She lay there a good long time before she reached for the nightstand and turned out the light.

In the morning they were overly polite with each other, behaving like awkward strangers with nothing in common and little to say. They got an early start, hitting the road shortly after seven, fortified only with coffee. Neither was hungry. If they rode hard, didn't take much time for stops, they'd reach San Francisco by evening, Josh told her. The minute they were on the highway, Gretchen could see that her escort was determined to be rid of her that day. He set a killing pace.

She sat stiffly behind him as they roared down the highway, doing her best to avoid touching him. He, too, was avoiding her. Unlike the previous day when he'd stopped every few miles to admire the view to give her the opportunity to talk, he pressed on with punishing determination.

When he did finally pull off the highway, it was to gas up. Although she didn't complain, Gretchen's entire body ached, especially her back.

He gingerly climbed off the Harley while she slowly eased herself from the seat and headed into the small mom-and-pop grocery for something to drink.

"Do you want anything?" she asked, making sure she sounded friendly yet reserved.

"Nothing." Then, as if in afterthought, he added, "Thanks."

Muttering under her breath, Gretchen walked into the store. After checking to be sure Josh couldn't see her, she rubbed some of the soreness from her buttocks and the small of her back. She stopped when she discovered the elderly male clerk eyeing her with appreciative interest. He had the good grace to look embarrassed when she glared back at him.

Doing her best to walk normally, Gretchen

made her way to the rest room, then stopped at the refrigeration unit, slid open the glass door and reached for a bottle of spring water. Her mouth was dry, her body was sore and miserable, and her heart was heavy. Not a good way to start the day.

As she stood in line to pay for her purchase, she noted the flashing red and blue lights of a police cruiser.

''What's going on?'' she asked the man at the counter.

The clerk craned his neck to see out the grimy window. ''Looks like they're arresting some young fellow. He damn well better pay for his gas before they haul him away. Otherwise I'm gonna confiscate his Harley.''

''His Harley?'' Gretchen repeated. Her heart, which had felt sluggish and lackadaisical only seconds earlier, shot into overdrive. The police were arresting Josh! Leaving her purchase on the counter, she raced out the door half a second in front of the clerk.

It was worse than she'd feared. Josh had his arms handcuffed behind his back and was being pushed toward the cruiser. Even from a distance of ten feet she could feel the anger emanating from him. His eyes were wild and his jaw so tight his face had gone white.

"What's going on here?" she demanded, outraged on Josh's behalf and not afraid to let it show.

The officer barely glanced her way. "Do you know this man?"

"I most certainly do." Gretchen's hands flew to her hips and she braced her feet, prepared to do battle. "Why is he handcuffed?"

The officer spoke without emotion. "He matches the description of a robbery suspect—age, height, clothes. Motorcycle." The officer met her eyes, silently daring her to challenge him.

Gretchen didn't doubt the patrolman would welcome an excuse to haul her away, too, but she refused to give him one. Josh needed her free.

"There's probable cause. I'm arresting him." The officer resumed shoving Josh toward the patrol car.

"What about his rights?" Gretchen cried, desperately trying to find an excuse to delay him.

"I read him his rights."

"Gretchen." Josh furiously whispered her name under his breath in warning.

"He has a right to an attorney." She looked to the clerk for confirmation.

"He owes me eight bucks for gas," the man said.

"I'll pay for the stupid gas!" Gretchen's heart hammered as she paced in front of the police officer. Josh was now sitting in the patrol car, his eyes closed as if he was mentally removing himself from the ugly scene.

"Do you have a license to drive that bike?" the patrolman asked her.

She glanced over her shoulder at the Harley. Josh's pride and joy. The symbol of his rebellion. "Yes, I've got a license," she lied, knowing that if she didn't, the police would impound it. Heaven only knew how long it'd be before Josh got it back, and she couldn't risk that.

"You'll take care of it then?"

Although she knew it was hopeless to protest, she did, anyway. "Look. Josh didn't commit a robbery. He was with me all morning. We left Newport Beach at seven. You can call the motel and they'll verify..." She trailed off, remembering that she was the one who'd registered for the room, not Josh. He hadn't spent the night with her. She couldn't account for his whereabouts every minute of the night. But in her heart, she knew Josh would never rob anyone.

"Leave it," Josh said, his voice low and tight, sharpened with frustration.

Gretchen clenched her hands into fists, finding it impossible to stand by and do nothing. She was the only one who appreciated how humiliating this was for him. How difficult. The pain in his eyes when he'd told her about his father in prison haunted her. Now to face jail himself for something he couldn't have done, wouldn't have done.

"Please," she whispered, feeling helpless and small. She wasn't even sure who she was asking for help.

"We were in Newport Beach last night," she said so fast the words ran together. She was willing to say anything, do anything, that would convince the officer he had the wrong man.

A sly smile lit up the patrolman's face. "Yes, I know."

Gretchen clamped her mouth shut, determined not to offer any more unsolicited information. She wanted to help, not hurt, Josh's cause. Her chest tightened painfully and she found it impossible to stand still. Nor could she seem to control her arms, which roved from her head to her sides and back again.

The patrolman opened the driver's side and

climbed into the vehicle. Gretchen planted her palms against the passenger window. "Josh!" she cried, wanting somehow to reassure him.

He turned his head toward her. Afraid she was about to erupt into sobs, Gretchen covered her mouth with her hand. Josh's eyes steadily held hers, and then he smiled. Through his anger, frustration and humiliation, he'd reached out to her. *He* was the one reassuring *her*.

Gretchen bit into her lower lip so hard she tasted blood.

"Miss, miss." The clerk took hold of her shoulders and pulled her away from the cruiser. She stood back helplessly as Josh was driven away, her gaze following the car until it was no longer in sight.

The clerk waited an impatient moment while she composed herself, then asked, "You going to pay for that gas or not?"

"Yes," she murmured, and stepped back into the store.

When she was back outside, she crossed to the Harley, donned Josh's leather jacket, dark glasses and helmet and swung one leg over the seat, pretending she knew what she was doing. Not only did she not have a license, she hadn't so much as twisted the key in the ignition. She felt like weeping.

Dragging in a deep breath, she squared her shoulders and decided then and there she would find a way not only to start the bike, but ride it. She had to do it for Josh.

He'd been there for her when she'd needed him, hadn't he? He'd taught her so much about herself in the past couple of days. She'd felt helpless and lost when they'd started out together. But he'd believed in her, restored her faith in herself. She wasn't going to let him down.

The bike felt enormous between her legs, a monster ready to overpower her. Gretchen's grip tightened on the handlebars. She refused to give in to anxiety. Refused to be intimidated.

It shouldn't be that difficult, she realized, forcing herself to think positively. After all, she'd watched Josh start the thing any number of times.

She twisted the key.

The engine didn't catch.

She tried a second and a third time with no results.

Breathing hard, she closed her eyes and reminded herself of everything that was at stake.

One more time, she decided, and this time, by heaven, the bike would start.

She turned the key. When the spark caught and the engine roared, the Harley vibrated with such force it nearly toppled her.

Releasing a shout of triumph, Gretchen thrust her arms into the air, feeling like an Olympic champion. She glanced over her shoulder to be sure the road was clear, then headed down the highway and into town.

It surprised her with what ease she drove the Harley. Anyone looking at her dressed as she was would assume she was a motorcycle mama. Let them! One thing was certain—she wasn't about to let anyone or anything intimidate her again.

For another, her father and brother were going to hear about this. Two of San Francisco's finest attorneys would make mincemeat of the charge against Josh. By the time the dust had settled, Josh Morrow would own this piss-ant town.

Rejuvenated, fire in her blood, Gretchen parked the Harley in the county courthouse lot. Head high and shoulders squared, she was determined to make an entrance that rivaled John Wayne in his finest.

"I'd like to see Judge Joseph Logan," she announced to the receptionist. Gretchen didn't have a clue who Judge Logan was, but if he insisted on having his name listed in the front of the courthouse, then he should expect to take appointments.

"I'm sorry, but Judge Logan died fifty years ago," the receptionist replied in a polished businesslike tone without cracking a smile. "We named the courthouse after him."

"Oh. Then who else is there?" Gretchen demanded, although much of the steam of her bravado had evaporated.

The woman looked sympathetic. "No one, I'm afraid."

"Ok. I guess what I really need is a good attorney."

The receptionist's face brightened. "I can help you with that. Janet Mercer's office is across the street. You tell her Maggie sent you, OK? Whatever's the problem, Janet can help you."

Gretchen was so grateful she could've hugged the receptionist. "Thank you," she said.

"No problem. Listen, I hope everything works out."

Heeding the woman's generous advice, Gretchen hurried across the street and found Janet

Mercer's name listed, along with three others, on the door outside a small brick office complex.

Apparently Janet didn't have a large enough clientele to warrant a secretary. Her office was simply a single room, with a desk, computer and one guest chair. A woman who didn't look much older than Gretchen glanced up when she entered the room.

"Hello," she greeted cheerfully. "I'm Janet Mercer. Can I help you?"

"Yes." At last. Without waiting for an invitation, Gretchen lowered herself into the guest chair. She spoke nonstop for five minutes, hardly pausing long enough to breathe. She told Janet everything.

"They took him to the jail?" Janet asked.

"That's right," Gretchen said, and nodded for emphasis.

"Well, in that case, I better get over there." She stood and reached for her purse.

The attorney led the way to the jail, asking a question now and then as they moved along the flower-lined sidewalk. Gretchen found the woman so warm and personable she wondered if the receptionist had steered her wrong. What she needed was a legal warrior who would fight for Josh, not a Mother Teresa!

Janet soon proved she was everything Josh needed. The mild-mannered attorney turned into a tigress the moment they entered the jailhouse. She announced herself as Josh Morrow's attorney, and as for Officer O'Malley's "probable cause" she laughed in the man's face.

Gretchen attempted to follow Janet into the interview room where Josh was being questioned, but was barred. With nothing else to do, Gretchen sat with her hands tucked under her thighs in a small waiting area, while Janet did battle alone.

A couple of times Gretchen thought she heard raised voices, but she wasn't able to make out the words or know who was speaking. About ten minutes later the door opened and Josh walked out of the room, freed from the handcuffs and rubbing his wrists.

Gretchen leaped to her feet, restraining herself from rushing forward.

Josh stopped when he saw her. And grinned. It was the biggest, most beautiful smile she'd ever seen. She felt her own mouth relax into one, too, and the next thing she knew they were hurrying toward each other.

She closed her eyes as Josh swept her into his arms. His hug was fierce. Speechless, they clung to each other as if they never intended to let go.

"Okay, you lovebirds," someone said gruffly from behind Josh. "Move it out, will ya? The last thing anyone wants to see around here is a little happiness. We don't know how to handle it." The officer chuckled.

Reluctantly Josh released her. Gretchen lowered her feet to the floor and smiled up at him, battling back emotion.

"Where's the Harley?" Josh asked, looping his arm around her shoulders.

"Where I parked it outside," she told him with more than a hint of pride.

"You rode it into town?"

"Yup. Ten miles over the speed limit, too. I was in a hurry."

Josh stared down at her and scratched his head. "I don't believe it."

"Believe it."

"All by yourself?"

"Yup."

"Clearly I underestimated you."

Gretchen grinned. "It would seem so."

Janet appeared. "You're free to go," she announced.

"He is?" Gretchen couldn't keep the delight out of her voice.

Janet nodded and strutted across the room like a peacock with feathers in full display. She was obviously very pleased with herself. "This calls for a celebration," she said. "I don't suppose you two have had lunch yet, have you?"

Josh looked at Gretchen. "As a matter of fact, we haven't had breakfast."

"Great. Then you'll be good and hungry. Lunch is on me."

Josh started to protest, but Janet stopped him, chuckling softly. "Don't worry about it. I'll just add it to your bill."

Gretchen wasn't sure where they were headed, but they laughed and joked like old friends as they walked outside. Janet led them to an outdoor barbecue place two blocks away. The aroma of pungent sauce, alder smoke and sizzling meat made Gretchen's empty stomach growl. She planted her hand over it, hoping to still the rumbling.

Josh glanced down on her and reached for her hand, lacing their fingers together. "I'm sorry," he said softly. They stood in front of the large printed menu posted on one side of the red building. Picnic tables in bright primary colors dotted the grassy area.

"For what?" Gretchen asked.

"Last night," he answered, keeping his gaze trained on the menu.

"Oh." Why he'd chosen now of all times to tell her she'd never know. Then again, maybe she did. By apologizing within Janet's hearing, she, Gretchen, couldn't very well question what had prompted his visit late last night. Or why he'd lied. And she knew he had, for the way he'd held her when he'd been released from custody, the way he'd pressed her close to his heart, contradicted everything he'd said.

They each ordered the barbecued-pork sandwich, with baked beans and corn bread. "This isn't the fanciest place in town," Janet said, "but I have my reasons for choosing it."

"What are they?" Gretchen asked.

"You'll see soon enough."

She was right. Halfway through their lunch several patrol cars arrived.

"I'd say those reasons are here," Josh said, then licked his fingers clean of barbecue sauce.

The attorney chuckled again. "Okay, so I like

to gloat now and again. It serves old O'Malley right. He hauled Josh in just so he could look good for Chief Davidson. I know his tricks, and I consider it my duty to make sure everyone else knows them, too.''

''You enjoy living on the edge, do you?'' Josh teased.

''Wouldn't have it any other way.''

Gretchen noticed how their newfound friend's gaze zeroed in on one particular officer. She recognized the longing in the other woman's expression; she'd felt the same thing herself in the past couple of days. Janet dragged her eyes back to her lunch with a resignation Gretchen could almost feel. Whereas the young attorney had been happy and animated moments earlier, she grew suspiciously quiet now.

''Someone you know?'' Gretchen asked, motioning with her head toward the tall athletic-looking officer.

''Yeah, I know him.'' Janet pushed aside what was left of her lunch. ''His name's Gary Foreman. Unfortunately we don't see eye to eye on a number of important issues and—''

''You like him, though, don't you?'' Gretchen asked. ''You like him quite a lot.''

Janet's face tightened "Does it show that much?"

"Yeah, it does."

"Oh, dear." Janet lowered her gaze. "We're constantly at odds with each other. At one time...well, never mind, it isn't important now. He's very good at his job and unfortunately so am I."

Gretchen stood, reached for her empty paper plate and Janet's almost full one. She walked over to the Dumpster and deposited them both there. On the return trip, she routed herself past the table where Gary sat alone, his back to Janet.

Boldly she slipped onto the bench opposite him. She'd say one thing for the attorney—she had excellent taste. Gary Foreman was exceptionally good-looking.

"Hello," she said, planting her elbows on the picnic table and cupping her face with her hands.

"Hi." He sounded hesitant, suspicious.

"I don't mean to butt into your private life, but how do you feel about Janet Mercer?"

Gary frowned, his thick dark brows drawing together. "Who the hell are you?" he asked, instead of replying.

She had his attention, Gretchen noted, and from

the quickly fired anger of his response, she also had her answer.

"Gretchen Wise. Janet's wonderful, you know."

Gary didn't respond.

"Don't you agree?" she pressed.

His frown deepened and she could see he wasn't keen on answering her questions. "Maybe I do and maybe I don't."

Gretchen laughed. "Oh, come on. Don't be coy."

"Listen, whoever you are—"

"Gretchen."

"Would you mind moving on? I've got thirty minutes to eat my lunch, and I don't want to squander it talking to you."

"Sure, no problem." She sighed expressively and happened to glance up in time to see Josh. He looked none too pleased with her. She smiled and waved to him. "Janet's crazy about you. I wasn't sure if you knew."

Gary's startled look clashed with hers. "You're sure about this?"

"Positive."

He didn't answer.

"It seems to me you and Janet have a lot more

in common than you give yourself credit for. If you worked together, perhaps you could find a way to make the system work better for you both." Having said her piece, she stood. "Listen, it was great chatting with you. I wish you the best of luck, even if you're silly enough to let a wonderful woman like Janet slip away."

She left him and walked back to the picnic table where Josh and Janet waited.

"What was that all about?" Josh demanded.

"Nothing important," she said, and winked at Janet.

Gary glanced over his shoulder, and Gretchen wiggled her fingers at him and sent him a bold smile.

"I think it's time we left," Josh said.

"I think so, too," Gretchen agreed.

They thanked Janet, and Josh wrote down an address where she could send him a bill. As they walked away, Josh started hammering Gretchen with questions. "What the hell prompted you to do that?" he demanded. "You don't even know the guy."

"Shh." Gretchen walked across the street and pulled him behind a huge fir tree. "Tell me what's happening back there."

Josh rolled his eyes.

"Josh, I'm serious."

"All right, all right. Gary's walking over to Janet's table."

"Great. Are they talking?"

"It looks that way."

"Hot damn!" She'd never done anything as bold or as crazy in all her twenty-two years.

"Well, I'll be," Josh muttered.

"What? Tell me!" Gretchen didn't want either of them to know she was watching.

"Janet just tossed my address in the garbage."

So Janet appreciated her little conversation with Officer Foreman. "Let's get out of here before someone else finds an excuse to arrest you."

"My sentiments exactly," Josh said. "Now, where did you say my bike was?"

"I parked it in front of the courthouse," she told him.

"I can't get over you driving the Harley," he said, and linked his fingers with hers.

"I couldn't very well leave it at the gas station, could I?" She reached into her jeans pocket and retrieved the key.

Josh walked across the street and stroked the motorcycle the way a man might touch the woman he loves and hasn't seen in far too long. He eased himself into the seat, inserted the key into the ignition and gave it a twist.

Nothing. Not even a cough.

He glared at Gretchen. ''What the hell did you do?''

Chapter 5

Josh was furious. He seemed to be accusing her of some unspeakable crime against his beloved Harley. "This is a delicate machine. You know next to nothing about an XLH."

"What the hell did I do?" she repeated with dead calm. "Let me see," she said, playing dumb and striking a thoughtful pose. She tapped her index finger against her cheek as she mulled over what terrible abuse she might have inadvertently heaped on his most cherished possession.

"You must have done something!"

That did it. Gretchen's temper had never been

explosive, but she'd had it. His accusation detonated her anger to such a degree she could feel her pulse pound like a hammer against an anvil in her temples. Her fists knotted into tight balls at her sides.

"Sure I did!" she shouted. "First of all I saved your precious Harley from being impounded. Then I made a raging idiot of myself in the courthouse, demanding to see a judge who's spent the past fifty years pushing up marigolds." She pointed at the building, in case he didn't appreciate her sacrifice, which clearly he didn't. "Then I found you the best attorney in three counties to get your sorry butt out of jail. And that's just for starters."

He tried to speak, but she wouldn't let him.

"Tell me, Josh, what have I gotten in exchange?"

"You shouldn't have done it."

"What? Ride your precious bike?"

"No, gotten involved."

"You honestly think I should have left you there?" He was being ridiculous.

Josh didn't hesitate. "Yeah, that's what I think. I told you before and I meant it."

"I heard you the first time—I'm not your type."

He was purposely picking a fight with her, and she

couldn't understand it. Minutes earlier they'd been joking and having fun. He'd hugged her as if she held the key to his sanity.

"The last thing I need is some society girl fawning all over me," he grumbled.

His words stung. "OK," she said. "If that's the way you feel, then I think it'd be best if we each went our separate ways. I'll find my own way home from here. Thanks all the same." Gretchen whirled around and started walking.

She was half a block away when he called after her, "I promised I'd get you to San Francisco and I don't make promises lightly."

Nonchalantly turning around, she waved an imaginary magic wand. "I hereby absolve you of your promise. You're free to go."

"I won't chase after you, Gretchen." His eyes were hard, his jaw tight and stubborn, and she couldn't doubt he meant what he said.

"I wouldn't want you to." With her back to him once again, she continued walking as if she was strolling through a meadow filled with wildflowers and hadn't a care in the world. Her pride got her as far as the city park, all of five blocks from the courthouse. By that time the sick feeling in the pit of her stomach had overtaken her. The knot in her throat had grown so tight it was all she could do to keep from weeping.

She found a picnic table and sat on the top with her feet resting on the bench. She reviewed her options. Normally, in volatile situations she was the one with a cool head. This simply wasn't like her. Her ability to remain calm in difficult situations had been one of her strengths as student-body president.

She emptied her lungs in a ragged breath and attempted to clear her mind. A pay phone near the refreshment stand in the center of the park appeared to be her only option. Her parents were due back in San Francisco that day, but she didn't know what time their flight arrived. If she called them collect, they could wire her the funds to see her home. But worrying them was the last thing she wanted to do. The minute they learned of her plight, her mother was sure to panic. Her father wouldn't be much better.

Three days after her college graduation and she was on the street, no better off than a bag lady. Jeez, worse than a bag lady. Everything she'd brought with her was stuffed in a pillowcase packed on Josh's Harley. She didn't so much as have identification with her.

She covered her face with both hands, questioning how she could have done anything as stupid as walk away from her purse, all her funds and clothes, and any chance she had of helping herself.

Janet Mercer would help her, Gretchen realized, but she'd feel foolish asking, after rushing in and extolling Josh's virtues to the attorney earlier. Well, she had no one to blame but herself. She'd gotten herself into this ridiculous mess, and by heaven, she'd get herself out. One way or another.

The thought had no more filtered through her mind when she heard the distinctive sound of a motorcycle. Her heart reacted with a wild surge of hope, but that quickly died. Josh had made a point of telling her he wouldn't chase after her, and she didn't doubt for an instant that he meant it.

Nevertheless it was Josh who slowly cruised past the park, his eyes searching the grounds. The temptation to raise her arm and wave him down was strong, but that thin layer of pride dictated she do nothing. If he was really searching for her, he'd see her. Still, she had to practically sit on her hands to keep from flagging him down.

Josh saw her, Gretchen was certain, and she tilted her head away, hoping to give the impression of royalty assessing her surroundings. But he didn't stop. Instead, he drove on past.

Perhaps he was expecting her to come rushing after him and beg him to take her home. Squeezing her eyes closed, she swallowed her disappointment. Josh Morrow's pride was legendary; he'd stood up to Dean Williams and hadn't flinched. He'd have no problem walking away from her.

Just when she was ready to swallow her dignity and go to Janet for help, she heard the motorcycle a second time. Her heart raced as she watched Josh approach. Straightening her spine, she sat up, refusing to allow him to see how distressed she actually was.

He pulled into an empty parking slot at the tree-lined curb and turned off the engine. He took his own sweet time removing his helmet and climbing off the bike. Fascinated, she watched how every movement he made seemed to be in slow motion. Not until he opened a saddlebag did she realize the reason he'd come back. At least he had the decency to return her belongings.

He approached her with all the enthusiasm of a man walking toward the electric chair. He could have been a robot for all the emotion he expressed. His gaze was as hard and unreadable as when she'd left him in front of the courthouse. Wordlessly he set the pillowcase on the picnic table beside her.

"Thank you," she mumbled. She bit her lower lip to keep from saying more.

"It was the electrical connector," Josh told her. "It'd vibrated loose."

She wanted to ask him if she'd somehow been responsible for that, but resisted. Most likely he'd be quick to blame her if she was, and reluctant to admit otherwise if not. His hesitation told her what she wanted to know.

The words hung between them like a thick London fog.

He glanced over his shoulder at the Harley as if eager to depart. Then he studied her for a moment. Was he assessing the damage his carelessly flung accusations had done? At last he said, "I meant what I said. I won't beg you to come with me."

"I know."

He cracked a smile, not one of amusement, but one tempered with chagrin. "You can be stubborn."

He hadn't seen the half of it.

He continued to study her, then his eyes softened. "Goodbye, Gretchen."

He started back to his Harley and Gretchen wound the pillowcase around her hand. "Josh!" she cried, leaping off the table and standing, her spine stiff and proud.

He turned back to face her.

She wasn't sure what she wanted to say. Even if she had known, she wasn't sure the words could have squeezed past the thickness in her throat. Earlier he'd clung to her and now he was walking away from her and showing no regret. Worse, she was letting him.

"Yes?" he said.

She bit her lip and shook her head . "Nothing."

His shoulders momentarily stiffened and then just as quickly sagged in defeat. "Gretchen, listen—"

"I'm not a society girl." Of all the ridiculous things he'd said to her, that one hurt the most. She shook her head and then said what was on her mind. "Why do you want to argue with me? Do I scare you that much?" Her gaze didn't budge from his. They'd come this far and she wasn't about to lose him now. Her heartbeat felt like a crash of cymbals inside her chest. She read the confusion in Josh's eyes, the restraint.

"Yeah, I guess you do," he admitted reluctantly. Then he held out his hand to her. "Come on, it's time we got back on the road."

"You're sure you want my company?"

He stepped forward and tenderly cupped her cheek. When he spoke again, his voice was low and gravelly. "Yeah, I'm sure."

She rewarded his honesty with a fierce hug. She was giddy with happiness.

When she climbed onto the Harley behind him, her arms wrapped around his middle. He placed his palm over her fingers and squeezed them.

When he turned the key in the ignition, the bike quickly roared to life.

As they pulled back onto the highway, she tried to analyze what had just happened.

With the wind pummeling her from all sides, and the sun beating down on her head, Gretchen kept her eyes trained on the passing scenery and her thoughts focused on the events of the past several days. Josh cared about her. He didn't like it, but he cared. She cared about him, too. So much that it sometimes hurt. She'd cared about Roger, too.

It troubled her that she hadn't recognized the kind of man Roger was sooner. The signs had been there. His lack of attention. His unexplained absences. The careless, almost lackadaisical attitude toward their meeting times. His frequent excuses.

She'd been blind to it all. Often she'd even been grateful when he arrived late, because she herself had been so busy. Her duties on the student council had demanded a great deal of time and effort, never mind her studies.

Then there was the matter of their parents. Roger's mother in particular. Stella Lockheart had done everything she could to encourage the romance, done everything she could to make matters easy for the two of them. Gretchen's parents had met Roger's, and the two couples had gotten along famously.

Another thing, Gretchen realized with new insight, was her complete unwillingness to become physically involved with Roger before they'd spoken their vows. While she believed strongly in the importance of waiting until after the wedding, it shouldn't have been that easy. They were two healthy young adults who were supposed to have been deeply in love.

If she'd been engaged to Josh, the physical temptations would have been far more difficult to withstand. She sighed at the thought.

Josh slowed the Harley, and Gretchen realized

they were stopping at the border between Oregon and California. The uniformed officer at the checkpoint asked them a few simple questions about transporting fruit before waving them through.

California. She smiled, knowing she was close to home. But she felt sad, too, for her wild adventure with Josh would soon be over.

At six they stopped for dinner, splurging on seafood at a glass-walled restaurant overlooking the Pacific. Although the view was breathtaking, Gretchen found her attention focused on Josh. She saw him in a fresh light. Not as the rebellious bad boy who went out of his way to challenge authority, but a man who welcomed the chance to prove himself. A man, filled with potential and intelligence, fighting his past, struggling to discover who he was and forge a promising future.

"Have you decided what you'd like to order?" he asked as he set aside the menu.

"Yes." She smiled at him.

The waitress appeared and Josh ordered the blackened salmon while she opted for crab Louie. Neither she nor Josh seemed to have much to say, but Gretchen was deeply aware of how much her heart was involved with him.

He held her hand, lacing their fingers in the middle of the table, until their dinners arrived. Although it'd been many hours since lunch, neither was particularly hungry. Gretchen managed to finish the crab and the hard-boiled egg, but the lettuce and olives remained untouched.

"Too bad they don't need a dishwasher," she said, reminding him of yesterday morning in Cannon Beach.

He grinned. "Or a waitress."

"Oh, I think they'd be grateful I'm not waiting tables."

Their eyes melded with their smiles.

"I suppose we should get back on the road," he said.

Gretchen wished they could have lingered, but knew it was best they press on. Unless they had to stop for gas, their next stop would be San Francisco and her family home. Gretchen nearly laughed aloud at the thought of introducing Josh to her family. Her parents wouldn't know what to think when they met him. Josh with his Harley and that chip on his shoulder. The last time she'd talked to her parents she'd been engaged to Roger.

When at last they rolled into the City by the Bay, it was after ten o'clock. Night had long settled, and the stars twinkled like fairy dust against the black velvet sky. It took another forty-five minutes to reach Daley City and her family home. As Josh parked the Harley in front of the curb, Gretchen removed her helmet and glanced toward the wide front porch of the three-story structure. Her parents had had the turn-of-the-century house extensively remodeled several years back by one of the city's most renowned architects. The renovation had enhanced the beauty, grace and flavor of a bygone era.

"Nice place," Josh said.

"I've always loved it."

"How long have you lived here?" He glanced around the upscale neighborhood.

"How long?" she asked, surprised by his question. "All my life."

He glanced at her and announced, in an aloof tone, "In my entire life, I've never lived anywhere longer than twelve months. I wouldn't know what to call home."

"It's where your heart is, Josh," she told him, repeating the adage.

He got off the Harley and opened one saddle-bag, then handed her the well-used pillowcase. It took her a moment to realize he had no intention of going inside with her and meeting her parents.

"Josh, what are you doing?" she asked. "You're coming in! You must."

He shook his head. "I don't think that's such a good idea."

"But my parents are going to want to thank you for helping me." She touched his arm. "I insist."

"Your parents will take one look at me and call the cops. I've had all I can handle with law enforcement for one day."

"Don't be ridiculous. Mom'll want you to spend the night. You can have your choice of bedrooms here."

"Yeah, right, Gretchen. You don't seriously believe your family's going to throw open their arms and welcome me, do you? That'll be the day."

"Would you kindly stop? You're going to meet my parents, and that's all there is to it."

Any further argument he might have offered was cut short when the front door of the house swung open and her father appeared on the front porch.

"Daddy!" Gretchen cried, and raced toward him.

Her mother wasn't far behind.

"Gretchen Marie, where in the love of heaven have you been?" Her mother all but broke into sobs of relief. Her recovery was quick, however, when she got close enough to get a good look at Gretchen. She gasped and covered her mouth. "Good grief, what have you done to your hair? Oh, my, your beautiful hair."

Gretchen had more things to concern herself with than her hair. She broke out of her father's embrace and raced back out to the curb to grab Josh's hand. She hauled him up to the front door. "Mom and Dad, this is Josh Morrow."

"Josh." Her father hesitated and then extended his hand. The two men shook.

"Mrs. Wise," Josh said, nodding stiffly to her mother. He stepped back a pace, indicating his desire to leave.

"I think it might be best if we talked inside, don't you, Mom? Dad?" Gretchen said.

"Of course," her father replied, eyeing Josh. "There appears to be a number of questions that need to be answered, and I don't think the front steps are the place to do it."

Josh didn't show any enthusiasm for going inside, but still he complied.

Gretchen watched his face when he walked through the front door and was greeted by polished woodwork done by some of the finest craftsmen at the turn of the century. The oak walls were adorned with several family portraits and some valuable artwork her mother had collected from around the globe. The stairway curved gracefully up to the second floor.

"Perhaps we'd best talk in the kitchen," Joan Wise said, leading the way through the oak archway. "I'll put on a pot of coffee and we can discuss this like four reasonable adults."

"Mother?" Gretchen asked, wondering what had prompted such a strange statement.

"You've given your mother and me quite a scare, young lady," her father said sternly.

Instinctively Gretchen moved closer to Josh. Not because she feared her parents' wrath, but because it appeared they intended to heap blame on his shoulders. She wouldn't allow it.

Before she could respond, Josh said, "Mr. and Mrs. Wise, Gretchen has done nothing wrong."

"We'd like to hear what she has to say for herself before we make any judgments." Her father, the attorney, was at his legal best.

"Who have you been talking to?" Gretchen demanded while her mother fussed with the coffeepot, spilling grounds across the counter because her hand was shaking so badly. Something was very wrong.

The four sat at the round table in an alcove off the kitchen. Gretchen reached for Josh's hand, making sure her parents realized she was allied with him. She wished now that they'd stopped and freshened up before pressing on to her family home. The day on the road had been brutal and they were both badly in need of a shower and rest.

"Stella Lockheart phoned…"

Ah. Roger's mother. "I can just imagine what she had to say," Gretchen said indignantly.

"Only the truth, Gretchen," her father said. "You ran off with another man." His gaze rested pointedly on Josh.

"Dad!"

Josh said nothing, but a shutter seemed to fall over his eyes.

"Stella said she felt Roger had no choice but to call off the wedding, and frankly, Gretchen, I couldn't agree more," her mother said, her voice quivering. "How could you have done that to such a fine young man? From what his mother said, he's fit to be tied. Hasn't eaten in days and blames himself."

As well he should!

"His father told us he's going to have to send Roger to a counselor." This came from her father.

How eager her parents seemed to blame her! She didn't think she'd ever felt so disappointed.

"Do you have anything to say for yourself?" her father demanded.

"You bet I do!" she cried, so angry she couldn't sit still any longer. "Counseling is exactly what Roger needs. I can't believe that the Lockhearts told you such a cockamamie story. I find it downright insulting that you'd believe them."

Raising her voice was out of character, enough to garner her parents' full attention. "What you heard doesn't even faintly resemble the truth."

"Tell us your version, then," her mother suggested, calmer now.

"*My version?* What I'm going to tell you is the truth." Gretchen didn't leave room for any misunderstanding. "You're both looking at Josh and me as if we did something terrible. I'll have you know if it hadn't been for Josh, I don't know what I would have done. I owe him more than I can ever possibly repay."

"What about the money we've sunk into this wedding, young lady?" her father asked.

"While I realize you've gone to considerable expense, I'm not willing to throw away my life and marry the wrong man. If that concerns you so much, Dad, I'll repay you myself."

"George, please," her mother said softly, and pressed her hand over her husband's. "Let Gretchen finish. I'm sure there's a logical explanation for everything."

"I don't suppose Mrs. Lockheart told you that Roger was with...that Roger slept with another woman the night before our graduation."

Her mother gasped and her father frowned.

"That wasn't the first time it'd happened, either," she added.

"Who told you this?" her father wanted to know.

"The other woman," Gretchen said, "and when I confronted Roger, he admitted it. Later I learned that she's pregnant."

"I thought there must be something more to this than what Stella Lockheart told us," Gretchen's mother said, sounding mollified. She tapped her index finger against the table, keeping time with the grandfather clock in the formal living room.

"Why didn't you *fly* home?" George Wise asked. He glanced toward Josh, and while he didn't say anything, his look indicated his disapproval.

"Because Roger's mother had my airline ticket."

"She wouldn't let you have it?"

Gretchen hesitated. "I...I didn't ask."

"Why in heaven's name didn't you?" her father barked. "Instead, you impulsively took off with a member of Hell's Angels and worried your mother and me half to death."

"I won't have you talk about Josh that way," Gretchen said angrily. She knew that her parents discounted Josh only because they didn't like the way he cut his hair and the fact he rode a motorcycle. "I don't know what I would have done without him."

Josh glanced at Gretchen and smiled apologetically, then scooted back his chair and stood. "Mr. and Mrs. Wise, it was a pleasure to meet you, but I don't believe my presence here is necessary, nor am I particularly welcome."

For one wild moment Gretchen was struck dumb. "No!" she cried when she found her voice. "I won't let you leave."

His eyes met hers. In that brief moment, she realized that nothing she could say or do would

change his mind. He'd seen and heard all he
needed to be convinced he didn't belong and never
would.

"Mr. and Mrs. Wise," he said, "forgive me. I
don't mean any disrespect." Then he reached for
Gretchen, catching her about the waist and hauling
her into his arms. His kiss was almost brutal.
"Goodbye, Gretchen," he whispered when he'd
finished.

Her mother gasped and her father's mouth fell
open in shock.

Gretchen was left speechless, stunned when
Josh hastily broke away and headed for the front
door.

"You aren't going to let him walk out of here,
are you?" Gretchen said to her parents, pointing
at Josh's retreating back.

Looking uncomfortable, her father cleared his
throat. "Frankly, yes, I think his decision to leave
is very perceptive of him."

Gretchen stared at her father and said, "Then
I'm leaving with him."

"Gretchen." The panic in her mother's voice
almost stopped her.

She placed her hand over her heart as she said
the words aloud for the first time. "I love him."

Her mother gasped.

"Gretchen, I forbid it," her father said.

"Oh, Daddy, I'm not a child. Please, trust my judgment. I know what I'm doing. I'm following my heart." She offered them both a quick apologetic smile. "I'll call you, I promise." And with that she raced out the door.

She heard her parents call after her, but she paid them no heed. She saw Josh already astride his Harley. She dashed down the steps and across the lawn to the curb.

Josh scowled when she reached him. "What are you doing here?"

She refused to be put off. "I'm coming with you."

His scowl deepened. "I don't think so."

"Listen here, Josh Morrow. I'm tired of playing games, of pretending. You pay attention now because I'm only going to say this once. You love me."

"I beg your pardon?" He made it sound as if it was all he could do to keep from laughing outright.

"You heard me," she returned sternly. "Furthermore, I love you. If you think I'm going to let you ride off into the sunset without me, you've got another thing coming! We're in this together.''

"Hold on." He held up his hand. "Don't you think you're taking a lot for granted?"

"Not in the least. You're going to marry me. My dad paid a fortune for that country-club membership and we've already got the date reserved. I don't believe anyone will mind that the groom has a different last name than the one I originally planned to marry."

Josh didn't laugh at her little joke. "Gretchen, there isn't going to be a wedding. At least not between you and me."

She blinked, uncomfortable with the alternative. "You want to live in sin?"

Pain flickered in his eyes. "I'd never do that to you."

Her relief was substantial. "Oh, Josh, I didn't think you would."

"I'm going to do you a bigger favor. I'm going to get out of your life before I screw it up along with my own."

"Oh, no, you don't," she said. "I've cast my lot with you."

"Goodbye, Gretchen." He revved the engine.

Where she found the nerve to leap in front of the Harley, Gretchen didn't know.

Josh looked stunned.

"I have one more thing to say and you'd better damn well listen." She'd never been more serious in her life.

Josh turned off the ignition. Now he looked uncomfortable. "All right, say it, but I haven't got all night."

"You've got the rest of your life. I...I talked with that policeman this afternoon, remember. It was so plain to me that Janet and Gary belong together I couldn't sit by and say nothing. It's even plainer that you and I should be together."

"No, baby, we shouldn't."

"Be quiet," she said, her voice trembling. "I love you and there's never going to be anyone I'll love more. If you leave without me, you're going to regret it the rest of your life. You'll look back to this time, this place, and wonder what would have happened if you'd let me come with you."

"You win some, you lose some," he returned flippantly.

"Don't you dare talk to me like that, Josh. Don't you dare treat my love as if it were something you can toss away without a care. You aren't fooling me. I know you. Do you think I've spent all this time with you and not know your heart?"

"Are you finished?" he asked grimly.

"No."

"Just how much longer is this going to take?"

"Not long." She swallowed tightly and began again. "You told me earlier today that you wouldn't chase after me. Well, I won't chase after you, either."

"Good. That relieves my mind."

Gretchen could see there was no cracking that stubborn pride of his. She stepped aside and watched helplessly as he restarted the engine.

Her hand covered her mouth to hold back the words to beg him not to leave her. With tears streaming down her face, she watched Josh ride off into the night.

Chapter 6

"That's not the end of the story, is it?" Carol Furness leaned back, bracing her palms against the concrete rim of the fountain, her eyes wide with dismay. A soft breeze rustled the leaves of the trees, and sunlight cut a pathway through the shade, splashing across the lush green lawn.

"Josh Morrow left you and rode off just like that?" This time the question came from Maddie Cobain.

"Yes, just like that," Gretchen whispered in a futile attempt to keep the pain out of her voice. Even after fifteen years she continued to feel that same crushing sense of defeat. On a starlit night one June fifteen years ago, Josh Morrow had left her standing alone at the curb, the sound of his retreating Harley drowning out her sobs.

Eventually her mother had moved from the porch and joined her, gently placing her arms around her shoulders.

"He didn't come back?" Carol asked, breaking into the flood of disturbing memories.

"No," Gretchen replied, staring unseeingly across the deserted campus. "He didn't come back."

"But that's terrible," Maddie said.

Gretchen was aware she was sitting in the very spot where her heartbreaking adventure had begun. Now Maddie's words brought her forward in time, and she glanced at her two friends, almost forgetting they were with her. "I loved Josh Morrow more after traveling with him for three days than I ever cared about Roger Lockheart."

"Perhaps it was for the best," Carol suggested, squeezing Gretchen's hand. "Josh always did have a chip on his shoulder."

"One about the size of Alaska," Gretchen said wryly.

"What happened next?" Maddie asked.

"Next?" Gretchen murmured, pulling herself away from the lure of the memories. "Well," she said, unsure where to start, "when it became clear I wasn't going to get over Josh as easily as my parents had hoped, my mother took me to Europe."

"Oh, how wonderful!" Maddie said.

"It was," Gretchen said.

"Do you ever wonder what happened to Josh?" Maddie wanted to know.

"And what about Roger?" Carol asked.

Gretchen leaned back on her hands. "I imagine the reunion will answer those questions. I saw both their names on the list of participants."

"Did you see Eddie Shapiro's name on that list?" Carol asked tightly.

"As a matter of fact, I did."

"That's right," Maddie said, straightening enough to meet Carol's look, "you were engaged to Eddie, weren't you?"

"Was," Carol repeated, anger flashing in her eyes. "He got rid of me soon enough."

A short awkward silence followed.

"I've told you what happened to me with Roger," Gretchen reminded her former sorority sister. "Now it's your turn."

Carol laughed ruefully. "If you think Roger was a jerk, just wait until you hear what Eddie did to me."

"I'm all ears," Gretchen said.

"I've got the afternoon to kill," Maddie seconded.

Carol

Chapter 1

Carol Furness fell in love with Eddie Shapiro the first time she saw him throw a football. It had been September of her freshman year at Nelson Lord University. Standing on the sidelines of the football field, she'd watched the pigskin ball sail effortlessly and gracefully thirty yards into the arms of the tight end. Eddie had made it look easy, his timing perfect, his throw masterful. In that moment Carol recognized that, with proper training and guidance, he was headed for the pros.

And she'd been right.

Growing up the youngest in a family of five,

with two older athletic brothers, Carol knew more about football than some coach's wives. She'd started cheerleading in junior high and had set her sights on making the cheerleading squad at Nelson Lord when she'd learned she'd been accepted there.

That first day on campus she'd set two goals for herself. Being head cheerleader by the time she graduated and marrying Eddie Shapiro.

She took over the cheerleading position her junior year and accepted Eddie's engagement ring the Christmas they were both seniors. They planned a July wedding, and while Carol was occupied with finishing the last of her credits for her education degree, something wonderful happened. Something terrible.

Eddie was drafted by the pros, chosen in the thirteenth round by the Denver Broncos.

"I never doubted," Carol reminded him as they hugged each other wildly and danced around the room. "Not once."

Little did she realize this was the beginning of the end.

"What do you mean you want to delay the wedding?" Carol cried, hardly able to believe what she was hearing.

Eddie lowered his gaze to the lawn outside her sorority house. He butted the toe of his shoe against a dandelion, breaking off the bright yellow blossom, crushing it. Crushing her. He apparently had nothing more to say.

"The wedding's less than six weeks away." Someone needed to remind him of that. Her parents had already spent a lot of money for the affair, not to mention the mental and emotional commitment she herself had made these past several weeks. Finishing her classes, studying for finals and getting ready for graduation had been more than enough for one person, but she'd taken on organizing their wedding on top of everything else. Now Eddie was telling her he thought they should wait. Carol hadn't slept more than four uninterrupted hours in a row in over two weeks. She was exhausted and cranky, and the last thing she needed was this.

"I can't help it, honey," Eddie said contritely. "I've got to start training early."

"Surely you can take one day for the wedding." She was willing to forgo the honeymoon. Besides, it wasn't as if the wedding date came as any surprise to Eddie. He'd been the one to choose July.

"I wish I could, but coach won't allow it." He

sounded flustered and apologetic, but Carol wasn't
buying it. She recognized that hurt-little-boy act of
his, the one he used when it suited his purpose.
Eddie had a way of getting what he wanted by
playing the misunderstood and abused hero. She'd
seen him do it any number of times, enough to
recognize the tactic when he attempted to work it
on her. Well, he could manipulate others, but not
her.

"Everything's different now," Eddie insisted,
his voice gaining strength. He looked up and Carol
watched the resolve strengthen in his face. In that
instant she knew the truth. There was more to this
announcement than met the eye.

That Eddie would purposely wait until after the
graduation ceremony to tell her didn't set well
with her, either. He must have known his practice
schedule with the Broncos weeks earlier. His agent
had worked out the details of the contract, and
although Carol was soon to be his wife, Eddie had
kept the particulars to himself.

That wasn't all. Carol had noticed that Eddie
had been less than attentive of late, but she'd at-
tributed that to the confusion of the final weeks of
school, exams, graduation, their wedding plans—
everything that was happening in both their lives.

His schedule was crammed as he prepared for his induction into professional sports. As crammed as her own.

As graduation approached it'd become increasingly difficult to get him to make decisions regarding their wedding. For weeks she'd been offering her mother excuses and had finally been forced to go ahead without his input. She needed his opinions, but it'd been impossible to catch him for so much as five minutes. When she did, his mind was on other matters, and so she'd given up.

Her list of excuses regarding Eddie's behavior had begun to sound hollow even to her own ears. Now she understood and wanted to kick herself for being so obtuse, so blind to what should have been obvious all along.

"Is there something you're not telling me?" Carol asked point-blank. She'd rather get things in the open now and be done with them.

Eddie shifted his weight and avoided eye contact. "Well...Mark warned me I was going to be exceptionally busy for the next several months with practice and the games and all."

Carol had never been keen on Eddie's agent, but her fiancé had argued that he was fortunate to have someone like Mark Raferty on his side. He'd con-

tinually discounted her objections and blindly allowed someone else to make business and now
personal decisions for him.

"How long?" she asked, keeping her voice firm
and strong.

"Long?" Eddie repeated. The confused I'm-
not-sure-how-to-tell-you-this gleam was in his
eyes.

"Before we can reschedule the wedding?"

He hesitated, and in that millisecond, in that half
a heartbeat, the truth reared its ugly head like a
sea monster rising from the waves. All at once
what Eddie was saying became clear. As clear as
clean glass.

"You want to *call off* the wedding." She said
it for him. Without emotion. Without censure. To
have the words in the open was a relief in its own
right.

"Honey, sweetheart, don't be angry," he
pleaded, sounding as if he was about to burst into
tears.

Amazingly Carol wasn't upset. It was almost as
if she was standing offstage and watching the
scene unravel between two strangers. Almost as if
she was a nonparticipant. What she should be doing was ranting and raving, giving in to hysteria

and dissolving in tears. Instead, a calm settled over her, a sense that this wasn't really happening, that everything would soon be set right. Eddie loved her and needed her. He'd always loved her, and she him.

It took her a moment longer to realize that Eddie was still speaking. "Mark suggested it wasn't a good idea for us to marry now, and I have to say that I agree with him. I'm starting a new life."

She blinked as the words came at her like sharp needle points. "A new life without me?"

"There's no need to take it personally, you know. I'm a professional athlete and I have certain obligations to my career and my team," he said, echoing the words of his agent, Carol was sure. "Certain...sacrifices." He appeared to have trouble remembering the next line of his speech. She strongly suspected he'd memorized and repeated it for Mark before confronting her. That sounded like something Mark would have him do.

Flustered, Eddie shook his head and asked, "Are you OK?"

"Fine. Wonderful." She felt light-headed and realized the color must have drained from her cheeks for him to have noticed. "You'll want this back." She slipped the diamond engagement ring from her finger and handed it to him.

He looked stricken, staring at the diamond in the palm of his hand. "I...I still love you and all, but it's...well, difficult, you see, me going into the pros and all. And...well..."

"It's okay, Eddie." It hurt to listen to him search for reasons to tell her he didn't want her in his life any longer. He was headed for the big time and she was just a cheerleader. An ex-cheerleader now. As far as Eddie was concerned, a wife would be an encumbrance to him in his new life.

"Okay? Really? You're not mad, are you, sweetheart?" How relieved he sounded!

"Mad?" she repeated, as if surprised he'd ask such a thing. "Not in the least." She brushed his cheek with her lips. "Good luck," she said brightly.

Her response appeared to stun him. She suspected he'd been anticipating a knock-down-drag-out confrontation. His timing was perfect. Perfectly awful. He'd waited until after the graduation ceremony and then opted to tell her in a public place.

Apparently Mark had prepared Eddie to expect yelling, cursing, hysteria and tears. To be fair, her complete lack of emotion came as much of a shock to her as it did Eddie.

"Mark thinks I have a good chance of making second-string quarterback," he explained hurriedly, looking to her for encouragement and approval, the way he always had.

"I hope you do." Carol realized she actually meant it.

Suddenly he looked uncertain. "We can still be friends, can't we? I'd like to call you now and again, if that'd be all right."

"Friends," she repeated, and laughed softly. Right. Eddie would do as Mark dictated and break the engagement, but he'd still look to her for emotional support. Because what Mark didn't understand was the vital role she played in Eddie's life. Eddie needed her.

In time Mark would know how much Eddie relied on her, and then Eddie would be back with his tail between his legs. It was only a matter of time, but until then she wouldn't make it easy for him.

"No, Eddie, I don't think it'd be a good idea if you phoned. If you want to break the engagement, then whatever we shared is over. Completely. Now if you'll excuse me, I'd better call my parents and do what I can to cancel the wedding.''

The least of Eddie's crimes was that he'd put her family through needless expense, allowing them to plan and pay for a wedding he fully intended to cancel. Right then and there, Carol decided she'd pay them back every penny even if it took her the rest of her life.

''Listen,'' Eddie said, taking a step toward her. ''I realize your family's sunk a lot of money into this wedding bit—I know I should have told you sooner. It's only fair that your father send me the bills. I'll make sure they get paid.''

''All right. And I'll make sure Dad forwards them to you.'' She turned and walked away. Pride was the glue that kept her from breaking into a thousand pieces.

When she got back to the sorority house, the place was buzzing with activity. Excited talk and laughter swirled around her like dust devils as her friends raced up and down the stairs, emptying their rooms. Boxes and suitcases littered the hallways. Silently Carol walked past her friends, up the staircase and into her room. Sitting on the edge of the mattress, she reviewed her options.

To save money for the wedding, her parents had

opted not to fly out from the East Coast to attend her graduation ceremony. By waiting until after graduation to break the engagement, Eddie had not only mutilated her plans for the future, but he'd cheated her out of sharing this special day with those who loved her and supported her dreams.

So while she had her teaching degree, Carol was without a job. She hadn't applied for a position in Washington, believing she'd be living with Eddie in Denver within a few weeks. And she'd decided to wait until after the wedding to apply for a Colorado teaching certificate. Eddie hadn't encouraged her to apply for work, but then, Eddie hadn't offered much in the way of advice for several weeks.

Not only had he pulled the proverbial rug out from under her feet, he'd single-handedly destroyed any chance she had of finding a full-time teaching position come autumn. Every teaching job would have already been filled by this late a date.

She could always fly home and live with her parents, but she had too much pride for that. Her family had helped her with her college expenses as much as possible, had sacrificed in order for her to attend Nelson Lord University. She wasn't going to take advantage of their generosity any longer. As an adult, she would find a means of supporting herself. While she might not find a full-time teaching job, she could always do substitute work.

Despite what he'd done, Carol still loved Eddie. She'd always loved him, even knowing he was weak. Even knowing how easily he could be swayed by others.

She held her breath and waited for the constriction in her throat to ease. The one thing that gave her hope was that she knew Eddie better than he did himself. It wouldn't be long before he realized how much he missed her, how much he needed her. Within a month, maybe two, he'd be back, pleading with her to marry him.

She could wait that long.

Three weeks later Carol found herself a studio apartment north of the downtown Seattle area. It was small but comfortable, and all she could afford.

Since graduation, she'd been busy submitting her teaching application to seven different school districts. Again and again she was told that the hiring process was complete, but that personnel would keep her name on file.

She made calls every day, and it wasn't long before her persistence paid off. She was asked to substitute for a physical-education teacher for summer school. A paying job, even if it was only for a week, was a start. A job was a job, and Carol was elated.

Summer classes weren't known for attracting the best and the brightest of senior high-school students, but Carol didn't let that dim her enthusiasm. Dressed in gym shorts, a whistle looped around her neck, she led a group of fourteen physically unfit students onto the Ballard High School football field. They whined all the way to the field, but Carol pretended not to hear.

As there were only a few years' difference between the age of her students and herself, Carol resembled a high schooler herself. Luckily she was tall, five-nine, with rich chestnut-colored hair that bounced against the top of her shoulders.

"We're going to run a mile," she announced.

A chorus of unharmonious gripes followed. One overweight boy fell to the ground and played dead.

"Hey, guys. This isn't a time test. Run, walk, crawl, I don't care," she said, laughing at their complete lack of enthusiasm. "All I'm asking is for each of you to complete a mile."

"You actually want us to crawl?"

"Whatever it takes, but the sooner everyone's finished, the sooner we can shower and go home for the day."

The words "go home for the day," captured the class's attention.

"The other teacher didn't say anything about making us do this," someone complained.

"Really?" Carol flipped back the papers on her clipboard. "Hey, you're right," she said, holding her index finger in place. "It says five miles here."

A short shocked silence was followed by a chorus of disbelief.

The boy who'd played dead miraculously recovered. He sat up and said, "No, it doesn't."

She thrust her right arm into the air. "How many of you would prefer five miles?"

Not a hand went up.

"One mile?"

Every hand went up.

"Then get to it."

With a dismal lack of enthusiasm, the teenagers started jogging toward the track. Being in top physical condition herself, Carol didn't understand their aversion to exercise. By the time they finished the mile—four laps around the track—she'd wager that each and every one of them would experience a surge of well-being.

Carol was wrong. When all fourteen had completed the required number of laps, they acted as if they'd completed the Bataan Death March in World War Two.

Six of the boys attempted to cheat by only finishing three laps, but Carol had kept careful count. Amid protests and threats, she'd sent each one back and penalized him an additional lap. It might not have won her an award for popularity, but she doubted anyone else would pull that trick.

To her surprise one of the girls jogged up to her into the change room. "Thanks," she said, grinning.

"For what?" Carol asked.

"For making Eddie, Jim and Charles do the complete mile. The other teacher probably wouldn't have noticed, and then they'd think they'd gotten away with something."

"They're only cheating themselves."

"I know," the girl said, her blond hair bouncing. "But they haven't figured it out yet."

It didn't escape Carol's notice that one of the boys was named Eddie. Like this high schooler, her Eddie hadn't discovered that by canceling their wedding, he was cheating himself, too.

Sooner or later he would want her back. She wasn't with him, wasn't there to listen to his tales of triumph on the playing field or have her rub the soreness out of his shoulder. He was sure to miss her by now. Sure to be thinking about her.

When he did phone—and he would, Carol was convinced of that—she would make him suffer, but for only a little while. Eddie had plenty of lessons to learn, and she was the woman to teach them. Her pride had taken a tremendous beating, and Eddie needed to understand she wouldn't allow him to treat her in that manner ever again.

At the end of the day, Carol walked down the high school corridor, the rubber soles of her tennis shoes making little sound against the floor. Her heart felt lighter than at any time since graduation. Substitute teaching helped keep her mind off Eddie and the fact she didn't have a full-time job.

She strolled past a line of classrooms and noticed another teacher writing on the blackboard at the front of one of them. Three rows of tables, topped with computers, stretched from one side of the room to the other. No students.

"Clark?" Carol did a double take.

Could it be possible Clark Rusbach was here in Ballard High School? Clark was Nelson Lord's computer wizard. A man so left-brain he walked with a limp. Throughout her college career, Carol had secretly admired his genius.

He was tall, on the lean side and fiercely intense. His thick dark hair, which needed to be cut, fell awkwardly over his forehead. Although it was a warm July day, he wore slacks and a sweater more suitable for autumn. But then, Clark never had been one to follow convention. In fact, what had always intrigued her about him was his complete lack of need to conform. A true individualist, he lived and breathed in a world foreign to her own.

Carol had hated the way Eddie made fun of Clark, calling him a nerd and making him the brunt of tasteless jokes. Clark had never reacted to Eddie's crude comments, which had earned him Carol's respect. It couldn't have been easy, but if Clark was bothered by any of it, he didn't allow it to show. His world consisted of bytes, bits and chips, and they appeared to understand and appreciate him far better than his fellow humans.

"Carol?" He'd turned to stare at the doorway. "Is that you? What are you doing here?"

She stepped into the room and said, "I was about to ask you the same thing." Shortly before graduation, rumors had abounded that Clark had been wooed by Softline, a big Seattle-based software conglomerate. Carol heard that the company's young ultrarich owner had personally courted Clark and offered him an employment package said to be a healthy six figures.

"I'm here as part of a community-service project for Softline. They said it's supposed to help us understand the frustrations of those just learning about computers." Absently he brushed the hair from his forehead. "I don't know about these kids' frustrations," he muttered, "but I experienced a few of my own. Were we this dense?"

Carol laughed. "I suspect so. At least I was." Although they'd taken a number of classes together, Carol and Clark had rarely exchanged more than a casual greeting.

Clark hesitated and then said, "I thought you'd be married to Eddie by now."

Embarrassed, Carol lowered her gaze, not wanting to talk about Eddie. However, it was only natural that Clark was curious. "I guess you didn't hear. Eddie broke off the engagement. He didn't think this was a good time to marry, what with him playing with the pros and all.''

Clark's thick dark eyebrows bunched together. ''He broke off the engagement?'' he asked, sounding incredulous, as if her former fiancé had made the biggest mistake of his life. ''Eddie might have a good throwing arm, but I guess I never *was* overly impressed with his brains. I don't see you two as a couple, really.''

His words soothed Carol's battered ego, and she smiled to show him she appreciated his kindness.

''Why are you still in Seattle? I thought your family came from the East Coast.''

''They do...but I like living in the Pacific Northwest and was hoping to get on full-time with the school district.'' Which was not the entire truth, she realized.

While she put on a cheerful facade, the past few weeks hadn't been easy. Talking about Eddie was like tearing away a half-healed scab. She discovered that tears were close to the surface.

''So how's the job hunt going?'' Clark asked.

Her only answer was a shrug.

''I take it that means not good?''

She tried to put on a happy face and failed. ''Not the best, but I'll be fine.''

An awkward silence followed. "Well, it was nice seeing you again, Clark," she said, eager to escape before she made a fool of herself by breaking into sobs.

"I don't know if it'd be much help," he said, stopping her, "but I understand Softline's hiring replacement help for the summer. It wouldn't hurt to put an application in there."

At this point she wasn't picky. Have rent payment, will work, was her motto. "Thanks. I'll give them a try."

A week and a half later Carol was being interviewed by a Softline human-resources manager. She'd already filled out an application form.

"I'm afraid all we have at present are several part-time positions," the woman told her. "I notice here that you've got a friend in the company."

Carol could feel the color creep up her neck. "A friend?"

"Yes, one of the young executives put in a good word for you. That helps."

"Well, I'm a hard worker."

"I'm sure you are. What I'd like to do is start out by having you fill in for support personnel who are out on vacations. I notice your secretarial skills are excellent."

"Thank you."

"Could you start first thing Monday morning?"

"That would be great." Carol didn't bother to disguise her eagerness. She could pay the rent and meet other expenses until school started up in the fall.

The woman punched a few keys on her computer screen and waited for the printout. "You'll be replacing an executive secretary who's away on vacation." She handed the printout to Carol, along with a list of other instructions.

Not until she left the building did Carol read the name of the person she'd be working with.

Clark Rusbach.

Chapter 2

Bright and early Monday morning, fifteen minutes ahead of schedule, Carol located Clark's office at Softline. Finding his name etched in gold on the door, she experienced a surge of pride that this incredibly brilliant man was her friend. And he was.

Knowing Clark, he hadn't anticipated that the woman who'd interviewed Carol would mention his recommendation. Her guess was he wouldn't want her to know what he'd done. Nevertheless it was sweet of him.

Carol traced her index finger over the raised letters of his name and smiled to herself. Just a month out of college and already Clark Rusbach had made his presence felt in the business world. He was also incredibly thoughtful. Eddie could stand a few lessons from Clark. When the time came, she'd be sure her former fiancé learned how good Clark had been to her.

Stepping into Clark's office, Carol paused and glanced about, soaking in the ambiance. Her smile widened. The one thing you could expect from Clark was the unexpected. While the outer office consisted of a desk, chair, filing cabinet and other secretarial paraphernalia, Clark worked in what might be best described as a research lab. Well, sort of. The large room off her own consisted of tables and chairs and no less than six computers in various stages of assembly. On the walls were diagrams that resembled road maps of China, and no less than three calendars, all with Monday the fifteenth—which was a week away—circled in red.

By the time Clark arrived, Carol had the coffee brewing and was humming softly to herself. She'd sorted through the regular mail, brought up his E-mail messages, printed them out and placed both stacks on his desk. One of the desks. He had five.

"Good morning," she said, feeling slightly awkward. Always before they'd been on equal footing, but now Clark was her boss.

"Mornin'."

"I'm taking Mrs. Derby's place while she's away," she explained unnecessarily,

"So I see." He shed his jacket and hung it in the closet next to her own cardigan sweater. "Do you have any questions?"

"Yes…several." She hesitated, not sure how to begin. "Do you want me to call you Mr. Rusbach? Would you prefer I pretend I don't know you from a past life?"

He chuckled. "Clark will do. Relax, we're friends. It was just the luck of the draw that you happened to be assigned to me right off."

"We are friends, aren't we?" Until her interview she'd considered Clark to be more of an acquaintance. "Thanks for putting in a good word for me," she said, forgetting that she'd decided not to mention what he'd done.

His shook his head as though to dismiss her appreciation and headed toward his own office.

"How do you like your coffee?" she called after him.

He reached for his mail and glanced toward her.

Carol stood in the doorway between the two rooms, rubbing her palms together, awaiting his response.

"Hot."

"You got it." She poured him a mug, and then carried it into his office and set it down on his desk. She started to return to her own room, changed her mind and abruptly turned around. "Clark?"

He glanced up, his gaze expectant.

Carol hesitated, then, "I'd like to ask you something...personal."

"Okay."

She hadn't intended to do this, but nothing ventured, nothing gained. "I signed up for line-dancing classes at the community center for Monday, Wednesday and Friday nights, and I was wondering..." She trailed off, wondering if it was wise to put him on the spot.

"And you need to leave the office a few minutes early those days? Sure."

"No," she said, surprised that he didn't understand what she wanted. "I'd like it if you'd come with me—that is, if you want to." It would be a lot more fun if she had a partner, although the instructor said she was welcome to attend without one.

"I'm not really the dancing type," he replied.

Carol thought she heard a bit of regret in his voice, as if he was halfway tempted. "But you could learn, and it'd be fun."

For a month she'd done nothing but sit in her tiny apartment night after night and feel sorry for herself. The dance classes offered a welcome respite from what was fast becoming monotony.

"Yes, but—"

"You could do it," she coaxed him, giving him a warm smile. "No one's going to laugh at you."

"Why me?" Clark asked.

"Well, because first off, I like you and there isn't any chance of anything romantic developing between us. I mean...well, you know."

"No. I don't know."

"Because of Eddie."

"What about him?"

"Any time now Eddie's going to want me back and the two of us will be married," she said.

"You mean to say you'd actually marry him after what he did to you?" Clark looked shocked.

Carol realized it probably sounded as though she had no self-esteem if she'd willingly forgive

Eddie when he'd treated her despicably. While she had every intention of marrying him—eventually—there would be a hefty penance she wanted paid first.

"Eddie's weak," she said, hoping Clark understood. "I know that about him and appreciate how easily led he sometimes is. I'll make the decision about my future with him when the time comes."

She could see that her response didn't please him. He said, "In other words, you're inviting me to these dance classes of yours because you consider yourself safe in the company of a nerd."

Carol didn't know how to answer.

"I see," he told her when she reminded silent. "Well, in that case, perhaps you should ask someone else." He reached for his mail again, effectively dismissing her.

Carol felt terrible. Obviously he'd taken her silence as confirmation of his statement. She'd been looking to thank him for being her friend and had ended up insulting him. Worse, she'd managed to start off the week on the wrong foot. Depressed beyond words, she slowly returned to her office and propped her forehead on the heel of her hand.

Before Eddie canceled the wedding, she'd been a confident and composed woman. Now, it seemed, words twisted themselves around her tongue, and she possessed all the poise of a four-year-old on roller skates.

That morning set the tone. Carol and Clark barely exchanged a word over the next four days. At first she assumed she'd insulted him so thoroughly he'd simply chosen to avoid her. Only later did she realize he was working hard. Every now and again he'd come into her office needing one thing or another. If she wasn't available, he left instructions on her desk. He arrived early and left after she'd gone home. If it hadn't been for the other secretaries in the department, Carol would have felt as though she'd been set adrift on an iceberg.

Mrs. Derby had thoughtfully prepared a list of instructions for her replacement and Carol followed them religiously. The other secretaries told her Clark was deeply involved in developing a revolutionary software, a project he'd first envisioned while still in college. On Monday the fifteenth he was scheduled to give a demonstration of the software's capabilities to Softline's board of directors.

That explained why Clark had basically ignored her.

Friday afternoon at closing time, she cleaned off

her desk and was ready to leave when Clark appeared and glanced about.

"Carol, could you—" He stopped abruptly when he saw her standing with her purse draped over her shoulder. He seemed surprised until he glanced at the wall clock and noted the time. "I didn't realize it was so late."

"Do you need me?"

He hesitated and then shook his head. "It's fine. You can go."

"Clark, please, I'd like to help if I can. If it wasn't for you, I wouldn't have this job."

"What about your dancing classes?"

"Oh. I decided to take them another time."

"Because you needed a partner?"

"No, not really. It just didn't turn out the way I wanted it to."

He ran splayed fingers through his hair. "I'll make a deal with you. If you can stay late and help me out here, I'd be willing to take those classes with you."

As far as Carol was concerned, this was the deal of the century. "You're on!"

"You're sure you don't have a date?"

She shook her head "Another relationship doesn't appeal to me at the moment." She was reluctant to admit that she still had faith that in time Eddie would come to his senses. But she didn't want Clark to remind her that such thinking was dangerous. She knew it was. Yet, hard as she tried, she couldn't make herself believe it was really over with Eddie.

She'd dated Eddie for almost four years. She knew him better than anyone—faults, foibles and flaws. They'd been a team, a couple, two of the most popular personalities on campus. Their love had been a storybook romance. The head cheerleader and the football hero. Their looks had complemented each other, too. She was tall and slim with rich chestnut-colored hair and deep blue eyes. Eddie was blond and gorgeous. A hunk.

Clark was nothing like Eddie. The computer wizard was perhaps the kind of hero you'd find in a spy thriller. His features were completely nondescript. Not one characteristic about him stood out and he blended into the crowd.

Actually, though, this was the first time she'd really paid attention to Clark's appearance, and she noted how attractive his eyes were. They were a soft brown, a shade darker than his hair. He was an inch or so taller than Carol, and while she wouldn't describe him as muscular, he looked as if he kept physically fit. Perhaps he jogged or enjoyed hiking.

"Then you've decided against dating anyone at the moment?" he asked.

"For now," she said. "It's too soon after Eddie." That was true. She missed her former fiancé too much to think about dating anyone else. "I'd like to stay and help if I could," Carol offered, "and really, you don't need to volunteer for the dance classes unless you really want to take them."

"You're sure?"

"Positive. I don't have any plans other than to veg out in front of the television." That was what she did most nights. She slept poorly, awoke at odd hours. In the long frustrating weeks since graduation she'd become personally acquainted with Jay Leno and come to appreciate his wit.

"I guess I should warn you," Clark said, "I've had an irrepressible urge to take up line dancing." His face relaxed into a rare smile. The transformation in his looks was amazing. His eyes changed to a warm shade of amber and a dimple appeared in each cheek. She was mesmerized. It demanded every ounce of control she possessed not to ask him to smile once more just so she could see those dimples again.

As it turned out, Clark needed her to transcribe his notes and then format them for his presentation. It amazed her that someone as familiar with the workings of a computer didn't think to use one himself.

It took her a couple of hours and when she'd finished, her stomach was growling. It'd been a long time since lunch and she was starved. Planting her hand on her stomach, she waited for the growling to subside.

"Do you like Chinese food?" Clark asked unexpectedly.

Carol looked over at him. "Chinese? Adore it. Why?"

"I'm ordering dinner. You interested?"

She nodded, returning her gaze to his meticulous notes. "Sure."

"Any preferences?"

"Hot, spicy and lots of it," she answered.

A moment later she heard Clark reach for the phone behind her. His conversation was followed by a call to alert security that their dinner would be delivered in half an hour.

By the time the food arrived, Carol had completed the formatting. Clark proofread the printout while she opened up the numerous white cardboard boxes and dug through the paper bag for napkins and eating utensils. The smell of chili peppers, ginger and vegetables made her mouth water. Sitting on the edge of the desk, she plucked a fat shrimp from the box and brought it, dripping hot chili sauce, to her mouth. Some of the juice rolled down her chin and she saved it from staining her blouse in the nick of time. As she set the napkin aside, she noted Clark's gaze had left the typed presentation and was studying her.

She froze. "Did I do something wrong?" Perhaps he'd ordered the shrimp for himself and hadn't intended on sharing. Feeling guilty, she lowered the box back to the desk top.

"No, no, you're fine."

Nevertheless she waited until he'd finished reading before she ate any more. Luckily it didn't take him long. He opted to sit in her desk chair, leaning it back as far as it would go and propping his feet on the corner of the desk. Both worked the chopsticks, too hungry to carry on a conversation.

Once the edge was off her hunger, Carol glanced at Clark. "If Mrs. Derby could see us now." Although she'd never met the woman, it didn't take Carol long to know that Clark's secretary was a neatness junkie, one who'd never risk tainting her workplace with soy-sauce stains.

Clark chuckled.

The chopsticks were poised in front of Carol's mouth. "Do that again," she instructed. At his puzzled look, she said. "I want you to laugh again." She finished taking her bite and waved him on with her chopsticks.

He frowned, but even that wasn't able to destroy the effect the short burst of laughter had had on him. His eyes warmed and he appeared more approachable, more human.

Four days earlier Carol had thought of Clark as nondescript, almost a nonentity. While she admired his genius, she'd viewed him as dull. But dinner together, sharing Mongolian beef, Szechuan shrimp and Chinese noodles, had altered her opinion. While Clark wasn't one to seek attention for himself, and in fact, avoided it, that didn't mean he was without personality. Like her peers at Nelson Lord University, she'd been blind to the warm generous man behind the brains.

"Carol?"

She lowered her gaze when she realized she was

staring. "Your face changes when you smile," she said.

"It does?"

"Yeah. It came as a surprise is all." How unnerving that Clark should have this effect on her! "Are you anxious about the presentation on Monday?" she asked as a means of changing the subject. The transition wasn't smooth, but he was kind enough not to mention it.

"Nervous? No, I can't say that I am."

Again he surprised her. She would have been a wreck knowing that her entire future with the company hinged on a one-hour presentation.

"I know this program. Door Handle is my baby." Door Handle, she knew, was the name of the software. "All I have to do is let the program do the talking for me. If I had any doubts about the performance, any qualms about the effectiveness, I'd be worried. But I have absolute faith in her."

"Her?"

"I think of Door Handle as female. At first she was temperamental and unreasonable, but after a while we adjusted to each other and now we get along great."

"You think women are temperamental and unreasonable?'' she asked, planting one hand on her hip and pretending to be offended.

"Not always," he said, grinning, "but on occasion." He went on to explain a number of bugs he'd worked out of the program, and as he spoke, he became more animated, more excited. Clark excited? This was a side of him she'd never seen. Much of what he said, she'd read as she'd transcribed his presentation. The words had seemed routine on the page, but when Clark said them, she could actually feel his energy and enthusiasm.

She couldn't help being impressed. Clark was nothing like Eddie, who was fond of boasting about his athletic skills, bragging about his accomplishments. Clark mentioned his own talents in passing. It was the program he promoted, not himself.

Their conversation evolved slowly between bites of food, and Carol found herself laughing again and again at his dry wit. When she was certain she would burst if she ate a single morsel more, she set her chopsticks aside and gave a satisfied sigh. "Thank you for dinner. I can't remember the last time I enjoyed myself more."

"I'm the one who's grateful. I appreciate your

staying late.'' Clark dumped the empty containers into the wastebasket.

''I was happy to do it.'' Now was the time to apologize. It was either take advantage of the opportunity given her now or regret it later. ''There's something you should know,'' she said, capturing his attention. ''On Monday I let you think that I'd consider myself safe with you at the dance classes because I saw you as a nerd. But I didn't—don't— see you that way, Clark. I see you as a gentleman—that's why I'd feel safe. And I also think you're...wonderful.''

He appeared confused, as if he'd put the matter out of his mind. ''Uh...don't worry about it.''

''But I have. Sometimes I do incredibly stupid things.''

For reasons she was hard-pressed to explain, Carol had the sudden urge to cry. It seemed his generosity of spirit had reduced her to this. And then she understood.

Just before graduation she'd been sitting on top of the world, and within a single afternoon, everything she'd considered important had come crashing down on her shoulders. This was the first time in weeks that she felt like her old self. It was thanks to Clark, and she was incredibly grateful to have him for a friend.

She hid the attack of emotions behind busy-work. Silently she gathered the leftovers and pack-aged them up for Clark, then removed any telltale evidence of their ''crime'' by wiping off the desk. As she reached for her purse, she glanced at her watch, uncertain of the bus schedule this late in the evening. While it was close to eight o'clock the sun had yet to set.

She lingered a moment, realizing she'd enjoyed their time so thoroughly she was reluctant to leave. ''Thanks again.'' She eased her way toward the door, taking small steps backward.

Clark nodded. ''I've got a few things to finish up here, otherwise I'd walk you to your car.''

She didn't correct him. ''Good night, Clark.''

''Good night, Carol.''

She left and the sound of her footsteps echoed in the corridor. Security let her out of the building. As luck would have it, she'd just missed the bus and was doomed to wait an hour for the next. Dusk was settling over the Puget Sound area and a breeze rustled through the trees, the wind weaving through the thick green branches, whispering se-crets.

Twenty minutes later a red Mustang passed the transit area, then stopped abruptly, tires squealing. Slowly the car backed up toward her. The passenger window lowered and Carol recognized Clark.

"You're taking the bus?" he asked, frowning. "Why didn't you tell me?"

"I was supposed to?"

"No...yes. Hop in and I'll give you a ride home." He leaned across the passenger seat, unlatched the door and pushed it open.

"Thanks," she answered, smiling to herself. After climbing in and giving him her address, she snapped the seat belt into place. When Clark merged with the freeway traffic, she leaned her head back and closed her eyes, lulled by the country music playing on the CD. This man was full of surprises. She would have assumed Clark was more of a classical-music fan. Russian or Italian composers whose names all begin with *P*. Prokofiev or Puccini. Men who'd suffered for their art. The mental picture she had of Clark didn't include Reba or Garth.

In her relaxed state, with her eyes closed, she grew brave. "I want to ask you something, all right?"

"Ask away."

''I want to know about the comment you made last week about not seeing Eddie and me as a couple.''

''I never did,'' he returned promptly.

''Why not?'' She'd always viewed them as perfect together. But she respected Clark and was eager to hear his reasoning.

This time her question gave him pause. ''Eddie was never right for you. He doesn't deserve you.''

While that might be true, she loved Eddie. Even now she found it hard to be angry with him. It wasn't Eddie who'd broken the engagement but his agent. Mark was the one who'd talked Eddie into canceling the wedding, and once Eddie came to his senses, he'd be back.

''You're wrong, you know,'' Carol felt compelled to tell him, irritated now that she'd asked. She had no one to blame but herself. Perhaps she was looking to have Clark reassure her that eventually her world would right itself. It was only a matter of time before Eddie recognized what he'd lost and want her back. She felt lonely and alone, and dammit, she missed him. Missed the life they'd dreamed about and planned together. It wasn't supposed to happen like this.

Clark's gaze briefly left the road as he glanced

at her. "You asked. If you aren't going to like the answer, then don't ask the question."

"Have you always been like this?" she demanded, gesturing with her hands, which refused to keep still. "It must be difficult for you," she added, not giving him time to respond, "seeing that you're such an expert on everyone else's business. Who died and made you king of the free world?"

"No one."

Her anger didn't rile him, but Carol was in rare form and wasn't about to end the conversation. Not until she'd gotten him to admit he was wrong. She *needed* him to admit it.

"If you know so much, then who do you think I should marry?" she demanded. There wasn't a single man in the entire campus she would love more than Eddie. The fact she recognized and accepted Eddie's flaws assured her.

The question hung in the air between them like a piece of spoiled meat. "You won't like the answer to that one, either."

"I asked, didn't I?" she insisted. "I'm a big girl, you can say it." She defied him to come up with a suitable candidate. She was meant to be with Eddie. While she didn't want to pin her hopes on her ex-fiancé's coming to his senses soon, she couldn't stop thinking about him.

When Clark wasn't immediately forthcoming with a response, she asked it again, this time with more feeling, more determination, more courage.

"Exactly who do you see me marrying if not Eddie?"

His fingers tightened on the steering wheel and Carol almost cheered. He was squirming in his seat. Carol loved it. Triumph oozed from her every pore. He couldn't come up with anyone better suited to her than Eddie.

Clark glanced at her again. "I could see you married to me," he admitted softly.

Carol gasped. It was as if someone had thrust a giant hose into the car's interior and sucked out all the oxygen. "You?" she repeated. "You and me? Together?" Oh, dear, she hadn't calculated he'd suggest something like this.

"I warned you that you weren't going to like the answer."

"You aren't serious." This was a joke. She should have known Clark was just like every other man. His ego demanded he come up with a response, even one as nonsensical as this one.

"I am serious."

"It's your ego, right?" she asked when he exited the freeway. "I realize men have a problem with pride."

"Men aren't alone in that."

"True enough."

Clark and her? She couldn't see it. They were about as different as two people could be. Not that there was anything wrong with diversity. But she wasn't right for Clark. He needed a woman, someone special, who understood him. Someone really wonderful.

He drove to her apartment building, parked and killed the engine.

Apparently he was waiting for an invitation. "Would you like to come inside?"

"Yes."

"Any particular reason?"

Again his answered with a terse "Yes."

She certainly had no objections to his company, nor to his seeing her place. The studio apartment was small, but she'd made an effort to decorate and was pleased with what she'd done. A few stuffed animals sat here and there on the sofa, mostly so she could hold them while she watched television. Her cheerleading pom-poms rested on the fireplace mantel along with the trophies she'd accumulated during her college years.

Clark stepped inside and glanced around appreciatively. "You've made this homey, Carol."

"Thanks."

She gestured for him to make himself comfortable and then walked into the kitchen and turned on the faucet.

"What are you doing?" he asked, following her.

"Making coffee."

He frowned. "Why?"

"I thought you'd like a cup..." Now that he'd asked, her making coffee made about as much sense as anything else that had happened that evening.

He moved toward her, his gaze holding hers. His eyes were dark and intense, keen and purpose-filled. He reached out and rested his hands on her shoulders. His touch was light, gentle and in a small way comforting. It'd been weeks since Eddie had held her, and she'd missed the closeness, the sense of belonging.

"I'd like to prove my point."

"Your point?" She wasn't sure she understood.

With his eyes imprisoning hers, he gently drew

her closer. Apparently he planned to kiss her, which was all well and good, but it wouldn't solve anything and was likely to embarrass them both.

He wrapped his arms around her and pressed her against the solid length of his body. What she'd suspected earlier proved to be accurate—he was both trim and muscular. Before she knew it, she was wrapped in the warm shelter of his embrace. He smelled of musk and spicy Chinese food, an odd yet pleasing combination.

Her heart pounded so loudly she was certain he must have heard it. She raised her head, anticipating his lips, wanting this over with so she could tell him that while his kiss was very nice, they would never be anything more than friends.

Then it happened. Something Carol could neither explain nor define. A yearning buried in the deepest part of her being broke free. If anyone had told her such a thing was possible, she never would have believed it. She'd been engaged, heavily involved with one man for years. A man she'd loved, loved still, despite what he'd done.

She was a woman who knew what she wanted and went after it. Never one content to wait patiently on the sidelines, Carol grabbed hold of opportunity with both hands.

That she should experience this...whatever it was, before Clark lowered his mouth to hers, left her feeling claustrophobic and fearful. Perhaps there was something to what he was saying, although she had trouble comprehending it.

Slowly, with deliberation that bordered on torture, Clark pressed his lips to hers. Carol's heart went into overdrive. She couldn't think to move. In that moment she was Clark's prisoner.

The instant his warm moist lips settled over hers, Carol was lost. No kiss had ever been more potent. A frightening kind of excitement took hold of her. She stood on tiptoe and slid her hands up his chest to link them behind his neck.

The kiss deepened as she opened to him the way an orchid does after a rainfall. She wanted more. Her breathing came fast and hard, and she was gratified to realize Clark's breath was ragged, too.

He demanded and she gave. Freely and without reserve. The heat of their kiss could have been hot enough to set off the kitchen smoke alarm as they angled and twisted their mouths, seeking to give more, to take more. To be more.

When Clark eased his mouth from hers, his shoulders were heaving. Clinging to him, Carol kept her eyes closed and forced air into her lungs.

Even now her heart clobbered her chest like a boxer's fist hammering a punching bag. Never in all her life had she experienced a kiss as profound as this.

She should have known it was too perfect, too beautiful. She should have known it would never last.

It didn't.

Within seconds Clark ruined the most beautiful kiss of her life.

"I was right, wasn't I?" he said. "You don't know yourself nearly as well as you think you do."

Chapter 3

Carol couldn't decide if she was relieved or disappointed when Clark's secretary returned from vacation. Mrs. Derby was exactly as she'd pictured her. Late fifties and meticulously groomed in a dark business suit with her gray hair primly pulled back in a bun. Punctual, precise and particular. Her personality meshed perfectly with Clark's. The two were said to get along famously.

Carol missed seeing Clark on a daily basis but at the same time was grateful they didn't spend time together. Not after what had happened when he kissed her. Especially when she considered her response. While she'd gone over that night count-less times, she had yet to make sense of it.

Ego had prompted Clark to kiss her. That part she understood. What she had trouble reconciling was her response. After a while she decided the best thing to do was put it out of her mind, banish that night and the kiss from her thoughts.

Fate seemed to be on her side. Clark didn't have a lot of free time on his hands. Door Handle, his software program, had received a warm reception from Softline's board of directors, and he'd been granted the additional funds he'd requested, along with a handful of staff.

Whenever Carol saw him, he was surrounded by others all making demands on his time and ex-pertise. His gaze would follow her and she made a point of greeting him with either a smile or a wave. He had to bow out of the line-dancing classes, and while she realized he regretted having to renege on his promise, he had no choice.

Every now and again they'd bump into each other in the cafeteria or in the huge parking lot outside the building. Clark would stop and ask how she was doing. Carol had the feeling the ques-tion needed to be rephrased: how are you doing *without Eddie?* Her answer remained the same.

"Good, really good." But she'd expected to hear from Eddie long before now.

Carol didn't need to ask Clark how *he* was doing; the answer was obvious. He worked too many hours, ate poorly and, from the darkening shadows beneath his eyes, she also suspected he wasn't getting enough sleep. While his poise remained unshakable, she instinctively recognized he was frazzled.

As for Carol, the job with Softline was ideal. She was able to substitute for a number of school districts as long as they were able to let her know in advance. The more time she spent in the classroom, the more she loved teaching. A natural with kids at any age, Carol proved to be a popular teacher. The reports on her had been full of praise, and she was convinced it was only a matter of time before she was hired permanently.

Teaching had been her dream from the time she was five when she'd lined up her dolls in front of a small chalkboard. Wearing her mother's high heels and a broad-rim hat her grandmother had given her, along with several long beaded necklaces, she'd lectured her rapt audience on vowel sounds and the importance of not eating glue.

Carol tried not to think about Eddie. But surely

he missed her. Surely he thought about her. Surely he wasn't so busy that everything they'd shared no longer mattered to him. She refused to believe it. After four years of daily contact, she'd assumed, hoped, Eddie would feel as if a part of himself was missing without her at his side.

The waiting was agony. The not knowing. Eddie haunted her dreams, and often she awoke with her heart heavy and her emotions raw. In the beginning it'd been much easier. Her anger and frustration had effortlessly carried her the first few weeks. Later she'd focused her fury on Mark Raferty, Eddie's agent. No one could convince her that Mark wasn't responsible for turning Eddie against her.

As August rolled into September Carol blamed herself for being foolish enough to hold on to any hope of Eddie's wanting her back in his life. Surely he'd have contacted her by now. Even with Mark's disapproval, he'd have found a way to reach her.

He hadn't, and that told her everything.

The first Sunday of September would either break her or make her, Carol decided. That was the day the Denver Broncos football team hosted the Seattle Seahawks in Mile High Stadium. The game was scheduled to be televised in Seattle, starting at eleven o'clock, Pacific time.

Carol assured herself she wouldn't so much as turn on the television. It was as simple as that. Why torment herself? Nothing good would come of seeing Eddie suited up in a Bronco uniform. Viewing him, even on television, was sure to make her heartache ten times worse. She'd be crazy to purposely make herself miserable.

It didn't take Carol long to admit that dementia was the least of her worries. On Sunday morning she dutifully sat in front of the television screen, dressed for the occasion in baggy jeans and a Nelson Lord sweatshirt.

The national anthem was playing when her doorbell chimed. She tore her gaze from the screen to run to her door and open it.

"Clark," she breathed, surprised to see him.

"How're you doing?" he asked, and looked past her to the television screen.

"I assumed you'd be at the office," she said. For a while she'd toyed with the idea of inviting him over just so she wouldn't turn on the football game. Knowing Clark, he would have felt obligated to accept, and she didn't want that. Not when he was so busy with his career.

"I *should* be at the office," he told her, and yawned, stepping into the apartment.

"Then why aren't you?"

His eyes were dark and serious. "You need me."

He removed his jacket and made himself comfortable on the sofa, stretching his arms out along the top. "I know you. Eddie's playing and you wouldn't be able to resist."

She couldn't very well argue with him.

He patted the space next to him. "Are you going to sit down and watch the game or not?"

"I wasn't going to watch the entire game," she rushed to tell him. "I intended on changing channels, but..." The lie died on her lips in midsentence when Clark's gaze swung from the television to her with laser-cutting accuracy.

"Okay, okay, so I thought I'd check it out. Eddie's the second-string quarterback, and it's highly unlikely he'll even play."

"You're still pining for him, aren't you?"

"Not as much." Embarrassed that what Clark said was true, she downplayed her feelings. Carol had never thought of herself as weak, but that was the way Eddie made her feel. Years ago in one of her psychology classes she remembered the professor explaining that a person's sense of emotional well-being was directly related to the amount of control they had in a situation. Eddie was the one in control of her, and it was time to let go. If only she could!

"Sit down," he said, and again patted the space next to him.

Carol did as he asked. Leaning against the thick cushion, she pretended to find the matter of football and everything that went with it exceedingly boring. It wasn't long, however, before she'd scooted to the edge of the cushion, enthralled with the game and clutching her teddy bear to her chest.

"You hungry?" Clark asked.

So intent was Carol on the action on the football field, she barely heard him. When the Seahawks completed a pass she leaped from the sofa and danced a jig in front of the coffee table. "First down. Did you see that?" she cried, thrusting her arm in the air. At Clark's blank look, she added, "We just made third and ten."

"Wonderful. What have you got to eat around here?"

"Not much." She sat back down and pressed her fingers to her lips as a Seattle running back carried the ball five yards, broke free and gained three more for a total of eight. It was highly satisfying to envision the Seahawks beating Denver on their own turf. Her heart would ache just a little less if that was the case. It was a matter of honor, of pride, of atonement for a man with a fickle heart.

In three months' time not only had she become deranged, Carol decided, but also petty and childish. She hadn't felt this good in weeks. Months!

Clark took it upon himself to examine the contents of her kitchen, which in her tiny apartment was directly behind the sofa. She heard him opening and closing cupboards and grumbling under his breath.

"I haven't bought groceries this week," she said over her shoulder. "There's some bread for a sandwich, though." If she remembered correctly.

She heard the bread box open and close, then Clark muttering something about preferring his bread white, not green-blue.

At last she heard a triumphant "Ah!" from behind her. She couldn't imagine what he'd found, but whatever it was appeared to satisfy him. He set the microwave to humming and soon the apartment with filled with the distinctive sound and mouth-watering aroma of popcorn.

Carol's stomach growled. She hoped Clark realized he was a dead man if he didn't intend to share. Her thoughts quickly returned to the football game when Seattle fumbled the ball on the kickoff on the five-yard line, setting up the Broncos for an easy score. Carol fell to her knees and pounded the carpet. "No, no, no."

"Something happen?" Clark asked.

She toyed with the idea of being flippant and decided against it. He just might get angry and decide to keep the only edible food in her entire apartment to himself.

"I don't know yet," she said, and sat down next to him, eyeing his bounty.

Unlike Carol, who generally ate directly from the popcorn bag, Clark had emptied the contents into a ceramic bowl. A paper towel protected his knee.

"You're going to share that, aren't you?"

He eyed her skeptically. "Do I have a choice?"

"No."

He chuckled. "That's what I thought."

Old habits being what they were, Carol rallied Seattle's team with a one-woman cheer, leaping high in the air when, several plays later, they scored the first touchdown of the game.

"You're rooting for Seattle?" Clark asked, apparently oblivious to anything but filling his stomach.

"Of course." His question irritated her. Naturally she'd cheer for Seattle. This city was her home, not to mention that her heartless ex-fiancé happened to play for the opposing team. She'd love to see the Denver Broncos get their butts kicked for having the audacity to draft Nelson Lord's star quarterback.

"What about Eddie?" Clark asked next, his words hitting her square in the center of her chest. Too close to her heart for comfort.

"What about him?" How well she could dupe Clark into thinking she'd completely forgotten Eddie remained to be seen. "Football's been a part of my life for as long as I can remember. You think I'm rooting for Seattle because of Eddie?" She made the question sound as ludicrous as possible. "You're probably unaware that both my brothers played high-school and college football. It's in our family's blood. It's only natural I should love the sport." Too late, she realized she'd given far more of an explanation than necessary. Clark *knew* and nothing she said would convince him otherwise.

Turning back to face the television, her eyes fell on the screen at the precise moment the camera focused on Eddie Shapiro. He stood on the sidelines, looking fit and muscular, and so handsome that merely seeing him produced a sharp unexpected jab of pain.

Pleased with the media attention, Eddie smiled into the camera. Only it wasn't just any smile; it was the special one that held deep meaning to her. It was the smile he'd directed at her on the sidelines after he'd completed a touchdown pass. The smile that reminded her of his love and the promise that they were a team and would always be together.

Yeah, right.

As if Eddie was looking directly at her, he winked. Too late to tame her reaction, Carol gasped. Pride demanded that she look away, but she found she couldn't. She broke into a cold sweat as if she was about to be violently ill, and still she couldn't force herself to stop watching.

Noiselessly Clark knelt beside her on the carpet and wrapped his arms around her, hugging her close.

Gripping his upper arms, her nails digging into his flesh, she waged a fierce inner battle between the demands of her pride and the intensity of her pain. She squeezed her eyes closed and trapped the emotion inside in her chest until she gasped for air. She was hardly aware of the tightening sensation in her lungs until they felt about to burst.

The release was instantaneous, and with it came a flood of tears. She didn't know which was worse—Clark witnessing this humiliation or requesting that he leave and bear her pain alone. She didn't want him with her, and yet she needed him. Needed to be held and reassured. Needed to be comforted.

Whispering soothing words of solace, he gently rocked her, the palm of his hand pressing the back of her head. With nothing left to hide, Carol slipped her arms around his neck and clung. Clark was her rock, her keel, her life preserver.

He brushed the hair from her cheek. "It's going to be all right."

She hated to argue with him, especially now when he was being so kind. "No, it isn't."

"Carol, trust me. It won't always be this bad."

"Yes, it will. I'll never get over him. The worm. It was my fate to fall in love with a worm, and dammit, I didn't expect this to happen."

"Eddie Shapiro didn't deserve you."

Carol ran the back of her hand beneath her nose. "I know that, everyone does...but that doesn't make me love him any less."

He spoke into her hair. "Someday you'll look back on this and wonder what you ever saw in him."

"I do already and it doesn't help."

She felt him smile against her temple. She was the undeserving one. She didn't deserve a friend as wonderful as Clark. That he put up with her was nothing short of amazing.

"Clark," she whispered, lifting her head from his chest and meeting his gaze through tear-filled eyes. "Kiss me."

He blinked as if he wasn't sure he'd heard her correctly. "Kiss you? Now? Why?"

"Because I want to feel something besides this pain. Please...you were eager enough not so long ago." The pain of actually seeing Eddie was bad enough. But that pain was only a small portion of what she'd experienced, and Clark had witnessed it all. She'd lain her soul bare, unable to hide behind a facade of disinterest. Unable to pretend it was only a game. So maybe kissing Clark wasn't such a good idea, but she certainly hadn't expected an argument from him.

Taking matters into her own hands, she removed the option of choice and kissed *him*. Her palms on either side of his head, she angled her mouth and firmly planted her mouth on his. He offered no resistance, fully involving himself in the exchange. As before, Carol was overwhelmed by her own heated response.

Clark moaned and, pushing his tongue into her mouth, gained control of the exchange.

Even as their bodies moved against each other, Carol didn't know what had prompted her to ask Clark to kiss her. Instinct, she suspected. Survival. He was the anesthetic, the drug that would help ease her through this agony. His kiss was the promise that she could, would, feel again. The reassurance her heart demanded and craved.

Again and again he kissed her. But then he seemed to pull back, as if easing himself away in a slow deliberate process before addiction set in, while she waged a silent war, seeking more, wanting more, needing more of him.

Clark was refusing her. Her pride might have been badly bruised if she had not been aware of how difficult it was for him to maintain control.

"No more," he gasped between labored breaths, sounding like a man on the rack, crying for mercy. He groaned and lifted his face toward the ceiling, exposing his throat. Carol kissed him there, pressing her lips to the underside of his jaw, her tongue exploring the taste and feel of his skin.

Clark rewarded her with a soft moan. He reached behind her, and she didn't know what he was doing until the television abruptly went silent. He held the remote control in his hand.

He set the remote aside, then glanced at his wrist and swore under his breath. "I have to get back to the office."

Carol barely recognized his voice. "Now?"

"Yes, now."

His rejection hurt, but she pretended otherwise. She dropped her arms and scrambled up from the carpet as though she hadn't a care in the world, as if this little interlude had been just the medicine she'd needed to see her through a difficult moment.

Clark stood with far less enthusiasm. "Will you be all right?"

"Me?" she asked as though it was a foolish question. "Of course."

He didn't believe her and his eyes said as much.

"I've got a million things to do. Groceries, errands...'' she said, counting them off on her fingers. ''I need to return a video and—''

''Carol,'' he said, stopping her. ''I mean it.''

''So did I. I feel great. You haven't got a thing to worry about.''

He held her gaze for a long time as if gauging the truth of her words. Good old-fashioned pride saved her. As she had for months, Carol pretended she was unaffected, unscathed and at peace.

She almost wished she hadn't.

He left soon afterward, and she moved to her window and watched him drive away. Using him as a buffer had been wrong. He deserved better. She liked Clark, always had. Even before they became friends she'd taken his side. Since working for Softline, she'd discovered she more than liked him. She'd come to appreciate him.

Clark Rusbach was quite possibly the best friend she had.

''Hi, Mom, hi, Dad,'' Carol chanted into the telephone. ''Happy Thanksgiving.''

''Carol, sweetheart. How are you?''

''Wonderful. Great.'' A small lie, but one she could rattle off without guilt. ''I'm subbing at Ballard High School this week, teaching English and PE the same as in the summer. I'm loving it.''

"What about your job at Softline?"

"I'm working there, too. They've been wonderful, giving me whatever days I need when the school district phones."

"You're spending the day alone? Thanksgiving?"

Her mother made it sound like a fate worse than death. "I already told you—Clark's family invited me over."

"Clark's your new boyfriend."

Carol had stopped counting the number of times she'd explained otherwise. "We're just friends." And they were. Good friends. She'd never experienced this kind of camaraderie with anyone else, male or female. While the Door Handle project continued to consume much of his day, he found pockets of time to be with her. Rarely more than an hour or two and often less, but he seemed to possess the uncanny ability to know exactly when she needed a friend most.

Following the September Sunday when she'd brazenly thrown herself at him, they both avoided any physical contact. She appreciated the wisdom in keeping their relationship strictly platonic. Nevertheless she couldn't help wondering...

"I like Clark," her father said.

"You've never met him," Carol said, taking delight in reminding her parent. Her father would champion Bozo the clown as long as it wasn't Eddie.

"I don't need to. I'm just grateful you didn't marry that bum."

"Harry," her mother chastised from the other phone.

"I know, I know, you don't want me to remind her of Eddie," her father muttered, speaking to his wife as though Carol wasn't there. "As far as I'm concerned, Carol had a lucky escape. I don't care how good of a football player he is, Eddie Shapiro is no gentleman."

While Carol agreed with him in principle, she couldn't force herself to admit it outright. Thoughts of Eddie still followed her like dark shadows. Try as she might to not think about him, a day didn't go by when he escaped her thoughts. Much of the anger had passed. She wished him well—at least she hoped she did. The only thing she hadn't been able to find was acceptance.

Each time the phone rang, her heart leaped and she prayed against all reason that it was Eddie. She stopped counting the times she was convinced she'd seen him on the street. Or heard his voice across a crowded room. Each time a small flicker of hope or joy would fire to life and then quickly fade as reality set in.

"Harry, please," said her mother. "Can we not talk about Eddie?"

Her father muttered something Carol couldn't make out. "I'm going to have a wonderful day," she said, forcing enthusiasm into her voice. "So don't worry about me."

"You'll be home for Christmas?"

"I'll be there." By hook or by crook she'd find a way to share the holiday with her family. "Give my love to everyone," she said, trying hard to remain cheerful. "And eat extra turkey for me."

The goodbyes were especially difficult. Carol had missed Thanksgiving with her family before. This wasn't something new. Only this year it was different, and her parents recognized it as keenly as she did herself.

Clark arrived just before noon to pick her up for dinner. He'd trimmed his hair and was dressed casually in an Irish cable-knit sweater and gray slacks. Carol did a double take, barely recognizing him. He looked good—different, although she couldn't say what it was. She found herself staring, perplexed by what was happening, and when he frowned, she quickly turned away.

"I made an apple pie," she said.

"I didn't know you baked."

Carol was pleased to see that she'd impressed him. "My mother insisted I learn two things before I left for college. How to bake an apple pie and the proper way of cutting up a chicken."

"The important things in life," Clark teased.

"They are!" she said, perhaps a bit too defensively.

"Hey," Clark said with a smile, and held up both hands. "I'm agreeing with you."

He opened the car door for her and then carefully placed the plastic-covered pie in the back seat. While Carol was grateful for the invitation to Thanksgiving dinner, she couldn't help being curious about Clark's parents. He rarely mentioned them. She suspected they were older versions of Clark. Successful, genius types. Her one fear was that the entire dinner conversation would revolve around topics with names she couldn't pronounce.

She couldn't have been more wrong. Clark's parents were as normal as her own. She might have suspected he was adopted, if it wasn't for the similarity in looks between Clark and his father.

Nadine Rusbach zeroed in on Carol's train of thought almost immediately. "I know what you're thinking," she said as she opened the oven door and tested the turkey.

"You do?" The comment caught Carol unawares, before she could disguise her thoughts.

"Don't worry," Nadine said, closing the oven door and removing the padded mitt. "Everyone wonders how it is that two perfectly ordinary people like Sam and me could have spawned Clark."

Carol was fascinated.

"We knew our son wasn't going to be like other children when he started reading at the age of two."

While Carol had never questioned Clark's brilliance, she hadn't been aware of how intellectually superior he actually was. Unlike Eddie, Clark didn't need to boast about his talents to anyone who would listen.

"He didn't fit in with the usual school crowd and he could have gone to college when he was thirteen, but we talked it over with Clark and decided against it. Sam and I wanted him to have as normal a childhood as possible."

Clark stuck his head into the kitchen. "Are you telling tales, Mom?"

Nadine smiled warmly at her son. "Of course. Why don't you take Carol downstairs and show her your first computer?"

"Mom, Carol doesn't want—"

"But I do." Computers weren't completely foreign to her, but she possessed little more than a nodding acquaintance with them, just enough to get her by in the office. Anything having to do with programming was light-years beyond her abilities.

"All right," Clark agreed. "Just remember, you asked for this."

He led her downstairs into the basement and flipped a light switch, bathing the area in warm light. Leading her past the washer and dryer, he escorted her into what might have been a workshop. Only it wasn't tools that lined the walls, but diagrams that resembled hopelessly entangled fishing lines. The workbench held a large, now obsolete computer.

"That's Melva," he said.

"You named your computer?"

"Doesn't everyone?"

Carol assumed he was serious until she saw the twinkle in his eye. "If I named mine," she said with a smile, "it would be something like Beel-zebub."

Clark chuckled. "Melba took on the personality of a demon more than once. When I built her for my sixth-grade science—"

"Sixth grade?"

Clark nodded and went on with his tale. While she listened, Carol's gaze roamed the workroom. Tucked between the diagrams was a small color photograph. There was something vaguely familiar about it.

"What's that?" she asked when he'd finished his story.

"What?"

"That." She pointed.

"Just a picture," he returned nonchalantly.

"Can I see it?"

Clark hesitated, something she had rarely seen him do. "I guess, although I don't understand why you're so curious."

Carol didn't understand, either, until he reached across the bench, unpinned the photograph and handed it to her.

Carol frowned as she stared into her own smil-ing face. She was on the football field, pom-poms in her hands. The camera had caught her in midair, arms and legs akimbo, her body like a giant X. The wind had whipped her hair behind her until it looked almost as if she were flying. "That's me," she whispered, completely stumped about when the shot was taken.

"Yes, I know." He sounded bored and eager to be on to another topic.

Carol stared at the photo. It wasn't recent. Not within the last couple of years, of that she was sure. Her freshman year? Sophomore?

"I took it," Clark admitted as if confessing to a crime.

She raised her gaze to his. "When?"

"The first time I saw you."

Although it was entirely possible that Clark had attended Nelson Lord's football games, she couldn't remember ever seeing him.

"When was that?" It embarrassed her to continue to be mesmerized by her own photograph, but Carol couldn't stop staring at her own innocence. How happy she'd been, carefree and full of enthusiasm for life and all that it held in store for her. Her eyes shone bright, her joy spilled over. She realized now that the photograph had been taken her freshman year before she'd started dating Eddie. Light-years ago.

"Did I really look like this?"

"You still do," Clark returned, seemingly surprised by her question.

"I do?" She wasn't fishing for compliments, but she no longer viewed herself in the same way. Eddie had robbed her happiness, stolen it like a thief in the night. If that wasn't tragic enough, she'd given him permission to do so. For each day, she allowed him into her thoughts, allowed herself to hope, to believe, he wanted her back. He'd robbed her of her appreciation for life.

"You're beautiful, Carol."

Clark wasn't a man who handed out compliments indiscriminately. She couldn't recall his mentioning how she looked one way or another in all the months they'd been friends. And now he tucked his finger beneath her chin and with maddening slowness lowered his lips to hers.

The kiss was gentle, devoid of passion. A friendly exchange. Nevertheless she felt its impact all the way to her toenails. Her eyes fluttered open when he raised his head. Releasing a deep sigh, she offered him a feeble smile.

"I think you might possibly be the best friend I've ever had," she said.

He smiled. A rare smile that lit up his eyes.

"We'd better get back upstairs before my parents decide to eat without us."

She nodded, and when Clark reached for her hand, their fingers intertwined.

Carol first heard Clark's parents when she was halfway up the staircase.

"I'm telling you, Nadine, she's the one."

"Sam, please, don't do or say anything to embarrass Clark."

"Me? I'd never do that." A short pause. "Not intentionally."

"Thank you for that."

"We're going to have magnificent grandchildren, sweetheart. With her athletic abilities and Clark's brains—what a combination."

Carol could feel her face growing hotter by the moment.

Clark stopped her on the stairs. "We better let them know we're coming," he said.

Chapter 4

When Carol booked her airline tickets to spend Christmas with her parents, her spirits lifted considerably. The holidays with her family and all that was familiar was sure to ease the disappointments and frustrations of the past year. It'd been far too long for her to be away from those she loved.

On a Tuesday a couple of weeks before Christmas, Carol sat in the Softline cafeteria finishing the last of her lunch. But her mind wasn't on her chicken-salad sandwich. It was on her two older brothers and their families. Both Jeff and Jerry were married and had children of their own. Carol enjoyed being an auntie to her two nieces and nephew. And although she dearly loved Seattle, it would be good to be home again.

Sipping the last of her tea, she was about to return to work when Mrs. Derby, Clark's secretary, approached her.

The older woman greeted her with a rare display of warmth. Mrs. Derby wasn't the chatty friendly sort. What made her such an excellent secretary was her dedication to duty. And to Clark. It went without saying that she had a specific purpose for seeking out Carol.

Carol returned her greeting, and for a moment, an irrational fear took hold that somehow Mrs. Derby had unearthed a soy-sauce stain on her desk. She smiled when she realized how ridiculous she was being. Clark would have covered for her.

Carol's thoughts brightened at the thought of her friend. They saw each other on a fairly regular basis these days. She'd come to rely on him for companionship, and he on her, although she recognized that she derived far more from the relationship than he did.

In her own way Carol tried to thank him for being her friend. She helped him Christmas-shop for his parents and Mrs. Derby, and he'd done the same for her. Shopping wasn't his favorite activity, but he'd been patient and helpful. They never did make it to the line-dancing classes. The one evening he was free to accompany her, Clark had arrived, looking tired and worn to a frazzle. He'd wanted to know how much it would cost him to get out of it. Carol had laughed, hugged him and let him off easy with pizza in front of the television.

It surprised Carol how often they laughed together. A few months earlier she never would have guessed Clark Rusbach had such a wonderful wry sense of humor. She appreciated his wit and wondered how it was no one else had recognized it during their four years of college.

Clark helped her in other matters, too. He diverted her thoughts from Eddie. Thoughts of him didn't plague her as they once had. She was no longer in a constant state of anticipation, sitting on the edge of her seat, waiting for him to phone, to knock at her front door. He hadn't and he wouldn't, she knew now. But her life had ceased to feel so empty without him.

She looked at Mrs. Derby, who seemed to be waiting as if uncertain she was doing the right thing. At last the woman spoke.

"I suppose you've noticed how late Mr. Rusbach sometimes works," she said.

"Yes, sometimes." Carol knew how deeply involved he was in Door Handle, but she hadn't really been aware he was working overly long hours. Of course, more often than not, she was in the opposite end of the building.

They saw each other once, sometimes twice, a week, but always on a casual basis. Carol didn't consider their outings dates. That would have been far too complicated. They were friends. Good friends. Nothing less, nothing more, nothing else.

"He's here all hours of the day and night!" Mrs. Derby blurted, and the outer rims of her ears turned crimson.

"I wondered..." Carol admitted, frowning. Clark *had* seemed overly preoccupied of late.

"He needs to take better care of himself." This last part was almost whispered. Mrs. Derby would rather die than be accused of unprofessional behavior. Discussing her employer's work habits bordered on conduct unbecoming to a secretary. "He'll listen to you," she went on, glancing over her shoulder to make sure no one could hear.

"So you want me to..." Carol trailed off, uncertain.

"You see, Mr. Rusbach forgets about the time."

That sounded like Clark, all right. The man was a computer genius, but time seemed to have no meaning for him.

"You'll come, won't you?" the silver-haired woman gently pleaded. "I don't mean every night, just some nights." She paused, looking flustered. "Like tonight."

Carol hesitated, still wondering exactly what it was Mrs. Derby wanted. "Are you saying you want me to tell Clark it's quitting time?"

"If you wouldn't mind. I worry about him. Mr. Rusbach's such a dear soul and you're such good friends. The nights he's meeting you, Mr. Rusbach can't get out of here fast enough. You make him happy, and I can see he does the same thing for you. I don't mind telling you how pleased I am with how matters are developing between you two. Lots of young women these days let their heads be turned by men with more brawn than brains." She pursed her lips, revealing her disapproval.

Apparently now wouldn't be a good time to mention that she and Clark were only friends. Other than the few times they'd exchanged kisses, nothing romantic existed between them.

"I've tried talking to him," Mrs. Derby said

with resignation. "Some of the other staff members have, as well. He listens, or at least it appears he listens. Sometimes he responds, then apparently forgets what was said, unless, of course, it has to do with the software program. This morning...I arrived for work and discovered Mr. Rusbach hadn't gone home."

"You mean he stayed the entire night?"

Mrs. Derby nodded and then worried her lower lip as if she regretted having said that much.

"I doubt I'll be much help. I—"

"Oh, but you will be," Clark's secretary insisted. "Mr. Rusbach listens to you."

Carol had trouble believing it. "All right," she muttered. She might not possess an IQ as high as Clark's, but she knew better than to get on the wrong side of a strong-willed woman like Mrs. Derby.

At five-thirty, as promised, Carol arrived at Clark's office. Mrs. Derby, who was cleaning off her desk for the night, glanced up and shared a conspiratorial smile with her.

"Everyone else has left for the night," she whispered.

"Go on home, Mrs. Derby," Carol said. "I'll make sure Clark leaves at a decent hour."

The secretary beamed. "I know you will."

Carol wasn't convinced she had as much influence on Clark as the woman believed. He revealed all the signs of a workaholic; even his mother had said so during Thanksgiving dinner two weeks earlier. It would take a lot more than a gentle prod to distract him from his mission.

Clark sat in front of a computer, fully involved with whatever he was doing.

"Clark," she said softly from behind him.

He glanced over his shoulder, and when he saw her, he frowned. "What are you doing here?" Not exactly the warmest of greetings.

It was all Carol could do to keep from glancing over her own shoulder and asking Mrs. Derby for the answer. As it was, she caught sight of the secretary giving her an I-told-you-so look on her way out the door.

"It's quitting time," she said.

"I know." He returned his attention to the monitor. "Had we planned to meet?"

"No...not really."

He glanced up at her. "Is everything all right?"

Carol faltered, unsure how to respond. This wasn't going well.

"Carol?"

''Everything's wonderful,'' she said too quickly. She had his full attention now when she was least prepared to deal with it.

Clark studied her, then blinked. In that split second she understood Mrs. Derby's concern. Something must have gone wrong with the software, some bug run amuck, or whatever the little darlings that infested complicated computer programs were called. Without leaking delicate information, Mrs. Derby had asked Carol for her help. The woman had been attempting to tell her that something was amiss, but dared not let on what.

In his effort to discover the solution, Clark had driven himself to the point of exhaustion. He desperately needed a break. Then and only then would the stress ease. Then and only then would his mind relax enough to release the solution. And there was one. Carol believed that with all her being. For every negative there was a positive, for every push a pull. She'd seen it happen time and time again.

Clark recognized it, too, and had worked himself into a frenzy, not sleeping, working twenty-four hours a day. Being the intense individual he was, he didn't have the patience to wait for the answer to reveal itself. He wanted a solution and he wanted it now.

"How about dinner?" she asked, saying the first thing that popped into her head.

"You're buying?" he joked.

"No, cooking." Every penny had been carefully budgeted over the holidays, and she had no choice. Her mind did a mental review of her cupboards, and she groaned inwardly while plastering a smile on her face. She was without a clue what she could possibly prepare that didn't come out of a can.

"You cook?" It wasn't such a ridiculous question, although he meant it as one.

"I've been known to," she said.

"What's the occasion?"

"Nothing special. I guess I didn't want to be alone tonight." She lowered her eyelashes for fear he'd see through her scheme to drag him away from the office.

Perhaps he wanted to believe her, Carol didn't know, but before she realized it, he'd turned off the computer.

"I'll need to come back," he said.

"Tonight? Here?"

He looked at her as though he hadn't a clue what she was asking.

"You're coming back to work after dinner?" she elaborated.

He didn't hesitate. "Probably."

She restrained herself from chastising him. He wouldn't listen and she doubted it would do any good. If anything, it might put a strain on their friendship, and she would regret that.

Carol needn't have worried. Clark sat in front of the television while she sorted through her cupboards in a futile attempt to scrounge up an appetizing meal. While deciding between Tuna Helper and boxed macaroni-and-cheese, Carol glanced into the living room, which was easily visible from the small kitchen. Clark was sound asleep on the couch. Obviously her company was less scintillating that she wanted to believe. If Mrs. Derby hadn't clued her in to his exhaustion, Carol might have been insulted.

Retrieving the afghan her mother had crocheted for her, Carol carefully placed it over Clark. He roused briefly, his eyes fluttering open, when she removed his shoes, but she could see it was too much of a struggle for him to stay awake.

"Rest," she whispered, and smoothed the hair from his brow. The idea of kissing him came out of nowhere. It amused her, tickled her fancy. Without stopping to gauge the wisdom of giving in to the impulse, she bent forward and gently pressed her lips to his.

The kiss was sweet, simple and wonderful. Her heart swelled with tenderness for Clark. He'd been such a good friend. She smiled, remembering their adventures while Christmas shopping and how they'd laughed over a delicate lacy nightie he claimed he was buying for Mrs. Derby. Then he suggested maybe he should purchase it for her and wiggled his eyebrows suggestively.

Carol straightened, then dimmed the lights. She couldn't seem to leave him alone and checked to be sure he was comfortable a number of times. She tucked the blanket more securely around his shoulders and ran her hand lightly over his brow. The urge to kiss him again was strong, stronger than it should have been. It worried her a little. The kiss earlier and the one she wanted to bestow now were meant to express her deep affection for him. An appreciation of all he'd done for her. Nothing more.

Suddenly she wasn't so sure of that.

What Mrs. Derby had said disturbed her. Clark's secretary had mentioned how pleased everyone was with the way matters were developing between them. At the time Carol had been tempted to ask *what* matters. Perhaps she was afraid of the answer. Then there was that time, ages ago, when she'd challenged Clark to name someone better suited to her than Eddie. Clark had suggested himself.

It'd been a joke, right? Ego and ego alone had prompted that. Even his parents seemed to believe she and Clark were an item. He'd never mentioned what they'd heard his parents say, but Carol understood that it embarrassed him and he wanted to spare her.

All right, so maybe a case could be built that Clark was actually in love with her. But she didn't want to believe that, because then she'd be forced to confront her feelings for him.

She liked him so much. She didn't know what she would have done without him all these months. He'd helped her through the most difficult time of her life, with warmth, understanding, compassion and humor.

Carol sat down and braced her elbows on her knees as she studied the sleeping Clark. His features had relaxed, the shadows under his eyes were gone, along with the worry lines that marked his forehead. In repose he resembled a choirboy, far removed from the computer genius.

Pressing her hands to her forehead, Carol held her hair away from her face as she mulled over her feelings for Clark. Did she love him? And if so, why was it so important that she deal with the notion now? He was by far the best friend she had, and it was common knowledge that friends often make the best lovers.

What about Eddie? Yes, he was a worm, and he'd hurt her terribly, but she wasn't convinced she didn't know how *not* to love him. Deep down she knew it was over, but he'd been a big part of her life for so long.

The phone pealed and Carol leaped to her feet, not wanting Clark to awake. Grabbing the portable, she pressed it to her ear. "Hello," she whispered fiercely into the receiver, annoyed with her caller's timing.

"Carol, is that you?"

"Eddie?" His whispered name rushed from her lips. Her knees felt as if they were about to give out. Bracing her back against the wall, she slid to a sitting position on the floor. For months she'd dreamed about this, been consumed by it. And now that he'd phoned, it didn't seem possible. She feared it was a hoax. Someone somewhere was playing a cruel joke on her. But it sounded like Eddie.

"Is it really you?" she asked, afraid to believe what her heart and head were telling her.

"How's it going, sweetheart?" he asked, as cheerful as a five-year-old.

"Good," she responded, without thinking. "How about you?"

"Fabulous. Fabulous."

She yearned to kiss him senseless and in the same breath, the same heartbeat, wanted to scratch his eyes out. How narrow the line between love and hate could be. Now that he'd phoned after all these lonely months, how quickly she was willing to forgive him.

Or was she?

The joy she'd experienced when she realized it was Eddie died a quick and sudden death. Eddie, who'd purposely waited until after graduation to cancel the engagement. Eddie, who'd led her to believe they were to be married until after they'd graduated. Eddie, who'd abandoned her without a qualm.

The line, charged with emotion seconds earlier, went strangely quiet.

"So, Carol," Eddie asked, forcing enthusiasm into his voice, "are you teaching?"

It was all she could do not to tell him she was a part-time employee, thanks to him. Even if she had said it, the comment would probably have flown right over his head. Eddie heard what he wanted to hear and nothing else.

"I know you must be a wonderful teacher," he added. But Eddie couldn't fool her. She knew him much too well. He was worried.

"I've been doing some substituting," she explained. "When I'm not working for the school district, I'm a rover at Softline."

"Softline," Eddie repeated. "Isn't that where... what's-his-name went?"

"Clark Rusbach," Carol said.

"Clark, the nerd?"

Eddie would never think of Clark in any other way. Everyone remained one-dimensional because Eddie was one-dimensional. "Clark, the nerd," she repeated, knowing it would do no good to explain otherwise. Clark was brilliant. It would take a dozen Eddies to make one Clark. No, a thousand Eddies.

The stiff silence hummed like a buzz saw between them.

"Does Mark know you're calling?" she asked bluntly. His agent wouldn't approve of his contacting her.

"No," Eddie admitted reluctantly.

"Then why'd you phone?"

Her former fiancé's laugh was forced. "What Mark doesn't know won't kill him. I've only got one more game till the season's over."

The football franchise was paying him megabucks to stand on the sidelines and be prepared to step in if necessary. After being the star player with Nelson Lord's football team for four glorious years, it must have been painful for Eddie to stand idly by and watch someone else collect all the glory.

In a blink of an eye Carol understood. His phone call made sense now, perfect sense. Eddie missed her all right, because she wasn't there to soothe his ego, to pat his back and tell him how wonderful he was. That was Mark's job now, but Mark wasn't her, and this was what Eddie missed. Carol's speciality—ego damage control. His poor ego must have taken quite a beating in the past several months.

He wanted her. He needed her, and by heaven being needed felt damn good just then.

"How'd you get my phone number?" she asked.

Eddie laughed. "I have my ways."

She bet he did.

"Are you glad I phoned?" he asked in a little-boy voice that told her he craved assurance. Not just anyone's, either. Hers. Only hers.

Poor guy. Poor, pathetic guy.

She delayed answering, wanting him to suffer. "It depends on the reason you phoned, don't you think?"

He hesitated and lowered his voice slightly. "I thought we could talk about that later."

"Really?" This was proving to be more interesting by the moment. "When?"

"Next weekend."

She held her breath while she debated what to do. She really should give him a piece of her mind right then and there. Tell him exactly what she thought about him, in small words so he'd be sure to understand. It was what he deserved. A swift kick in the butt and then she would be done with him once and for all.

But she didn't.

"Dinner," he added, his voice dipping to a

husky murmur. "Just you and me the way it used to be."

She wasn't even tempted. Her head snapped up and she inhaled sharply when she recognized the truth. She was free. Free from Eddie. Free from the endless waiting. Free to move on with her life.

All the weeks, all the months, of mourning her lost love were for naught. Her father had insisted she'd made a fortunate escape, and for the first time she acknowledged he was right.

Eddie was selfish and egotistical. She wanted no part of him. Not now. Not ever.

"What do you say, sweetheart?" he prodded gently.

In the nick of time she bit back the words to tell him what he could do with his invitation. He wanted things to be the way they used to be. He wanted her back and was willing to sweet-talk and coax her if necessary.

Well, by heaven, she'd let him. He could talk all he wanted, get down on his knees and grovel, but it would do no good. She'd take pleasure in laughing in his face.

"Dinner?" she asked, wanting to make sure they were meeting in a public place with lots of witnesses.

"Sure—anyplace you want. Anyplace," He murmured. "I've missed you, Carol. Tell me you've missed me, too."

"Why?"

"I need you to say it. I need you to tell me you've thought about me."

She hesitated, almost choking on the words as they slid past her tongue. "I've missed you," she said, and while it was the truth, it wasn't the whole truth. In the beginning, she'd missed him desperately; her heart had been breaking. Not any longer.

"Wear that blue dress I used to love, will you?" he asked with the same breathless quality he'd used when he'd first seen her in the skintight satin dress.

"All right, I'll wear the blue dress," she said, smiling. She had every intention of doing as he asked. Every intention! She wanted the drool to leak out of the side of his mouth when she walked into the room. Wanted Eddie to know exactly what he was missing.

"Will there be champagne?" she asked softly.

"Anything you want, sweetheart."

"Where are we eating?" Wherever it was had to be expensive. Very expensive. Not only would she derive a great deal of delight in flaunting herself, but she wanted to be sure she ordered the priciest meal on the menu before she walked out on him.

He named one of the best restaurants in town. "Is that good enough for my sweetheart?" he asked.

"That's perfect." Lots of people would be there while she made a fool of him.

This was too good to be true. After all these months she was going to have her revenge. If she was noble and mature, she'd be frank but kind and tell him there was no hope of their ever getting back together. She toyed with the idea for perhaps two seconds, then rejected it.

She wanted to see Eddie squirm. It was what he deserved, and she was looking forward to making sure it was talked about around town.

"Saturday, then," Eddie said.

"Saturday."

A moment later Carol turned off the phone. With her eyes closed she contemplated the conversation. This was good. Better than good. This was what she'd been waiting for.

She went into the kitchen and threw her arms into the air with silent shouts of triumph. Joy all but exploded inside her. She was free, finally, finally free, and damn, it felt good!

So involved was she in celebration that she didn't realize Clark was awake, sitting up and watching her antics in the kitchen. His face was devoid of emotion, as if he'd only just awoken. She sincerely hoped that was the case.

"Clark," she said, so excited it was all she could do to keep from telling him what had happened. He wouldn't understand her need to see Eddie one last time, and if she told him, he'd feel bad. "You're awake," she said, hoping her voice didn't betray her.

He nodded, and his eyes seemed to look straight through her. "I thought I heard the phone."

She glanced down at the receiver in her hand as if she'd never seen it before. "Yes...it did ring." Then, attempting to gauge if he'd heard any part of the conversation, she said, "I hope I didn't disturb you."

He ignored that and asked, "Anyone important?"

She bit the inside of her lip, undecided how to answer. When she did, she spoke the truth. "No."

He didn't say anything for a long moment.

Carol was grateful because it gave her time to

collect her wits. "Dinner's almost ready," she announced as though she was serving a culinary masterpiece. "Tuna casserole. I hope you like tuna? I would have asked, but you fell asleep and..." The words tumbled out of her mouth like bowling pins struck by a thirty-pound ball. When she realized she was talking too fast, too excitedly, she shut up.

Rubbing the sleep from his face, Clark sighed heavily. "Who was that on the phone, Carol?"

Chapter 5

"Who was that on the phone?" Carol repeated slowly, giving herself time to debate how much she should tell him. Clark deserved the truth, but he wouldn't understand her need to see Eddie.

"Carol?"

"A friend," she hedged.

"You seemed to be in a good mood when I awoke," Clark commented. "I looked up and saw you waving your arms as if you were celebrating something. Whoever it was must have relayed good news."

The time to tell him was now, but Carol still

hesitated. Eventually she'd explain everything. But all in good time, when she could gloat and they could laugh about it together. She'd fill in every detail and announce that once and for all Eddie Shapiro was out of her life. Then she'd look at Clark and suggest that perhaps it was time for them to be more than friends.

The timer dinged and, grateful for the distraction, Carol took the tuna casserole out of the oven and set it in the middle of the table. They ate in companionable silence. If Clark was quieter than usual she didn't notice. Her own thoughts were humming along at high speed as she replayed the phone conversation in her mind again and again, savoring every word.

All at once, for no apparent reason, Clark leaped to his feet, almost toppling his chair.

Carol gasped. "Clark?"

He said nothing, only stared directly ahead as if her cupboards contained the answers to the universe's most complex questions.

"What's wrong?" she asked. "What is it?"

"I've got to get back to work."

"Now?"

"Now," he said, and cast her a look so full of joy it was almost blinding. He caught her by the shoulders, half lifting her from the chair, and soundly kissed her. Carol was certain he'd meant it to end there. Just a happy excited kiss.

But it didn't. Instead, Clark kissed her a second time, his lips hungry and urgent. Carol responded in kind, her inhibitions gone. Oh, this was wonderful. More than wonderful. Why had it taken her so long to discover that everything she'd ever wanted was well within her grasp?

Carol clung to him, her fingers buried in his thick sweater. She felt as if she were on a carnival ride, ascending higher and higher, afraid to open her eyes for fear of what she'd find.

At his unspoken demand, she gave him what he wanted, her tongue mating with his in an endless game of desire. A roaring sound filled her ears, and she realized it was her own blood, her own heart, racing with happiness.

They'd exchanged kisses in the past, but these were different.

Clark felt it, too. He eased his mouth from hers and stared at her, his eyes somewhat dazed, as if he were trapped with one foot in heaven and another in hell. Carol herself was winded, although she continued to breathe normally. This feeling, this sensation, was new and she reveled in it. Marveled that she would share this wonder, this excitement, with Clark.

She slid her fingers into the hair at the nape of his neck and urged his mouth back to hers. The kiss sent her senses reeling once more. After a few long moments she tore her mouth away and whispered, "Clark?" She wasn't sure what to make of what was happening between them.

Clark braced his forehead against hers and inhaled sharply, the way a drowning man gasps for air when he breaks the surface.

"That answers my question, doesn't it?" he said softly.

"It does?" Her eyes were still closed.

"Yes. About who was on the phone." He released her and her eyes flew open. "Eddie Shapiro," he continued, and she felt a sudden chill at his tone. "I know. I heard far more of the conversation than I wanted to hear. You told him you were working at Softline with the nerd—who can only be me."

He'd heard that? Oh, no! "Clark, I know what you're thinking, but it wasn't like that."

"I asked, but you weren't exactly forthcoming with information, were you? You'd rather I didn't know you'd talked to Eddie."

"Well, yes, but there's a reason for that, and if you'd give me a chance, I'd—" She wanted to say more, but he wouldn't let her.

"Isn't there always a reason, Carol?"

"Oh, Clark, don't make this difficult. You're right. It was Eddie. He wants to see me and—"

"I know. I heard. He's taking you to dinner and he wants you to wear your blue dress. And you're happy about it."

She hesitated, then confessed, "Yes, but not for the reason you think."

His laugh was short and devoid of amusement. "Carol, please, I'm not stupid. Be honest—you're thrilled. Don't try to fool me. I saw you dancing around the kitchen like you'd won the lottery.

"This is what you've been waiting for all these months. Eddie wants you back, and you couldn't be happier. Otherwise you'd never have responded to me the way you did just now. What was that, your swan song, to let me know what I've been missing?"

"No!" That he'd suggest such a thing was truly insulting.

"Then you weren't pleased to hear from Eddie?"

He was trapping her with logic, damning her

with her own responses and not allowing her to explain or untangle this mess. "Maybe in the beginning, months ago, I longed to hear from Eddie, but that's all changed."

"When?"

"When did it change? Heavens, I don't know. It was a gradual thing. I'd pined after him all those weeks and then one day I realized I didn't. I can't tell you when, because I don't know."

"That isn't the impression I got. You sounded absolutely delighted when you realized Eddie was on the other end of the line."

She groaned. He was right. If she claimed otherwise, he'd know she was lying. "Okay, I'll admit when I first answered, there was a certain excitement there. I'd been anticipating Eddie would call me all these months, and then it finally happened, but...my delight was more a sense of being right. Knowing that eventually he would need me, then hearing from him."

She paused and held Clark's gaze. "I don't want to talk about Eddie right now," she said. "I want to know what happened just now between us."

"Nothing happened."

"Don't kid yourself. We've got something precious and wonderful, I know it. I don't want to ruin it by dragging Eddie into the middle of it.''

A sadness leaked into his eyes. "Yes, I know. But unfortunately, whatever it is, it's too late. You've got your precious Eddie back." Abruptly he turned away and without looking back walked out the door.

Carol followed him outside, her emotions whirling like dry snow whipped about by the wind. "Clark!" she called after him. A chill raced up her arms and she folded them tightly about her abdomen. The cold that struck her had nothing to do with the temperature, and everything to do with Clark. "Please listen to me, I'm only planning to see Eddie this one time!" she cried. If Clark would give her a chance to explain, then he wouldn't be in such a hurry to walk out on her.

"So I understand," he said as he opened his car door.

"Clearly you don't, or you wouldn't be doing this. I need closure with Eddie. It has nothing to do with you and me."

He climbed into his car and started the engine.

Carol couldn't believe he was actually going without bothering to hear her out.

Her anger carried her for nearly twenty-four

hours. This unreasonable side to Clark was one she'd never seen before. The man was both stubborn and irrational. He'd refused to listen. He'd heard what he wanted of her telephone conversation and discounted everything she'd tried to tell him afterward.

For three days she didn't hear from him. Three of the longest days of her life. Seeing that this entire matter was utterly ridiculous, Carol stopped in at his office a few minutes before quitting time on Friday.

When Mrs. Derby saw her, she smiled warmly. "Hello, Carol."

"Hi," Carol said, looking past Clark's secretary, hoping to catch a glimpse of Clark. Dammit, she'd been miserable, and she'd be leaving soon to spend the holidays with her parents. She needed this matter settled before she left.

"I don't suppose Clark's around?" she asked, elevating her voice, hoping he'd know she was there.

"Oh, sure, go right in." It surprised her that Mrs. Derby didn't choose to announce her the way she did everyone else.

Carol hesitated. "How's he doing?" Her guess was that he was staying late again, working himself to the point of exhaustion and not eating properly. Worrying about him had been a convenient excuse to rationalize this unexpected visit.

"Mr. Rusbach's doing much, much better," Mrs. Derby surprised her by saying.

"He is?" Carol's ego appeared to be in for a beating, along with everything else. Clark walks out on her and it seems he's never been happier!

Mrs. Derby's smile revealed her approval. "Whatever plagued him earlier has worked itself out. Mr. Rusbach is his old self and I can't credit anyone but you."

Carol wanted to believe it, but she knew otherwise. Clark wasn't the kind who ranted and raved. Oh no, that would be much too uncivilized for Clark. Instead, he kissed her until she'd practically fainted, said things that made positively no sense and then walked out on her.

She needed to see him, to talk to him and tell him she'd received a wonderful job offer—a full-time teaching position. The only problem was, she'd need to move to Alaska, but the pay was excellent. She couldn't afford to turn it down. She would, though, in a heartbeat, if Clark asked her to stay. Surely that wasn't so much to ask of him. He'd been tired and had overreacted, and she'd allowed the squabble to escalate. This evening they could laugh about it, put the matter behind them.

Wearing a smile, Carol walked toward Clark's office. The door was open enough for her to see him. He sat at his desk, shuffling paperwork. He knew she was there, Carol was convinced of that, and had opted to ignore her.

This wasn't looking good.

She glanced over her shoulder, a smiling Mrs. Derby urged her forward with a wave of her hand.

"Hi, Clark," she said.

He glanced up and revealed no emotion. "Hello, Carol."

"I'd like to talk to you if I could."

"Sure." He gestured toward an empty chair.

Carol sat on the edge of the seat. "I think we should discuss what happened the other night, don't you?"

"Not particularly."

So he wanted to make this difficult. "We're too good friends to let this happen, Clark."

"I assumed we were friends."

"We are," she insisted. "Good friends." She couldn't have survived the past six months without him. He'd lent her confidence and support. Held her when she'd wept, encouraged her, helped her find a job. The list was endless. "You're probably the best friend I've ever had," she reiterated.

He looked bored.

"I know you're upset about me seeing Eddie again, but it isn't what you think." She smiled, wanting him to hear about the dinner date, convinced that once he understood what she planned he'd laugh with her.

"I heard everything I needed. Spare me the details. You want to have dinner with an old lover, that's fine. I don't have any claim on you. I'm just the nerdy guy who kept you entertained until Eddie Shapiro wanted you back."

"That's not true!" Knowing how much being called a nerd offended him, she wanted more than anything to correct the impression. "And only Eddie called you a nerd."

"And you agreed with him."

"No, I repeated it, for which I'm very sorry. The only reason I did was because I didn't want to argue with Eddie. You and I both know Eddie's no rocket scientist. He referred to you that way, and rather than take the time to argue with him, I agreed. Okay, okay, I realize how it must have sounded from your end, but please, Clark, let's put this behind us." She waited for what seemed an eternity before he spoke.

"Apology accepted."

She heaved a giant sigh of relief and planted her hand over her heart. "Thank you. You don't know how badly I've felt about all this. I've got so much to tell you. Has it really been just three days since we talked? It feels like three years." She paused to inhale a deep breath. "Clark, I was offered a teaching position."

"That's wonderful."

"It's one of those 'good news, bad news' situations. I was offered a job, which is obviously the good news," she said gesturing freely with her hands. "But the bad news is I'd need to move to Alaska. It seems the second-grade teacher has developed a heart problem and has asked for a sabbatical, and you know me and kids—I love that age group. What do you think?"

"Think? What's there to think about? I suggest you take it."

"You do?" The happiness drained out of her like water swirling down a drain.

"This is what you've been waiting for, isn't it?" Clark asked her, smiling briefly.

"But it means I'll be leaving Seattle." *Leaving you,* she added silently.

"So it seems, but that's progress for you."

She was on her feet, but couldn't remember standing. The room felt cold suddenly. "I guess that settles that, doesn't it?" She forced an air of breathless enthusiasm into her voice.

"Settles it?"

"You and Eddie are more alike than I realized. Neither one of you has a clue of what it means to really love someone. I...I assumed you were different, but I was wrong. Goodbye, Clark." She was too hurt to say anything more. Clutching her purse to her side, she started to walk away.

Then her steps slowed, and with her back to him, she said, "Before I leave I'd like to thank you. I mean that sincerely."

Her words were followed by a painful silence. She waited a moment with her eyes closed, praying he'd say or do something to stop her.

He didn't. She had no choice but to leave.

With her head held high, she walked out of Clark's office and out of his life.

Chapter 6

"That's it?" Maddie asked, incredulous. "Clark actually let you leave?"

Carol nodded, and her gaze drifted across the square to the Rusbach Science Building. The bronze plaque outside the building stated that Clark Rusbach had donated the funds for the structure. He'd done well for himself. Very well. His computer company was said to be worth millions. Fifteen years earlier he'd designed software, and these days his computer systems were known worldwide.

"How sad," Gretchen said, and gently squeezed Carol's hand.

Carol hadn't known either Gretchen or Maddie well in her college days, and realized now it had been her loss. She could have used friends like these two. Then and now.

Even after all this time, the pain of that last confrontation with Clark was fresh and sharp. She'd honestly believed, naive as she'd been back then, that Clark had loved her. She'd believed he'd have taken whatever measures necessary to keep her in Seattle and in his life. Instead, he'd taught her one of the most valuable lessons of her youth.

"What about Eddie?"

"Yeah, Eddie," Gretchen put in. "Did you have dinner with him, after all?"

"Oh, yes," Carol whispered, and laughed at the memory. "Only it didn't turn out the way I'd planned."

"The dress didn't fit?"

"Oh, it fit just fine, but I was so miserable without Clark that it was all I could do to even look at Eddie."

"You fell in love with Clark, didn't you?"

"Oh, yes," she said again. It amazed her how long it took her to recognize what should have been apparent. Instead, she'd allowed her experience with Eddie to cloud her judgment, and by the time she recognized the truth it was too late.

"Tell me what happened when you met Eddie," Maddie insisted. "Did he want you back?"

"I think so, but actually I never gave him a chance to ask. The entire evening was a disaster. All I could do was talk about Clark. It was Clark this and Clark that until Eddie tossed his napkin on the table and claimed he wasn't going to waste his time on a woman who was hung up on another man."

Both Gretchen and Maddie laughed.

"It serves him right," Maddie said. "It feels good when someone who's done you wrong gets his comeuppance."

A silence fell between them. "Are you speaking from experience?" Gretchen asked.

"You could say that," Maddie admitted reluctantly. "You probably remember me as something of a bad girl. I said and did some outrageous things in my college days, but I only did them to attract attention."

Gretchen chuckled. "I seem to recall more than one of your stunts. You were crazy, girl."

"You can say that again," Maddie said, and

smiled. "But the craziest trick I ever pulled was falling in love with John Theda."

"Professor John Theda?" Gretchen had heard the rumors and remembered they'd caused quite a stir—a student capturing the heart of a faculty member!

"Yup. I had one class with him and it was love at first sight. I worked my butt off to gain his attention, and then we started seeing each other on the sly."

"Oh, Maddie."

"I knew it wasn't the smartest thing I've ever done, but I was in love. What can I say? He wanted to marry me—or so he claimed—and like a fool I believed him. After I graduated it was a different story. He couldn't be rid of me fast enough."

"He hurt you, didn't he?"

Pain flashed in Maddie's eyes. "Yes, I won't lie about that. He did hurt me, more than I thought it was possible for any man to hurt me. Eventually I got back at him."

"You did? How?" The bad girl had Carol's full attention.

"You sure you want to hear this?"

"I'm sure," Gretchen said.

"Me, too." Carol wouldn't miss this for the world. Professor Theda had given her a C on a paper she'd written in order to get out of the final. Eddie had handed in the exact same paper the following quarter—she'd let him copy hers—and had been given an A. She'd love hearing how the professor got what he deserved, and if she remembered Maddie correctly, Maddie was just the one to do it.

Maddie

Chapter 1

Maddie Cobain enjoyed her bad-girl image. She thrived on letting others believe she was a sexual tigress on the prowl, changing bed partners as often as she changed her underwear. Her clothes and hair were outrageous. Her thick auburn curls plunged all the way down her back, bouncing against her shapely buttocks. Her skintight pants and thigh-high leather boots attracted plenty of attention along with her more-than-adequate bustline. That she would end up at a classy private college was a fluke, a gift from a rich uncle, which in fact was the truth, although she let her classmates assume otherwise.

Maddie was thrilled by her notoriety. Men paid her attention, women envied her, and she lapped it up, becoming more and more outrageous. That was until she met her Waterloo. Who'd have believed that an advanced-mathematics class would change her life? To be accurate, it wasn't the class, but the man who taught it. John Theda. For the first time in her life Maddie Cobain fell head over heels in love. Her college career had been marked with average grades. She wasn't stupid, but good grades conflicted with her image; therefore she tended to downplay her brains.

Until she met John.

It hadn't been easy to garner his attention. She'd done everything but drape herself naked over the top of his desk. He wasn't like other professors she'd known. They seemed old and stuffy. Not John. He was only thirty and handsome as sin. Half the females in class were in love with him, and the ones who weren't were either brain-dead or blind. It was a wonder anyone managed to keep their minds focused on the subject matter.

Because he was outgoing and friendly, John flirted effortlessly with his students, refusing to play favorites. After class the female members would flock around his desk like bees seeking nectar. It was apparent her peers knew nothing about the art of subtlety. Unlike the others, Maddie bided her time and found far more astute methods of calling attention to herself. Instead of revealing her interest in John, she cozied up to the subject matter itself. Clearly mathematics was a subject near and dear to John's heart. If she was going to have any success with the man himself, she had to play his game. And play she did, as if her very life depended on it.

Maddie studied as she never had before, poring over books, memorizing everything she could about math concepts. She'd always been good with numbers, mathematical theories and concepts. To her, mathematics was poetry without words. Numbers were precise, rational and real, much easier to understand than people. Numbers she understood. Numbers weren't unreasonable. Numbers were fun.

Before long she had top marks. Still John Theda didn't reveal an iota of interest in her. By midterm Maddie was convinced nothing she said or did would attract her teacher.

But she was wrong.

Her plan of action was to dazzle him with how well she did on the midterm exam, so far the biggest test of the year. She studied half the night, falling asleep at her desk in the early-morning hours. To her horror she overslept and raced around like a madwoman, arriving late for the test. Breathless, her hair a mass of curls, wearing the same clothes she'd worn the previous day, she crashed into the classroom convinced she'd blown it. Everyone else sat at their desks huddled protectively over the exam sheets. Their attention swiveled to her as if she'd purposely disrupted them. Maddie even thought she heard someone whisper about her being up half the night with some guy.

Standing in the doorway of the classroom, she looked to John for guidance. He smiled sweetly, told her to sit down and handed her a test. The first page was easy. Kid stuff. She whizzed through that and the second sheet, as well. Then she hit a wall. The last page consisted of one problem.

Maddie read it once. Twice. Three times, and felt herself starting to panic. Closing her eyes, she cleared her mind and focused all her energy and reasoning abilities on the problem. By the time the test period was nearly over, Maddie was the only student left in the room.

With one eye on the clock and another on the

empty sheet in front of her, she bit into her lower lip, hating to turn in an incomplete test. The others had gotten it apparently. She'd watched as the student next to her had scribbled in an answer.

Then it came to her. The method, the answer, the theory. Scribbling as fast as her fingers would allow, she worked out the problem and handed the completed test to John Theda with a full thirty seconds to spare.

To Maddie's delight her plan worked. John sought her out after the test, complimented her on her class work, and invited her to coffee in an out-of-the-way café. They saw each other frequently from that point forward.

Because John wasn't a full professor yet and because the school would have frowned on his dating a student, they kept their growing attraction for each other a secret. John hated it as much as Maddie. Meeting on the sly, pretending they meant nothing to each other, was hell for them both. As graduation grew nearer, Maddie found it impossible to hold the news of their engagement inside her any longer.

She told Janice Hailey, a sorority sister. The news spread like wildfire across campus. People she hadn't spoken to in all four years stopped and asked her if it was true. Maddie refused to lie. She was madly in love, and it was either speak the truth or burst. Her sorority sisters had already guessed she was in love; they said she glowed with happiness. Maddie was happy, blissfully so. Although John had never said anything to her about the way she dressed, she knew as a professor's wife she'd need to tone down her flamboyant style. She was willing to do whatever was necessary to be the kind of wife who would make him proud.

With graduation upon them, Maddie could see no reason to continue the charade. It wasn't necessary to hide how they felt about each other any longer. They were free to share their feelings. Free to express their love. Free to tell others.

John, however, wasn't pleased when he learned what she'd done. They routinely met at his place when he was finished with his classes for the day. Maddie hurried there and found him pacing the kitchen, waiting for her.

"You couldn't have waited until after graduation?" he demanded, slapping his hand on the table. He hit it hard enough to upset the napkin holder.

Maddie flinched, and then because she realized she should have talked it over with him first, apologized. "I'm sorry, but I only told Janice." Maddie had purposely chosen the one person in her sorority house who didn't know how to keep a secret. After months of sneaking around on the sly, Maddie was tired of games. Tired of excuses.

"You could get me fired," John said, walking to the kitchen sink and staring out the window.

Maddie wrapped her arms around his waist and pressed the side of her face against his back. "Don't be mad, Bunny Toes." He loved her nickname for him. If anything would get him out of his bad mood, it was a little baby talk and some tender loving attention.

"What am I supposed to do if Dean Williams hears of this?"

It didn't look like much of a problem to Maddie. "Marry me sooner." She wrapped her calf around his thigh and slid her bare foot down the inside of his leg. She felt him tense, and she knew he was fighting the strong physical attraction between them. If past experience was any indication, it wouldn't be long before he forgave her. She decided to make it easy for him to absolve her from her sins. It took some doing, but she managed to get him out of his jacket and unbutton his shirt. Then she spread moist spongy kisses across his naked chest. He smelled of cologne, but tasted salty and sweaty. His hands bit into her shoulders.

He kissed her hard and she kissed him back, arching against him. This was better, much much better.

Then without warning, he pushed her up against the wall so hard she could hardly breathe. But she didn't care, giving herself over to his masterful lovemaking. But that, too, had changed. His mouth was hard, painfully so. Suddenly he was all lips, teeth and anger.

"Johnny," she whimpered, twisting her face away from his. "You're hurting me."

"Good."

His response shocked her into passivity. Her arms fell limply at her sides as she attempted to convince herself she'd misunderstood him.

"You're a fool. Did you know that?" He laughed harshly, the sound echoing in her ear like distant thunder.

"What's wrong?" she pleaded. "Tell me what's wrong!"

"You. That's what's wrong. Get out."

If he'd stunned her before, this last comment paralyzed her with shock and disbelief. This was John, her Bunny Toes. He'd never talked to her like this, never raised his voice to her, never said or did anything to hurt her.

Backing away, John rammed his fingers through his hair. He surveyed her and his gaze held undisguised contempt, as if merely having her in his home was more than he could tolerate.

"What is it?" she asked, fighting back tears. "Tell me what it is I've done that's so wrong."

"Everything," he answered with a sneer. "Now get out."

Pride rescued her. "Fine," she said, sitting on the floor and reaching for her boots. Before long she was outside. Hardly aware of the fresh sweet air, scented with cherry blossoms and sunshine, Maddie walked back to the campus.

Instead of returning to the sorority house, she found an isolated shady spot under a fir tree and sat, hoping to collect her chaotic thoughts. John's behavior made no sense. Until now, he'd been loving, gentle and good-natured.

True, she'd broken her word by letting Janice know they were engaged, but graduation was less than three days away. It shouldn't matter if anyone knew they were in love. Especially now. For all intents and purposes classes were over. Graduation was a formality.

Maddie closed her eyes. John had made her feel dirty and ugly. The cool grass and the gentle breeze off Puget Sound helped ease the ache in her heart.

Three senior men strolled past and Maddie defiantly raised her chin. She knew one of them. Steve Malcom had made numerous attempts to date her. Because she was involved with John, she hadn't been interested. Even if she hadn't been dating John, Steve wouldn't have interested her.

Unfortunately Steve Malcom couldn't take no for an answer. He had a reputation as a ladies' man and her rejection had tarnished his image. A friend had warned her recently that Steve had promised to make her his final college conquest.

The last thing she needed just then was to deal with Steve's libido. Despite her lack of welcome, Steve broke away from his friends and headed in her direction.

Maddie groaned inwardly, but rather than lower her gaze, she met his in open defiance. Steve had an irritating way about him but, she silently promised herself, she wouldn't allow him to dent her composure. Not this time, when she was vulnerable and confused.

His gaze slid over her appreciatively. His look made her uneasy, but she said nothing.

"Sweetie pie, what are you doing here all by yourself?" Steve asked.

"Enjoying the solitude."

"I've come to help you," he said, leaning against the tree trunk, his hands buried in his pockets. He crossed his ankles in the practiced pose of someone modeling for a catalog.

If she hadn't been depressed and miserable, Maddie might have laughed, but her head and heart ached, and she needed to reason out what had happened with John.

"Is it true?" Steve asked.

She looked at him and blinked, her thoughts racing like a hamster's exercise wheel. "Is what true?"

"That you and John Theda are engaged?"

In light of what had happened earlier, Maddie wasn't sure how to answer. She neither confirmed nor denied the rumor. "It could be," she returned.

"Either you are or you aren't," Steve pressed.

"Let's put it in terms you can understand, then," she offered. "It's none of your damn business."

Steve laughed sharply. "That's what I thought.

A mathematics professor isn't your type. Oh, he might let you think so, seeing the benefits you offer," he added, snickering. "But you're not the marrying kind, and Theda knows it."

That did it. She roared to her feet, knotting her fists at her sides, forgetting her resolve to not allow him to rile her. "I love John and he loves me. We're going to be married as soon as I graduate."

"Really?" Steve made it sound like one big joke.

"Really!" Her tone had an equal measure of confidence.

"You and a math professor." He laughed and shook his head.

"I don't need your approval and neither does John." The anger burned inside her, but she wasn't going to let Steve know that. Her composure was partially back, and she pretended he was nothing more than a pest she was forced to endure. Fortunately he'd soon be gone.

Steve rubbed the side of his jaw as if giving the question serious consideration. "You know, you've got me curious."

She had no intention of asking him what had garnered his interest. She'd endured quite enough of this mindless conversation, and she turned away.

To her surprise Steve captured her arm and pulled her toward him. With her momentum carrying her, her body collided against his. Not giving her a chance to recover, he kissed her, rubbing his moist sticky mouth against hers.

It required one swiftly delivered jab to the right area to convince Steve Malcom to release her. Not waiting to give him ample opportunity to repeat the action, she reeled away from him and hurried across the campus.

She hadn't gone far, her head down and walking as fast as her feet would carry her, when she ran, literally, into Brent Holliday, another senior. Mumbling an apology, she hurriedly crossed the lawn toward the sorority house. As she walked, she felt Brent's scrutiny and disapproval burning a hole in her back.

Once inside the safety and familiarity of her room, she sat on her bed, her back against the headboard, legs bent, her face buried in her knees. It didn't take long to convince herself she'd hear from John that night. He was probably trying to phone her that very moment. He might even come for her, although he never had before, anxious to apologize. Until that very afternoon he'd always been loving and generous with her. They'd spent as much time together as possible. Because he'd taken up so much of her free time, Maddie's grades had slipped since the midterms, especially in classes other than math.

When she didn't hear from John by the next morning, she mulled over what to do. John had been angry with her, angrier than she'd ever seen him, but when they married, they would face this kind of situation again and again. It was important that they learn to resolve their problems. By noon she'd decided that, if he wouldn't seek her out, she'd confront him.

Her guess was that John was embarrassed by the things he'd said and done. He'd appreciate the fact she loved him enough to come to him and settle this matter once and for all.

As for her part in their disagreement, she wasn't blameless. He was right—she shouldn't have told Janice about the engagement. But John needed to realize that his behavior had been unacceptable. He owed her an apology, as well. Having made the decision to seek him out, Maddie felt worlds better.

Unfortunately, before she could confront John,

she was required to attend practice for the graduation exercise. As luck would have it, she was paired up with Brent Holliday. He didn't like her. That much had been apparent from their brief encounter the afternoon before.

He didn't look pleased to be assigned her partner. She wasn't exactly overjoyed, either.

"You can always request a change," she muttered under her breath as they lined up two by two, a male graduate on the left and a female on the right.

"I already tried."

Despite her hard outer edge, Maddie flinched, surprised that his words had the power to hurt her. She didn't know Brent well and had no desire to. From what she understood, his degree was in criminology. He'd already been accepted into the Seattle Police Academy. A fitting occupation for the son of one of Seattle's best-known pastors. The Reverend Earl Holliday faithfully preached fire and brimstone every Sunday morning at eleven. Not that Maddie was interested in attending church services.

"One would assume a preacher's son would have a more charitable tongue," Maddie said, favoring him with a saccharine-sweet smile.

He chuckled softly as the processional music blared from the speakers set up on the stage. "Don't make the mistake of confusing me with my father," he warned under his breath.

"I don't think there's much worry there."

They marched silently up the aisle. With someone else Maddie would have joked and teased. Not with Brent. He'd made no attempt to be friendly, and she couldn't help wondering what she'd ever done to him. He didn't know her any better than she knew him.

As sophomores they'd had a couple of classes together, if she remembered correctly. Her degree was in history, and she'd rarely seen him once she'd declared her major. She'd chosen history for her uncle Alfie, because it was his passion, his love.

It was because of her uncle that she'd enrolled in Nelson Lord University. Although she'd made jokes about her rich uncle, Maddie loved him dearly. Her own father had died when she was seven, and she could barely remember him. Alfie was her father's oldest brother, and he'd taken it upon himself to see that his brother's two children were properly cared for and educated.

Although he was getting on in years, Uncle Alfie had insisted on attending her graduation. Maddie wished now that she'd worked harder, attained better grades. Uncle Alfie was a sweetheart and she owed him more than she could ever repay.

After practice Maddie couldn't escape the school gymnasium fast enough. The last hour had dragged like a dredge scraping the ocean bottom. Sitting though the interminable practice had been pure torture, so great was her need to talk to John. And all the while she'd waited, she'd prayed that he'd cleared up in his own mind whatever had plagued him the day before.

Rushing across the campus, she found him alone in his classroom reading a scientific journal. When he saw her, he quickly closed the magazine and stuffed it into his briefcase.

Maddie relaxed. All was well.

She soon discovered that her assumption was premature. His eyes hardened, and her heart went still.

"John?"

"Get out."

"What?" She couldn't believe what she was hearing. This was the man she loved, the man she planned to marry!

He stood, and his face darkened to a scowl. "You heard me. Out."

It was almost comical that John believed he could intimidate her with a few angry words. She'd stood up to bigger men than John Theda. "You owe me an explanation," she said. "What's going on?" Ignoring his command, she marched into the classroom, then stood her ground, refusing to move until she discovered what was wrong.

John stood and snapped his briefcase closed. "I've had a change of heart."

"Like that?" she snapped her fingers.

"Just like that," he agreed. "I can't trust you."

"But...that's ridiculous!"

"I relied on you to keep delicate information regarding our relationship private, and you blew it."

"But surely—"

"That isn't all." He looked as if the mere sight of her was enough to make him sick to his stomach. "Do you seriously think I don't know what's going on between you and Steve Malcom?"

"Steve Malcom!" That was almost as ridiculous as his previous statement.

"I understand the two of you were kissing in full view of the entire student body."

Maddie opened her mouth to defend herself, then promptly closed it. The kissing incident had happened following the ugly confrontation with John. And now John was using it as an excuse to give credibility to his behavior.

"It's over," he announced as if they were talking about something as mundane as a television movie, instead of their lives together.

Maddie's knees felt like they would no longer support her. "I don't understand," she said, and her voice, faint as a summer breeze, wobbled with shock and dismay.

"I don't expect you to. Goodbye." With his spine ramrod stiff, John Theda stalked out of the classroom and out of the building.

In all her life, Maddie couldn't remember being more hurt. For almost twenty minutes she sat and waited for the worst of the pain and disappointment to pass.

Uncle Alfie, so kind and wise, had told her that the measure of maturity could be gauged by how quickly a person bounced back from a disappointment. John's rejection was more than a disappointment. A numbness that refused to go away settled in the area of her heart.

She'd learned her lesson, though, and it would

take one hell of a long time for her to risk her heart again.

One hell of a long time.

The graduation exercise was a blur. The one thing Maddie remembered was walking across the stage and being required to pose, briefly, for the camera. Knowing John sat somewhere in the front three rows with the other staff members gave her the necessary incentive to act as though she hadn't a care in the world. She dazzled Dean Williams with the brilliance of her smile, accepted her diploma and walked down the stairs.

Following the graduation exercise, Uncle Alfie and Maddie's mother met her on the lawn outside. The glorious sunshine made Maddie squint as she stepped out of the gymnasium. Ellie Cobain hugged her and wiped a tear from the corner of her eye, then turned to exchange pleasantries with a friend.

Uncle Alfie hugged Maddie next. "Your father would have been so proud of you," he whispered close to her ear.

Humbled, Maddie pressed her head to his shoulder. It was then that she saw Brent Holliday with his family. His gaze, dark and full of disapproval, lingered on her. To hell with him. She refused to allow him or John Theda or anyone else to destroy her enjoyment of this day.

Uncle Alfie insisted on taking Maddie and her mother to dinner at one of his private clubs. They sat at a corner table in an elegant dining room, where the walls were made of dark polished wood and the distinguished gold-framed portraits resembled the waiters.

"I can't tell you how pleased I am," Maddie's mother said as she set aside her menu. There were only a few selections, and the prices were outrageous, but Maddie knew Uncle Alfie wanted her to ignore them.

Ellie Cobain had never remarried. In many ways Maddie felt as if she'd lost both parents the day her father died. Her mother had withdrawn from life, shriveled up and surrendered to her grief. Maddie's world was forever changed.

"I'm pleased you chose Nelson Lord University," Uncle Alfie said, breaking into Maddie's thoughts.

She smiled, distinctly remembering that her sweetheart of an uncle had helped her make that choice. "I am, too," she said, pushing all thoughts of John from her mind and heart. After four years at Nelson Lord, she'd miss the school, miss shaking up a few sensibilities, miss the few friends she'd made.

"It's a good school," her mother inserted.

Maddie agreed with a nod.

"From what I understand, one of your mathematics professors recently made a name for himself in the history books."

"Really." She hadn't heard anything about that. Maddie reached for a dinner roll and a pat of butter in the form of a tiny rosebud.

"John Theda's his name, if I recall correctly," Uncle Alfie continued.

Maddie dropped her butter knife. It hit the edge of the gold-rimmed plate with a clang. Hastily she apologized and stared at her uncle. "Say that again?"

"I read about it in the *American Scientist Journal.*"

She continued to stare at her uncle blankly. "I don't understand."

"The quadratic quandary," Uncle Alfie said. "He solved it. It's been unsolvable for fifty years, probably longer. It's been years myself since I wrestled with it. Every student does, you know."

"When did this happen?" she asked. One thing

Maddie had learned about John in the months they'd dated was that he was basically lazy. He did exactly what was required of him to teach class and nothing beyond that. If he'd worked on solving the quadratic quandary, it was news to her.

"This April," her uncle explained. "It's big news."

"What *is* the quadratic quandary?" Maddie asked next.

An engineer by trade, Uncle Alfie removed a pad and pen from his inside jacket pocket and wrote out the equation. He stared at it for a couple of moments more, shook his head and scribbled a note, then handed it to her.

Maddie studied the equation and then looked up. "This isn't it."

Uncle Alfie frowned. "It is, as I recall."

Maddie scowled. "I had this problem on a mid-term test."

"Yes, that's quite common. I told you that almost every mathematical student is given the opportunity to solve it. Fifty years or more and it's never been done. That's why the Nelson Lord teacher is making a name for himself."

"But..." The room started to swim and she gripped the edge of the table.

"Maddie—" her mother gently touched her arm "—is everything all right, sweetheart?"

She couldn't answer, the anger bubbling up inside her until it threatened to explode. John Theda hadn't solved the quadratic quandary. She had. And he was accepting the credit.

Chapter 2

Maddie didn't mean to stop in the church. Eaten up with anger and frustration, she started walking aimlessly, with no real destination in mind. Two months had passed since graduation, she'd found a decent apartment and a good job with an insurance company, and had tried to make a life for herself. Outwardly she was doing well, but inwardly the turmoil brewed like malted beer. Nights were the worst. Try as she might, she couldn't get John out of her mind. The love she felt for him had festered like an infected sore. Bitterness ate at her. Anger. Frustration. She had no peace, no sleep, no comfort.

John had used her, and she'd been too blind and stupid to realize it. Used her, and while he was busy accepting credit for her accomplishment, he'd made sure she hadn't a clue what he was doing. No one would believe her if she had the audacity to claim she'd solved the quadratic quandary. That was exactly what John Theda was counting on her doing. Nothing.

It took her almost a week to realize how it'd happened. She remembered how she'd arrived for the exam late and therefore hadn't been there to hear him explain that the problem on the final test sheet had never been solved. If ever there was a testament to positive thinking, this was it. Maddie believed this was just one more problem on an already difficult test, and so she'd raced, full steam ahead, thinking the others had worked out the solution and so she could, too.

Later, when he handed back the tests, John had called her to his desk and apologized for having lost hers. He'd smiled, and because she'd been so infatuated with him, she'd accepted him at his word. As a means of making it up to her, he'd invited her to have coffee with him. She'd practically fallen all over herself in her eagerness to accept. Thinking about it now made her feel ill.

Everything would have gone smoothly for him if she hadn't blown the whistle and announced their engagement before graduation. His plan was to be long gone before she learned what he'd done and how he'd done it. From what she understood, he continued to live in Seattle and would for what remained of the summer, but he'd accepted a position at a prestigious university and been granted a full professorship.

The bitterness, anger and frustration made it impossible to hold still, and so she walked, often late into the night, until she was too exhausted to do anything but fall into bed and sleep.

This evening she stopped at the church. The door was unlocked, an unexpected surprise. She wasn't sure what had led her to this particular church or why she felt drawn inside. What she sought, Maddie suspected, was peace.

Slipping into the last pew in the darkened church, she bowed her head and closed her eyes. She hadn't done a whole lot of praying in her life, but she did now, silently pouring out her heart, grateful that the church was deserted. She wasn't sure how long she sat there in the solitude. Perhaps she even dozed. The next thing she knew someone said her name.

"Maddie?" The voice held evident surprise.

Flustered, Maddie glanced up, her heart pounding. Brent Holliday. He was the last person she wanted to see. How amused he must be to find her in a church.

Without waiting for a sarcastic comment, she grabbed her purse and leaped to her feet. She was half-out the door when he said, "Don't go."

She stopped midstride, her back to him. She said nothing, but she didn't turn around, either. Not sure what had prompted her to obey his command, Maddie closed her eyes, willing this to be over quickly. What John had done to her was humiliating enough.

"Church was the last place I expected to find you." Although the words cut, they lacked his usual biting sarcasm.

"I bet. Well, don't worry, I won't make attendance a habit. Nice seeing you again, Brent," she said, mocking him, and then stepped into the night, unwilling to linger. Unwilling to pretend they'd once been friends or could be now.

"Maddie."

She raced down the stairs, her feet bouncing against the concrete steps in her rush to escape.

That he'd hurry after her, his footsteps echoing

hers, was a surprise of its own. Walking swiftly, Maddie buried her hands in her pockets and forged ahead, pretending she hadn't heard him.

"Wait, Maddie. Please."

It was the "please" that did it. She paused beside a light standard, exhaled sharply and lifted her chin. "What?" she demanded, giving the impression she had places to go, people to see.

Brent stood about four feet away. He didn't say anything for a long time, and when she shifted her weight from one foot to the next in a silent hint of impatience, he spoke. "I owe you an apology."

"Several, I'd say." She wasn't making this easy for him, not that she was particularly angry with him. Any irritation with him paled next to what she felt toward John Theda.

"All right, several," he agreed. "I regret the things I said during graduation rehearsal—and other times too," he added, lumping his offenses together in one fell swoop.

She blinked twice, remembering how his attitude and his words had bit into her ego and how she'd pretended otherwise. Brent had never made a secret of his contempt for her.

"Don't worry about it." Her forgiveness came easily. It was unlikely they'd meet up again and she wasn't one to hold grudges. Then again maybe she was. She'd like nothing better than to find a way to hurt John.

Brent hesitated and she wasn't sure if he wanted to say more. She was about to leave when he asked gently, "Are you okay?"

She bristled, damning her luck for being found praying in a church. By Brent. "Of course I am. Why wouldn't I be?" Her tone was harsh.

"You tell me. You aren't exactly the first person I'd think to find in a church at night." He sounded edgy himself, irritated, which was exactly what she wanted to happen. If she got him angry enough, maybe he'd leave her alone.

Still she didn't look at him. Not directly, anyway, for fear he'd notice the shadows beneath her eyes or the weight she'd lost. Afraid he'd ask questions she didn't want to answer.

The silence stretched tautly between them. Maddie was eager to be on her way, yet reluctant to leave, which made no sense. But she felt there was something more Brent longed to say and was holding back. Not that she'd encouraged him.

"I...I've got to get home," she blurted, although it was a small lie. No one awaited her return. No one worried if she was home or not.

"Yeah, me, too. Do you want a ride?"

"No, but thanks." She stepped away from the light standard and then hesitated, remembering he'd been a criminology major. It was only polite that she inquire how life was treating him. "Everything going okay at the police academy?"

"Great."

She offered him a brief wobbly smile. "I'm pleased to hear it. Good to see you again, Brent." Surprisingly she meant that.

"You, too, Maddie."

For some unexplainable reason, Maddie thought she heard a hint of sadness in his voice. Perhaps it was something more. Well, if he suffered a few regrets, then so did she, but her regrets were bogged down with self-recriminations for allowing herself to be used by someone who didn't deserve or appreciate her love.

"Good night," she added companionably. Brent wasn't so bad, and she wished now that she'd made more of an effort to get to know him when she'd had the chance. She'd gone no more than a few steps when he called out to her once more.

Hands in her pockets, she turned around, poised in the middle of the sidewalk.

"If you ever need someone or something, call me."

"You?" She wasn't sure she'd heard him correctly. Only a few months earlier he'd mocked her. Now he claimed he wanted to help her.

Brent cocked a smile, one side of his mouth riding up with amusement. "Yes, me. You're not doing my ego any good, you know."

She chuckled softly and it felt good. The last time she'd had reason to laugh had been too long ago to remember. She'd buried herself in recrimination, doubts and regrets. It was a tight fit, leaving little room for humor or frivolity.

By the time she'd walked back to her apartment, it was well after midnight and she was exhausted. After a long hot shower, she climbed into bed and slept the night through, something she hadn't done in weeks.

She awoke refreshed and eager for a new day. It took her some time to realize she felt better and why. Brent Holliday. Whatever had happened to cause him to apologize she didn't know. It didn't matter. She was grateful to know she had at least one friend in Seattle.

The idea didn't come to her until the following afternoon. While she didn't know Brent Holliday well, she felt strongly that he'd meant what he'd said. If she needed someone or something, all she had to do was give him a call. The lyrics to the old Carole King hit "You've Got a Friend" played through her mind the rest of the day. She wanted to believe Brent's offer of friendship was sincere and so decided to test it.

Maddie hadn't told anyone what John had done. What good would it do? she reasoned. No one was likely to believe her. No one would expect her to be capable of such an achievement. What irked her the most was that she'd done this to herself. She'd played this silly game, dressed and acted like a "bad girl," a brainless twit. An aptitude for numbers didn't fit in with her carefully constructed image.

Her mistake had been that, in assuming the role she had, she'd almost lost her true identity, forgotten who she really was. Well, no more. She'd packed away her thigh-high leather boots, tamed her hair and lengthened her skirts, then stared at the stranger in the mirror. The Maddie who'd been so hungry for attention was forever gone. The one who grieved over the loss of her emotional innocence had laid claim to her soul, and the real Maddie Cobain had stepped forward.

It'd taken her the better part of the summer to discover who the real Maddie Cobain actually was, and Maddie learned that she liked this person. The woman without pretensions. The woman who had no need to impress others. The woman willing to risk the chance on being herself.

Brent couldn't really have noticed the differences in her in the dark and when she'd been dressed for a cool stroll. But he would. She'd make sure of it.

Phoning him, suggesting they meet for coffee, had seemed like a simple plan. All she had to do was get his phone number from his parents—they were in the book—and place the call. But even that first step required courage.

When she finally managed to dredge up the fortitude, she dialed, closed her eyes and waited. To her surprise and relief Brent was the one who answered.

"Hello," he grumbled as if picking up the receiver had inconvenienced him greatly. In her surprise she didn't speak right away, and he said hello again with a more pronounced tone of impatience.

"Brent?"

Silence, then, "Maddie."

He'd recognized her voice. "I... Could you meet me for coffee?"

"Sure. When? Where?" he responded with no hesitation.

She decided on the Java Joint, a coffeehouse not far from the Nelson Lord campus, and named a time in the evening she felt would be convenient for them both.

"Fine, I'll see you then."

His eagerness was a balm that helped ease the ache that had held her heart prisoner all these weeks.

Brent had arrived ahead of her, and he waved when she entered and glanced around. He'd chosen a booth in the back of the room and she was grateful for the limited privacy it afforded them.

The coffeehouse was a leftover from the early sixties when beatniks played bongos and recited poetry. Maddie resisted the urge to snap her fingers and say words like "groovy" whenever she stopped by for a latte.

The walls were black with brightly colored geometric designs in red, orange, yellow and blue. The counter was decorated with polka dots of different colors and sizes, and the room was filled with the pungent aroma of coffee.

"Thank you for coming," she said, scooting onto the wooden bench across from him.

Brent stared at her as if seeing her for the first time. "Maddie?"

"Yes, it's the new me." She beamed at him. Her auburn hair was tied at the base of her neck with a yellow ribbon. She wore loose-fitting jeans and a sleeveless blouse. Cotton, white and plain with an eyelet collar.

His mouth opened and then slowly closed as if whatever he'd wanted to say had gotten lost somewhere between his mind and his lips.

"I imagine you're wondering why I suggested we meet," she began after the waiter, a college student, had taken their order.

He nodded. "I'll admit to being curious. About that and other things." But he appeared patient enough to wait until she explained matters to him in her own time and in her own way.

"I don't know if you heard or not, but I was dating John Theda in the spring." With effort she managed to keep her voice even and reveal none of her feelings. The waiter returned with their order and she smiled her thanks.

Brent waited until the college student left before

he responded, "I heard you and Theda were an item or something to that effect."

"I thought you might have." This was where it grew difficult. If Brent didn't believe her, she didn't know what she'd do. "We didn't exactly date," she told him. "Oh, he took me out to dinner now and again, but always at an out-of-the-way place. His biggest fear was that someone from the school would see us together."

"I think you should know up front," Brent said, stopping her. "I'm not much of a Theda fan."

She laughed. "Neither am I."

A heartbeat later he asked, his voice gentle with concern, "Are you pregnant?"

"No!" she cried, angry that he would assume such a thing. After a moment she realized it was a logical conclusion after finding her in a church, clearly troubled. His willingness to meet her held greater significance. Even now she wasn't sure she was doing the right thing. She wouldn't if she hadn't been so desperate for a friend.

"Sorry, I shouldn't have asked," he said, gesturing for her to continue. "I won't interrupt again."

"Do... How comfortable are you with math?"

His gaze searched out hers. "Comfortable enough to balance my checkbook."

His smile caught her off guard, and for a moment, perhaps longer, she was held captive by it. Men often grinned at her, but generally they were looking for something she wasn't willing to give. Brent's eyes held warmth and genuine concern. Friendship.

"As it happens," she said, forcing herself to look away, "I'm quite good with numbers."

"That doesn't surprise me."

"I'm more than good. I'm competent enough to have solved the quadratic quandary." She waited a moment for that to sink in. Either he believed her or he didn't. She had no way of proving it. No way of supplying irrefutable evidence that would convince him, the school or anyone else.

Brent frowned, then shook his head as if to clear his thoughts. "Are you saying what I think you're saying?" His left hand tightened around his coffee cup until his knuckles whitened.

"Yes. It was me who calculated the correct answer, not John."

"And Theda claimed the credit." Brent flexed his right hand as if itching to plow it into the professor's face.

"You believe me?"

"Yes." His emphatic reply removed all doubt.

"Why?"

"Why not?" He met her gaze steadily. "You said it, and that's good enough for me."

If she ever fell in love again, she thought, it would be with a man who cared this deeply that she'd been wronged. A man whose belief in her didn't waver.

"That was the reason he...he asked me to marry him. But it was all a ruse. With my head and my heart preoccupied, I paid no attention to anything else. John knew he couldn't allow a word to get out until after graduation. He counted on my not knowing what I'd done." She explained the circumstances, how she'd arrived late for the exam and so didn't understand the significance of the last problem.

"It isn't just that he's taking credit," she said. "It's that he used me, hurt me. I'm convinced he never loved me, never intended for us to marry. He played me for a fool." Her voice shook with the fervor of her emotions. "I want him to know what it's like to be embarrassed in front of one's peers. I want him to feel the same humiliation."

"And you think I can help?" Brent asked.

"Yes."

Brent didn't look convinced. "How?"

"You know people. You have connections. Surely if I talked to a detective, he might be able to do something. If nothing more, I'd like to file a complaint."

"And claim what? That he stole your thought process?"

"He took a lot more than that," Maddie returned heatedly.

"I'm sorry, Maddie." He sounded as frustrated as she felt.

"I know."

"Did you talk to Dean Williams about this?"

"No." It would do no good, for it would be John's word against hers, and it went without saying who the dean would choose to believe. "I want him to suffer," she mused aloud.

"I wish there was something I could do."

Maybe it'd been a mistake to tell Brent, but telling someone else what had happened eased the tension in her stomach considerably. She'd known for a long time that life was unfair. Not only had John Theda hurt her pride and her heart, he'd stolen her work and claimed it as his own. And now

he was responsible for what she was sure would
end up as a stomach ulcer.

"Well, I appreciate being able to talk to you
about it," Maddie said. "So in a way you've already done something."

"Who else have you told?"

"No one."

"No one?" He sounded incredulous. "Why'd
you choose me?"

The answer to that wasn't as simple as it
sounded. "I'm not sure. Because...well, you
seemed approachable when we met at the church.
Nice."

"Hey, don't sound so shocked."

She laughed softly.

"What made you—" he studied her a moment
"—you know, change...clothes."

"I didn't want to be stupid any longer."

"Stupid?"

"The woman you knew in college was playing
a game. I'm through being the bad girl."

His gaze held hers. "You never fit the part."

Oh, but she had, Maddie thought. She'd grown
comfortable with the role, high on the attention she
received. Daring and bold, wild and fun. That was
her, willing to try anything once. Twice if it

caused a commotion. Three times if a crowd gathered and someone phoned the police.

"I knew otherwise," Brent continued, "and that was what troubled me most. I wanted to shake you, demand that you stop and reveal the real you. Let go of the outrageous persona and that hard-edged facade."

Maddie couldn't stop staring at him. He'd believed her when she'd laid claim to the unbelievable, and she could offer him no less than her trust. What he said was equally true. He'd known. He'd always known.

"So, what about an attorney?" he said now.

She'd thought of that, too. "I'd need the money to pay a retainer, money I don't have. Besides, I don't have any real proof."

He closed his eyes and exhaled forcefully. "The guy's a slimeball."

"I appreciate you hearing me out, Brent, I really do. It's helped tremendously."

"I'm glad. I know it's going to be difficult for you to let this go."

"Let it go?" She had no intention of doing that.

His gaze narrowed. "You *are* letting this go, aren't you?"

"No way!"

"What do you intend to do?"

"I don't think I should tell you."

"Why not?"

Maddie grinned, hope stirring her senses alive once again. "It's illegal."

Chapter 3

"I'd be more comfortable if I knew what you were thinking," Brent said, frowning darkly.

Maddie shook her head. "It's better that you don't."

Despite her protest, Brent picked up the tab for their coffee and followed her outside. The night was warm, despite the breeze coming off Lake Washington. Maddie had taken the bus to the Java Joint, and now she walked toward the transit waiting area to catch one home.

"Maddie!" Brent was beginning to sound irritated as he caught up with her. "Come on, I'll give you a ride."

She giggled, and oh, how good it felt to laugh again! "You don't know where I live."

"You can tell me. *And* you can explain what you've got up your sleeve."

"Really, Brent, it's best you don't know."

"I'll be the judge of that!" Putting her hand in the crook of his elbow, he led her across the street to where he'd parked his car, then unlocked the door and helped her inside. Such a gentlemanly thing to do, Maddie thought. The men she'd dated weren't inclined to open the door for her. Not even John.

"Tell me what you're thinking of doing," he demanded once he was in the driver's seat. He put the key in the ignition but didn't turn it.

"I'm going to break into John's house and find my test paper."

Brent's hands folded around the steering wheel and he glared straight ahead. "You're right, I don't want to hear that."

"I won't involve you."

"Maddie, this is craziness. Pure craziness. You could get thrown in jail for a stunt like that."

"I know." It was incredible how good she felt now that she had a plan of action. It felt as if the heaviest of burdens had been lifted from her shoulders. For weeks she'd wallowed in self-pity, moping around crying about how she'd been misused and abused. Well, no longer. She'd find a way to prove John was a thief and worse. Even if that meant risking jail time.

"Maddie—"

She interrupted him. "Don't try to talk me out of this. I'm serious. I'm going to find that test paper. John must have it somewhere. I know him."

"He'd be a fool to keep it."

"My point exactly. John Theda is a fool." Brent didn't understand. The least she could do was try to prove her case. She'd never be able to live with herself if she stood by and did nothing, which was what had made her so miserable until now.

"When do you plan to do this?" he asked, heaving a huge sigh of resignation.

"Tonight," she returned, giving no thought to the matter. Why not? She'd waited this long, and now that the decision was made she could see no reason to delay it. As for her odds of locating that test paper, she hadn't a clue More than likely Brent was right, but she had to discover that for herself.

"How are you going to get there?" he asked, starting the ignition.

"Bus." It was the only means of transportation available to her.

He turned and stared at her. "You're going to take Seattle Transit to commit a felony?"

"That's what I said."

He wiped his hand down his face. "I can't believe I'm hearing this."

Maddie giggled, feeling almost giddy with happiness.

"What if he's home?" Brent asked, as if this hadn't occurred to her.

"On Thursday night? Nope, I know him. He's with his card-playing buddies, unless, of course, it's his turn to host."

Brent pounded his forehead against the steering wheel. "You can't do this."

"I don't have any choice."

He exhaled a deep breath as if he'd reached an important decision. "Then I'm coming with you."

Now it was Maddie's turn to be concerned. "Oh, no," she said, and shook her head. "I won't hear of it."

"You can't stop me any more than I can stop

you.'' His grin was wide, triumphant and sly. The kind of grin that demands a response.

''But—''

''Turnabout is fair play,'' he said. ''If you're going to risk your future on something so incredibly—''

''You'll stay in the car?'' she demanded, cutting him off. Yes, there were risks, she knew that, but she didn't dare look too closely at them or she'd talk herself out of it, which she didn't want to do. Although she put up a fuss, she was pleased that Brent would be there. If for nothing else but moral support.

He backed out of his parking space, then finally answered, ''Probably.''

''Probably? Not good enough. You have to promise. Give me your word as a gentleman that you'll stay completely out of sight. Otherwise I'll do it alone some other time without telling you.''

From the intense color his eyes turned and the ferocity with which he pulled out onto the road, she knew he wasn't keen on the alternative. Good. If he was caught with her or anywhere close to her, Brent's career with the police academy would be over. She didn't need that on her conscience.

''All right, I'll stay in the car and wait.''

"On your word as a gentleman," she prompted.

"On my word as a gentleman," he said. His promise seemed to lack sincerity, and Maddie was tempted to challenge him further, but she had other matters to consider, the least of which was whether John Theda was home or not.

They stopped off at a pay phone and Maddie called John's house. The answering machine clicked on after four rings and, not bothering to listen to the message, she replaced the receiver. Smiling triumphantly, she gave Brent a thumbs-up and headed back to the car. Brent looked almost disappointed.

As they approached John's neighborhood, she had second thoughts about involving Brent. She tried to talk him into simply dropping her off. If he drove away now and she was caught and arrested, no one could accuse him of aiding and abetting. Even if he was seen, all he'd need to do was claim he was unaware of her intentions. No one would doubt him. He was the son of a preacher, and his word was good as gold.

Brent, however, would have none of it. He was not going to leave her on her own.

He parked half a block down the street from

John's rental house, but in full view. He kept the engine running.

"John's car is missing," Maddie said. She started to open the car door, but Brent stopped her by grabbing hold of her arm.

"Could it be in the garage?" he asked.

She shook her head. "It could, but I doubt it, seeing that the garage-door opener has needed a new battery from the moment I met him. It isn't likely he's changed it now." Not when he was said to be moving within the next couple of months to another university.

Brent continued to grip her forearm. "How do you plan to get inside the house?"

That seemed a silly question. "The key."

"You have a key?" he asked incredulously.

"Well, not exactly, but I know where one is."

Brent's eyes widened even more. "You mean to tell me he keeps a spare key tucked under a flowerpot?"

"No, it's hidden in a fake rock in his flower bed." Brent's fingers loosened enough for her to free her arm. She got out, then bent down to look through the window and offer Brent a reassuring smile. "Wish me luck."

"I wish to hell you weren't doing this."

''Hey, this is gonna be a piece of cake,'' she said, feeling lighthearted in her eagerness to prove how easy this would be. Why, oh, why hadn't she thought of this sooner? She'd endured weeks of mental turmoil, refusing to seek any solution of her own. Brent's wisdom had empowered her, and she was grateful.

''Come on, wish me luck,'' she said again.

He offered her an all-too-brief smile. ''Good luck.''

''Thanks.''

From experience Maddie should have realized that often the thing that looks the easiest proves to be the most difficult. She walked up the cement pathway to the house, something she'd done a thousand times before. None of John's neighbors were out or about, watering their lawn, talking across fences, that sort of thing, and Maddie was grateful. She hoped to nonchalantly slip inside John's house without a suggestion of a problem.

It didn't happen.

First she couldn't locate the fake rock. Squatting down in the flower bed, she picked up rock after rock, shaking each one. When she'd checked them all, she made a second go-round, this time placing each stone close to her ear, certain she must have overlooked the obvious.

She glanced up once to discover that Brent had eased down the road and had parked much closer to the house than was advisable. Damn him. Now he'd be watching her every move. No doubt he'd already figured out she'd run into a hitch.

Okay, so maybe John had done away with his fake rock. But even so, it was only a small detriment. There were other ways to get into the house. As she started toward the back, she noted that the lawn needed to be mowed. Perhaps John was out of town, which was all the better. Stopping abruptly, she reconsidered. Before she changed plans, she'd better tell Brent what she was doing; otherwise he might follow her. Bringing along a silent partner was becoming a hassle! Muttering under her breath, she trotted back to the car. When she approached the driver's side, Brent rolled down the window.

"Thank God," he breathed.

"Thank God for what?"

"You're giving this up, aren't you?"

The man obviously didn't know her very well. The phrase "give up" wasn't in her vocabulary. Good grief, how did Brent think she'd solved that silly math problem? Anyone possessing the qualities of persistence, tenacity and the will to succeed wasn't going to let a little thing like a missing key distract her from her goal.

"I haven't even been inside yet," she informed him, growing impatient with his attitude.

"Then why'd you want to talk to me?"

"To tell you I was going around the back of the house and—"

"I could see that," he muttered.

"—and to tell you to move the car," she finished.

"Why?"

"Because you're too close to the house. People can see you. Go down a block, maybe two. I'll find you when I'm finished."

"Maddie—"

"Please, Brent. You promised, remember?" This wasn't his battle, it was hers, and she didn't want him up to his armpits in trouble because of her.

"All right, all right." She could tell he didn't like it.

Maddie smiled and impulsively leaned into the car and kissed him full on the lips. She hadn't planned that, the action was purely instinctive.

Purely natural. A means of thanking him for giving her back a part of herself. A piece of her soul. Her serenity. His immediate response surprised her, delighted her. He took control of the exchange and threaded his fingers into her hair, holding her a willing captive.

Twisted as she was with her head inside the car, the kiss was awkward. But even that didn't distract from the pleasure of it. Maddie was the one who broke it off. For a long moment, she kept her eyes closed and remained silent. Brent's fingers remained in her hair, and he propped his forehead against hers.

"I...I won't be long," she promised when she found her voice. She stretched out her hand and pointed at John's house without looking to see if she'd aimed in the right direction.

"Be careful."

"There's nothing to worry about. Knowing John, he won't be home for hours. All I want is to see if he was stupid enough to leave my test paper lying around. I'm not interested in anything else."

"Get in and out as fast as you can."

"OK, partner."

Brent smiled and kissed the tip of her nose. "Hurry."

Her senses reeling thanks to Brent and the kiss they'd shared, she practically staggered back to the house and went round behind. And then she saw it. The fake rock was parked on the top step on the back porch. Maddie nearly laughed out loud. Set off by itself, without the camouflage of the other rocks, it looked exactly like what it was. John couldn't have made it any more apparent if he'd tried.

Maddie picked it up and removed the key. The door lock clicked open, and she went inside without a problem. Not risking any chance of someone walking in on her, she locked the door behind her. She'd tiptoed two or three steps, then paused and strained to hear any out-of-the-ordinary sounds. Anything that would indicate she wasn't alone.

She heard nothing.

The tension eased from her limbs and she made herself at home the way she had so many times before. The anxiety of the moment had made her parched; she opened the refrigerator and removed a can of soda. The six-pack she'd brought here months earlier was still there. John wasn't much of a pop drinker, so she'd supplied her own.

She took a swallow, then clutching the soda can, moved into John's office, or what he referred to as his office. Actually it was the formal dining room, but he'd set up his desk and bookcases there.

For someone who routinely worked with numbers and the sense of order that implied, John was incredibly disorganized. She'd tidied his desk a number of times and devised a simple filing system for him. But in the months since she'd been away, it didn't look as if he'd bothered to file a single paper. Clutter obliterated the top of the desk. Unopened mail was stacked in one corner, and it looked as if he'd made only a halfhearted effort to sort through it. Halfhearted and several weeks ago.

She eased herself into his leather chair and leaned back as she had so often. She'd loved his office, loved sitting in it and reading. Loved the smell of leather and old books. She felt a pang of regret, but it was brief. Any genuine regrets she harbored had more to do with her own witless behavior than missing John, or the man she'd believed him to be.

Opening the bottom desk drawer, she leafed through the files she'd taken such time and care to organize until she found one labeled TESTS. Her fingers froze, not because of the subject matter, but because the label was one John had made himself. He wouldn't keep her test there, she reasoned; that would be much too obvious. Too stupid. But then again, it was exactly what he would do.

She reached for the file and held it in her lap, prepared to sort through it, and would have if she hadn't been distracted by a loud discordant noise coming from the direction of the bathroom.

Was John home, after all? Had he slipped and fallen in the shower? Her mind and heart raced at the speed of light. Should she investigate, or get out of the house and leave and leave him to his fate? Should she—

"Maddie!" She recognized Brent's voice. "Theda's coming."

Her heart, which was already racing at double time, nearly exploded out of her chest. John must be about to walk through the door at any second, otherwise Brent wouldn't have risked everything to warn her.

She dropped the file on the desk and nearly fell off the chair in her rush to escape. She took three steps in the direction of the back door and then abruptly changed course, afraid John would use that entrance. Her heart was jammed in her throat and she was halfway to the front door when she heard movement on the front porch.

Oh, no. John was going to walk inside and catch her red-handed.

"In here," Brent whispered urgently. He appeared out of nowhere, grabbed her hand and jerked her toward the narrow hallway that led to the bathroom and two bedrooms.

"Wait," she whispered, spying the file on the desktop. She refused to leave that behind, not when she'd come this far.

"There isn't time," Brent warned. "He'll be inside the house any second."

"I won't leave it." She raced across the living room toward the office and realized Brent was right—there wasn't time. She turned back and made it into the hallway and out of sight just as the front door burst open.

Brent pulled her into the bathroom and stepped with her into the tub behind the shower curtain. Maddie prayed that the thick floral print would conceal them. She'd noted that the window was open and realized that this was how Brent had gotten into the house in time to warn her. He'd risked everything for her, including physical harm, which was minor compared to everything else. He'd put his life on the line for her. The chance he took left her trembling.

Maddie heard John speak and then a second voice followed. So John wasn't alone. That didn't surprise her. Neither did the fact that the other voice was a woman's. The words were too low for Maddie to understand. She didn't need to, for the woman's sultry tone told her everything. It was the tone that belonged to a woman who knows what she wants and is convinced she's about to get it.

While Maddie wasn't especially shocked, she did experience a stab of pain. She bowed her head and covered her mouth with her hand. She'd been so foolish, so incredibly foolish to believe John had ever loved her.

Hardly breathing for fear of being discovered, Maddie instinctively leaned toward Brent. He stood behind her and braced his hands on her shoulders, urging her closer, lending her his strength.

Maddie felt Brent stiffen and a heartbeat later realized why. John and his friend were in the hall-way outside the bathroom. She couldn't see what was happening, but from the sounds coming from the hallway it was clear the two were heavily involved with each other. Kissing, groaning, whispering, panting. The sound of their sexual eagerness rang as loud as church bells. It was abundantly clear where they were headed, and it wasn't the bathroom. Too bad, because Maddie would have loved shoving aside the shower curtain and giving them both the shock of their lives. But common sense and the fact that Brent was with her kept her still.

The distinguishing sounds of their foreplay continued.

Maddie's stomach churned. Unable to stop herself, she turned around and buried her face against Brent's chest. His arms closed protectively around her, and he placed his chin on top of her head. How gentle he was, how caring.

The sounds moved into the bedroom, and Maddie flinched when she heard the mattress springs squeak.

Brent pulled the shower curtain aside and motioned toward the window, gesturing for Maddie to go first and he'd follow.

She shook her head vehemently. She wasn't leaving without that file, and she let him know with hand gestures and pleading looks.

Brent's eyes almost bugged out of his head and

he shook his head furiously as they continued their silent but impassioned argument.

Maddie realized she needed to change tactics. Forcing herself to relax, she smiled sweetly and attempted to assure him in charade-style motions that he didn't have anything to worry about. John and his friend were so wrapped up in each other they'd never hear a thing.

Brent rolled his eyes to the ceiling in a display of frustration.

Her mind made up and not wanting to waste precious moments in this fruitless "discussion," Maddie carefully climbed out of the tub and moved toward the bathroom, her footsteps muffled by the thick bath mat. Brent was right behind her. Although she hadn't thought it probable, it would have been best if he'd left by the same means he'd entered.

The sounds coming from the bedroom were more distinct now. She peeked down the hallway and was greatly relieved to find the bedroom door half-closed. Holding her breath, Maddie shot across the open space and into the living room, her steps muffled now by the broadloom—not that the preoccupied John was likely to hear. The intensity of her anger at the man for his treachery was enough to make her want to throw something, knock over furniture. But once again common sense prevailed. There was nothing to be gained by such an action and everything to lose.

Brent's hand reached for hers, and he silently led the way into the office. Maddie grabbed the file off the top of the desk and grinned triumphantly.

They tiptoed to the back door, and when Brent opened it, the hinges squeaked. They both froze, held their breaths and waited, for what Maddie wasn't sure. Retribution. To be discovered and arrested. Fear kept her immobile for a moment longer than Brent, who urged her forward. Then he closed the door with great care.

Once outside, Maddie removed the key from her pocket and locked the door, then carefully replaced it in the fake rock. The sun had long set, and the lack of light was a welcome cover. The moon afforded them enough illumination to find their way across the back lawn.

Feeling as though she'd made the escape of her life, Maddie sprinted with Brent into the dark alley.

"I'm parked down here," he said, pointing the

way with his free hand. His other continued to grip hers.

"You should never have come," she said as they hurried along.

His face was softened by the moonlight. "If I hadn't, he'd have found you. I couldn't let that happen."

She sobered, deeply moved. She'd be forever in his debt for the terrible risk he'd taken on her behalf. What would have happened had she been caught didn't bear thinking about.

"I was an idiot, though," he went on, "to allow you to do it in the first place."

"Do you honestly think you could have stopped me?"

"Yes! If I'd had my wits about me I could have. Should have. I need to have my head examined."

They were nearly at the car and Maddie said, "I guess all's well that ends well."

"You mean to say Theda actually saved your test?" he asked, glancing at the file she held.

"I don't know," Maddie told him. "I didn't have time to look."

They reached the car. He opened the door for Maddie and helped her inside. She waited until he'd joined her to open the file. She didn't have far to look. Her midterm test paper was right on top.

Maddie's gaze found Brent's.

"That's it?" he asked.

She nodded. John had saved it.

"Great!" The excitement in Brent's voice said everything they'd gone through was worth it.

As Brent drove the car out of the alleyway, Maddie continued to stare at the test paper. It seemed unreal. She'd actually done it. And now, here was the proof of John's treachery and fraud.

Suddenly she cried, "Stop!" and grabbed his arm.

Brent slammed on the breaks and stared at her.

Maddie cast him a panic-stricken look. "We have to go back."

Chapter 4

"Go back?" Brent continued to stare at Maddie as if she'd just escaped a mental institution. "Back where?"

"To John's house." The man was being purposely obtuse. "I left my soda pop behind."

His head moved back slightly as if somehow that would help him assimilate her words. "Your soda pop?" Each word was said slowly and distinctly.

"Yes." Clearly he didn't understand the significance of what she was saying, and if he'd stop asking her silly questions, she'd explain.

"Where in the name of heaven did you get a soda pop?"

"Where else?" she cried, growing more frustrated by the moment. "Out of John's fridge!"

"You were thirsty and so you helped yourself?" His mouth fell open in disbelief.

"Yes, but—"

"I'll buy you another," Brent offered carefully as though speaking to an unreasonable child.

"You don't understand!" she all but shouted.

"I'll admit there appears to be a missing piece of information."

"Of course there is. Did you honestly believe I'd risk everything because I was thirsty?"

"To be honest, the thought *had* entered my mind."

"John doesn't drink pop. He prefers bottled water or white wine. He considers pop unhealthy. I can't tell you the number of times he lectured me about its evils."

"And?" Brent prompted.

"And...well, I really didn't care what he said. The decision was mine and I like my soda every now and again. So I brought my own and kept a supply at his house. This evening, after I got inside the place, I realized I was thirsty. I looked in the fridge and sure enough there was my six-pack.''

"If he had such a dislike of the stuff, why didn't he throw it out?''

"Because he's basically lazy.''

"Okay, okay, continue,'' Brent said, urging her to explain further.

"I took the soda can to John's desk, and in my panic, I left it behind. The minute he sees it there he'll know something's not right. He'll guess it was me and he'd know why I'd been there. My fingerprints are all over that can.''

Brent groaned.

"We have to go back,'' she insisted, furious with herself for being so careless. "I can't believe I did anything so stupid.''

"You honestly think he'll notice?''

"Yes. But probably not until morning.'' Not while he was wrapped up in his current preoccupation, which from the look of things, would keep him engaged well into the night.

"Maddie, I know what you're saying, but we can't risk returning. Not now.''

Part of her realized he was right, but another part was chomping at the bit to remove the one damning piece of evidence that clued John in to

the realization she had his test file. "Maybe he
won't contact the police," she suggested hope-
fully. All she'd removed from the house was
something that belonged to her. But John would.
Deep down, Maddie knew it. This wasn't something he'd be willing to overlook. Not when she
held the one damning piece of evidence that would
show him for the fraud he was.

They drove out of the neighborhood in silence.
All at once Maddie was exhausted, both mentally
and physically.

"You okay?" Brent asked when he stopped at
the first red light.

She smiled weakly. "A little tired."

"Close your eyes and put your head on my
shoulder," he said.

She did as he advised and was comforted by his
solid strength. "When I was a little girl, my dad
used to sing me that song when he carried me up
to bed."

"What song?"

"Oh, an old Paul Anka one. My dad loved to
sing. I do, too, sometimes." She wasn't sure why
she felt the need to chatter. Rarely did she mention
her father. After his death, she'd learned not to
because it upset her mother. Later, it seemed more

important to hold the memories close to her own heart, as though exposing them would water them down, weaken them in her own mind. She'd been secretly engaged to John for almost two months, and except to say that her father was dead, she never mentioned him. Never told John how she grieved for her father to this very day.

Maddie didn't want to evaluate her reasons for sharing this favorite of all memories with Brent. If she stopped to think about it, she was sure to find some profound significance, but she was too tired. Too tired and perhaps a little afraid.

Brent started to hum, the sound low and melodic. Tears formed in the corner of Maddie's eyes when she recognized the tune. Brent was humming "Put Your Head on My Shoulder."

Rather than let him see her tears, she closed her eyes and pretended to be asleep. Pretended she was a child once more, protected by someone she loved and who loved her. The fantasy worked far too well, because the next thing she knew they were parked outside her apartment building and Brent was whispering her name.

"Maddie." His voice seemed to come from a great distance. "You're home. Don't you want to go inside?"

She made a soft protesting sound, too warm and comfortable to do what he asked.

"If you want, I'll walk in with you and check behind the shower curtain to be sure no one's hiding there."

"Okay." She didn't hesitate to accept—and not because she was afraid of a robber taking up residence in her apartment. Truth was, she wasn't ready to be separated from Brent. It was too soon and she didn't want him to leave. She suspected he felt the same way about leaving her. In the short hours since they'd met at the Java Joint, they'd bonded. Brent had risked everything for her. His reputation, his career, his future. And all to warn her she was about to be caught. No one had ever cared that much for her. No one had ever put so much on the line for her. She snuggled closer to his warmth, and he stroked his chin across the top of her head.

After a moment or two his shoulder rose and fell with a deep breath. "Maddie, look at me." His words were little more than a wisp of sound.

Slowly she lifted her head and their eyes met. He wanted to kiss her. She wanted it, too, and when his mouth swooped down on hers, she felt as if she were being lifted up, transported to another sphere. After the initial contact, he kissed her again, slowly, carefully, as though he feared his need would frighten her. His teeth tugged at her trembling lower lip and then he introduced his tongue, delicately pushing it into her mouth.

It didn't take Maddie long to respond and kiss him back, catching his lower lip with her own teeth, nibbling on his tender flesh and then teasing him with the tip of her tongue. Kissing had never been this good. Not with anyone.

At one time Maddie had considered herself an expert in the art of kissing. She'd been tutored by some of the best, but what she'd learned was technique. What she experienced with Brent was a tenderness, a purity of emotion that pierced her soul.

He broke off the kiss and, after claiming a moment to compose himself, he escorted her to the door of her apartment. She discovered that her hand was shaking too badly for her to insert the key into the lock.

Brent did it for her, though his hands didn't appear much steadier. He turned the knob and opened the door for her to enter. Maddie walked in, clutching John's file to her breast. When she realized Brent hadn't followed, she turned around.

"Are you coming in?" she asked, mildly surprised that he remained in the hallway.

He shook his head.

She frowned. "Why not?"

He hesitated, as if weighing his response. "Because if I do, I won't be leaving until morning."

Hot color roasted her cheeks and she lowered her gaze. He reached out and brushed the soft skin of her face with the back of his hand. She closed her eyes and covered his fingers with her own. She yearned to thank him, to tell him that his honesty, his restraint, his generosity in refusing to use her had renewed her faith in men. She'd known Brent four years and yet had never really known him, the same as he'd never completely known her. But then no one at college had. Maddie hadn't allowed anyone close enough to see her as she actually was.

Until now.

Brent's kindness when he'd found her in church deeply affected her. Less than forty-eight hours later he'd jeopardized everything for her. No one had ever cared that much. That alone had rejuvenated her belief in human goodness and kindness. Now he was admitting a desire to make love to her, but because he was an honorable man, he wouldn't place either of them in the path of temptation.

Moisture filled her eyes.

He seemed to think she was asking him to explain himself because he said, "You trust me, Maddie. I'm not willing to destroy that."

She did, would always. Completely. Utterly. With everything there was in her to trust. Again and again he'd proved himself. In the past two days he'd revealed the true depth of his character. By contrast, John, whom she'd dated and loved and trusted, had used her, belittled her and broken her heart.

"I'll call you in the morning," Brent promised.

She smiled and nodded, reluctant for him to leave.

He turned to walk away, then abruptly turned back and hugged her fiercely. "Don't ever sell yourself short again, understand?"

"Never," she promised.

His hold relaxed. "Good night, Maddie."

"Good night."

Maddie awoke feeling refreshed and alive. The sun shone through her bedroom window, glorious and bright. She rolled her head to one side and groaned when she realized the time. If she didn't rush, she'd be late for work.

Tossing aside the covers, she hurried into the bathroom, showered and dressed. Breakfast consisted of an English muffin, which popped up from the toaster at the precise moment the phone rang.

Brent. It had to be him. He'd promised to call her in the morning.

She almost tripped in her eagerness to get to the phone. "Morning," she greeted cheerfully.

Cold silence slapped her in the face.

"Hello," she tried again, and a chill scooted down her spine.

"You were in my house."

John.

A breath jammed in Maddie's throat before her defenses snapped into place. "I don't know what you're talking about," she returned indignantly. "As I recall, you asked me not to contact you again, which I haven't. I expect the same courtesy from you." With that she replaced the receiver in its cradle. Hanging up on him might have been childish, but it sure felt good. Damn good. Besides she had nothing more she wanted to say to him unless it was in a court of law, and she'd let an attorney do the talking for her there.

The phone pealed again, and she jumped back as if she'd received an electrical shock. Fearing it might be John again, she allowed the answering machine to pick up the call.

"Maddie?" Brent asked. "Are you awake?"

"Brent." She leaped for the phone, saying his name even as she brought the receiver to her mouth. "Good morning."

"Morning." He sounded groggy and relaxed, as if he'd just awoken.

"Did you sleep well?"

"As well as can be expected," he murmured, and she could hear the smile in his voice.

"Me, too."

He yawned. "Are you doing anything special this evening?"

"I...no, nothing." If she was, she'd cancel it.

"No bank robberies or any other crimes plotted?"

"No," she said, and laughed, giddy with happiness. John could call and say whatever ugly things he wanted, but he couldn't destroy the joy she felt being with Brent.

"Do you think you could pencil me in for dinner?"

"I'll have to check my day planner, but I believe it could be arranged.'' Her feet floated several inches above the ground.

"Six o'clock?"

"Perfect." That gave her enough time to arrive home, change and freshen up.

"My parents want to meet you."

His parents! Maddie nearly dropped the phone. Brent was joking, he had to be. He was playing a trick on her. A silly prank to pay her back for the craziness she'd subjected him to earlier.

"You're not serious, right?" She tried to make light of it.

"As a matter of fact, I am."

In all the years she'd been dating, no man had taken her to meet his parents. And Brent's father was a minister, and his mother...well, she was a minister's wife. Until she'd dated Brent, ministers and minister's wives had never shown any interest in knowing her.

"Uh...why?" She wanted to suggest it was a bit early for her to meet his parents, but stopped herself. For that would imply Brent was serious about her and it was much too soon for them to be serious. Wasn't it?

"Why?" Brent said. "A number of reasons. I'd mentioned you earlier in the week and—''

"You mentioned me?" Oh, no, she wished he hadn't. "What did you say?"

When he didn't answer right away, Maddie was sorry she'd asked. She said quickly, "That's all right. You don't need to tell me." He must have done what she feared most—relayed to his parents the stories about her that had circulated around campus. The men she'd known, slept with, entertained. Her wildness, her antics, pranks.

"I told Mom I'd run into you recently," he explained, "and I mentioned that I'd never really known you and was sorry I hadn't made the effort while we were in college—because I find myself completely enthralled with you now."

"Oh, Brent." She closed her eyes and pressed the phone hard against her ear.

"Mom seemed to think I'd been given a second chance and I should make the most of it."

"We've both been given a second chance, don't you think?" she asked.

"Yeah, I guess I do. Now, are you coming to dinner or not?"

She needed time to mull over this invitation to his parents' home. It was such an important step...

"Maddie?" he asked when she remained silent. "It's my parents. They won't bite, I promise.

Well, not unless provoked." He paused. "There's no need to be nervous."

"Oh, all right," she said, tossing out her acceptance in a less-than-gracious manner. "I mean… tell your mother I'd be honored to join her and your father for dinner."

"If it'll make you feel better, I'll hold your hand the entire evening."

"I don't need anyone to hold my hand," she assured him, though his offer filled her with pleasure.

Brent responded with a hearty laugh. "OK, we're on. I've got to get going or I'll be late for the academy. I'll see you tonight at six."

"I'll look forward to it." Not so much the dinner, because she knew she was going to be poked and prodded with questions, but being with Brent.

The workday was over before Maddie knew it. She was never quite sure why the large downtown insurance agency had hired a history major. She suspected Uncle Alfie had something to do with it. He had his connections and didn't hesitate to use them. But Maddie was happy to have the job and worked hard to prove herself.

At five o'clock, spirits high, she breezed out of

the office and was back at her apartment in plenty of time to be ready when Brent arrived.

He was prompt. When she opened her door to him, he took one look at her and his eyes widened with appreciation. "Hi," he said and whistled softly. Maddie had chosen to wear a short-sleeve ankle-length summer dress in a pastel floral print. It was the most demure outfit she owned.

"Hi." Maddie had never been shy around men, but she felt so now. Her eyelashes fell, fanning her cheekbones.

"Have you thought about me as much as I have you?" he asked, his words low and raw.

She wouldn't have admitted it if he hadn't spoken first. All day Brent had been on her mind and in her heart. Earlier, too. From the moment he'd found her in the church, he'd dominated almost her every waking thought and ventured into her dreams, as well.

"I've thought about you, too," she admitted, afraid to let him know how much and saying too little. She'd didn't want to discount their attraction, nor did she want to build it out of proportion. This was all happening so fast.

Brent slowly expelled his breath, reached for her and pulled her into his arms. It didn't take him long to claim her mouth with his own. The kiss was infinitely tender and prolonged, as if this was the reward he'd been waiting to collect all day and he refused to be cheated by his own impatience.

Maddie's heart was spilling over with joy. And once more she experienced that incredible urge to weep, which she fought. For tears made you weak. Tears made you vulnerable and were to be avoided at all costs.

"Mom and Dad are eager to get to know you," he said as he escorted her outside.

"If you're telling me this to make me feel less nervous, try something else, all right?"

He chuckled. "It's the first time I've ever brought a woman to meet my parents."

"Knowing that doesn't help, either, Brent," she told him in a singsong voice, her teeth clenched.

He chuckled again. "At one time you infuriated me more than any woman I've ever known," he said as he eased the car into the heavy flow of traffic.

"That I can deal with," she announced, then relaxed and smiled at him. "I'm accustomed to irritating others. I guess that's why I'm so good at it."

"Mom found your picture in Nelson Lord's yearbook."

Maddie's spine went ramrod straight. Not the yearbook! Anything but the yearbook! She'd dressed and behaved in the most outrageous and irreverent manner to get her photo in it; there hadn't been much hope of making it through the traditional channels. Clubs didn't exactly clamor for her to join. It'd taken her most of her teen years to perfect the skill of being a misfit. That was the skill that had earned her a place in the pages of the Nelson Lord University yearbook.

Remembering the photo, she groaned. "Please don't tell me your mother found the picture of me streaking at the football game last October."

"That's the one she liked best."

She groaned more loudly.

"You had on flesh-colored underwear beneath the trench coat." It was true, despite the rumors she'd been in the buff.

"Take me home. Just turn around and take me home." No one needed to tell her how this evening would go. No mother would want her son to date someone like her—the someone she'd once been.

Her demand appeared to amuse him.

"Brent, I'm serious."

"I know you are," he returned calmly, "but there's no reason to worry."

Maddie didn't believe that for a moment.

"My mother looked at the photo, and after her initial shock, she told me..." He paused.

"Told you you're a fool to so much as talk to me."

"No," he returned forcefully. "She laughed and confessed to appreciating your individuality and grit. She knew about the incident."

"So you told her about me way back last fall."

"Just what you'd done. As I recall I was rather put out about it myself. I thought it was just plain stupid."

"It was." Maddie would be the first one to admit that now.

"My mother said anyone who would do something that bold is..."

"Nuts," Maddie supplied.

"Brave, I believe was her word."

"But it isn't the type of girl a mother is anxious to have her son date."

Brent reached for her hand and squeezed it. "On the contrary. My mother is a very special woman. It didn't take her long to see past that bad-girl act of yours.''

"Brent, I'm nervous." The woman who'd raced across a football field in front of the marching band wearing little more than a trench coat was afraid of meeting a preacher's wife.

"Don't be."

As it turned out, he was right. The dinner, the evening, everything was perfect. Brent's parents were gracious and warm. In retrospect, it made sense they would be. They were the ones who'd shaped Brent into the person he was, weren't they? Brent Holliday was by far the most honorable man she'd ever known. Honorable, kind and good.

After dinner Brent took her to his apartment, which was above the family garage. They sat at the kitchen table while their coffee was brewing, and at his insistence, Maddie worked through the quadratic quandary on a piece of paper. He watched and declared her brilliant. Then they sat side by side on the sofa, drinking espresso and listening to a Beatles CD, holding hands and frequently kissing. Maddie couldn't remember spending a more enjoyable evening.

"Are you free tomorrow night?" he asked when he dropped her off at her apartment. Before she could tell him she was available *every* night, he kissed her, and then kissed her again.

"I'm free," she whispered, her eyes closed, her lips moist and slightly swollen from his kisses.

"What about the night after that?"

"Free."

"Good." He eased away from her with a reluctance that made her heart sing. "I'll call you in the morning."

"Please." She smiled and leaned against her open apartment door as he walked backward, taking small unwilling steps.

She blew him a kiss and he grinned and did the same. She didn't close the door until he was completely out of sight. Then she raced to the window and stared down on the street watching till his car turned the corner and was gone. Never had she felt so giddy or so young. Like being fifteen all over again. In love, truly in love, for the first time in her life.

She walked around her apartment as if in a dream. None of this seemed possible. Only a few days earlier she'd been in a pit of despair, certain life had done her wrong. Now she was so much it was almost frightening.

The test paper that proved she'd solved the

quadratic quandary didn't seem important any longer. John Theda was a fraud and sooner or later others would learn that, too. Still, she fully intended on setting the record straight. If he got away with this with her, he might try it again with another student. He might use another unsuspecting female student the way he had her, and Maddie couldn't allow that to happen.

First thing in the morning she would contact Dean Williams. Brent had talked it over with her that evening and was in full agreement. He felt strongly that now that she had the proof she needed, she should use it.

She smiled as she recalled his reaction to her showing him the solution to the quandratic quandary. Not only had he claimed she was brilliant, but he'd talked about her future and all the things she could do, growing more excited and animated by the moment. Maddie had laughed off his praise, embarrassed by it. The only way to stop him had been to kiss him, and so she had, again and again, loving him for believing in her, for encouraging her to be all she could be.

The phone rang and Maddie looked at it, hesitating. It couldn't be Brent—he wouldn't be home yet. She hadn't told Brent about John's call earlier in the day. It would have alarmed him, and anyway, she could handle John.

"Hello," she said, her voice cool and even.

"That was a touching little scene."

She squared her shoulders. "What do you want, John?"

"You mean you haven't figured it out?"

"I told you this morning and I'll say it again—don't contact me. It won't do you any good. I'm having my phone number changed first thing in the morning."

He laughed, and the sound was cold and heartless, sending chills down her spine. "I said you're a fool and I meant it. Don't try to play games with me, Maddie. I'm the master, and you'll only end up getting hurt."

"Goodbye, John." She wasn't waiting to listen to any more of his threats. She had the test paper in a safe place, and she wasn't going to allow him to intimidate her.

Almost as soon as she replaced the receiver, the phone rang again. This time Maddie let the answering machine take it.

"You didn't give me a chance to mention something important," John said. "Something you should know." A pause. "I talked with Mrs. Johnson this morning. You remember Mrs. Johnson, don't you? She lives next door.'' He paused again, as if to give his words time to sink.

"It seems that Mrs. Johnson saw something rather unusual the other night. It's actually rather humorous.'' He chuckled. ''Apparently I was just pulling into the street when a young man, a former student of mine, she guessed, launched himself over her fence and all but broke speed records in an effort to get into my home. When the back door was locked and he couldn't find the key, he hauled himself through my bathroom window. No easy task, as I recall.

"Being the concerned neighbor she is, Mrs. Johnson went into the alley and wrote down his license-plate number.''

Maddie's blood went cold.

"I had a friend run the number, and it seems the car belongs to Brent Holliday. He's a good friend of yours, I take it. A very good friend. I imagine the police academy would be interested in knowing young Holliday's nighttime activities, don't you?''

"No!'' Maddie cried although there was no one to hear her.

"Pick up the receiver, Maddie," John ordered. "We have something important to discuss."

She hesitated.

"Now!" he shouted, then more calmly, "Before you force me to do something you and your boyfriend would find very...uncomfortable."

She flinched and with a trembling hand did as he requested.

Chapter 5

"I don't understand," Brent said, studying her. "I thought we'd already talked this out." They sat at the kitchen table in his apartment drinking tall glasses of iced tea. All Maddie had wanted to do was explain she'd changed her mind about reporting John to Dean Williams and then be on her way, but Brent had refused to let her leave.

Maddie felt his disappointment as keenly as her own. This wasn't what she wanted, but she had no choice. John hadn't given her any alternative. Only, Brent didn't know that and never would.

"I've changed my mind," Maddie said in what

she hoped was a convincing tone. She downed the last of her tea and set the empty glass on the tabletop, signaling that now she really had to go. "I've already canceled my appointment with Dean Williams."

"Why?" Brent's eyes narrowed.

Maddie had known it wouldn't be easy to fool Brent with this apparent change of heart, but she'd hoped she could pull it off and leave him thinking she'd come to the conclusion that was best for everyone involved. A nearly impossible task when she had trouble believing it herself.

"Why'd you cancel the appointment?" Brent pressed a second time.

"Dean Williams won't believe me." She tried to make it sound as simple as that. "The date on the top of the test is May sixth. Unfortunately I wrote it in the European style—the day first—so it could just as easily be read as June fifth."

"But it was a midterm test and it says so. Dean Williams knows when midterms were given. You shouldn't have to prove a thing. It's all there in black and white for him to read. That sounds like a convenient excuse to me. Come on, Maddie, what's up?"

She was afraid of this. Feared Brent would use

logic against her. In reality she had no reason for canceling the appointment other than to keep John from reporting the burglary. He had more than enough evidence to have Brent and her arrested. If she'd acted alone, Maddie would have willingly called his bluff, but she refused to drag Brent's good name through the mud. Nor would she allow John to destroy Brent's future. Not when it was within her power to prevent it.

"Nothing's up," she insisted. "I thought everything over and decided it didn't matter what John claimed. I know who solved the quadratic quandary, and that's all that really matters. Setting the record straight, embarrassing John...well, it isn't worth the hassle."

Brent's eyes told her he didn't believe her. He went very still. "What happened?"

"What makes you think something happened?"

"You." His face tightened until his mouth formed a pinched line. "You're different."

"How could I be different," she said, attempting to make a joke of it. "I'm the same person I was a couple of days ago. Just remember, what you see is what you get."

"That wasn't the way it always was."

His words suggested something she didn't like. "What do you mean by that?"

"Just what I said. You wore a facade for years. It's back, Maddie, and something's happened that you're not telling me about. I know you and I want to know you better, but I can't do that when you put up a steel gate locking me out."

"Don't be ridiculous."

"Am I?"

She needed something, anything to distract him. "Is this what you're going to say every time we have a disagreement?" she demanded. "Accuse me of blocking you out? Dredge up the past and throw it in my face?"

"I want the truth."

"You got it." She stood and walked over to the kitchen sink with her glass. She'd downed the cold drink so fast she'd developed a headache. Her temples throbbed and her heart was fast sinking. Dear heaven, how she hated deception. But she had no choice.

"I have to go," she whispered.

"Where are you headed?" he asked with more than a hint of accusation.

"You mean a few kisses gives you the right to

demand my whereabouts twenty-four hours a day?''

Looking ashamed, Brent buried his hands in his pockets. ''I apologize. I had no right to ask you that.''

''True, but I'll tell you, anyway. I'm meeting a friend.''

The question all but burned from his eyes, but he wouldn't ask, and wanting them to part on good terms, Maddie sighed and hugged him. ''OK, if you must know, I'm having lunch with Susan Cabot. We grew up together. Now stop, please. What I do or don't do about that test paper is my decision.''

He said nothing, but she felt his disapproval as keenly as if he'd spoken. He followed her outside to where she'd parked her bicycle in the driveway. ''The person you're cheating is yourself, Maddie. That's what bothers me most.''

''It's my decision, Brent,'' she reminded him again.

''You're giving Theda a license to hurt someone else. By not reporting him, you're giving him the impression he can get away with fraud.''

''He won't need me to prove anything. John will do it to himself. His type always does.

Haven't you ever heard the expression 'Time wounds all heels'? John's a first-class heel and in time it'll catch up with him.'' When it did, Maddie would love to be around to witness it. The man was a major jerk and deserved everything he had coming to him.

"Fine," Brent said resignedly. "If that's what you want."

"It is." The words nearly stuck in her throat. As hard as she'd argued, as hard as she'd worked to convince Brent this was the best way, she didn't believe it for a minute. But she couldn't, wouldn't, hurt Brent, not when all she really wanted was revenge. The trade-off was fair. In exchange for serenity, she gave the file back to John and nothing would be said either way.

Brent kissed her lightly and stepped back while she climbed on her bike.

"You'll call me?" she asked, needing to know he wouldn't allow a disagreement to stand between them.

He hesitated, smiled briefly and then nodded. "Sure. You want to catch a movie later?"

Her relief was palpable and she smiled back, loving him so much it was all she could do not to throw her arms around him and explain every-

thing. Instead, she said calmly, "That'd be great."
Her heart swelled with emotion. Brent was disappointed in her, discouraged, too, but he'd work his way through it. By inviting her to a movie, he was telling her that, despite this, the two of them as a couple would continue. He hadn't liked what she'd had to say, but he'd accepted it.

Early in her dating career Maddie had discovered that often a man's pride was wrapped around his advice, and if she refused to do as he suggested, it deflated his fragile ego. Brent's sense of self was strong.

"I've got to return a book to the library this afternoon," he said, "and I'll give you a call when I'm back. How does that sound?"

"Come here," she instructed, holding on to the bike's handlebars.

"Come here?" he questioned as he advanced.

Maddie looped her arms around his neck and, standing on tiptoe, the bike balanced between her legs, kissed him. When she pulled away, Brent's breathing was ragged and so was hers.

"Thank you," she whispered.

"For what?" He seemed to have a problem finding his tongue.

"Just because."

He grinned, his look almost boyish. "You can thank me again later, all right?"

"Any time you want."

He chuckled, then watched her ride down the driveway, waving when she entered the street. She smiled and waved back. But her smile faded as she rounded the corner. Maddie had never really hated John Theda. He'd hurt and disappointed her, broken her heart and used her, but she'd never hated him. She was close to doing so now, however. How she could have been so blind before, she didn't know.

Maddie hadn't lied to Brent about her appointment. She was having lunch with Susan Cabot, all right, but afterward she was meeting John. It wasn't a confrontation she looked forward to, but it was necessary. One last meeting, and then it would be over once and for all.

Her lunch with her childhood friend went well. "You've changed," Susan noticed almost immediately. "What happened to my friend, the rebel?"

"I fell in love with a man who turned out to be a rat," Maddie explained sheepishly. "And the rebel in me died. I discovered I didn't like the woman I'd become and decided it was in my power to change that."

"You look terrific." Susan's enthusiastic smile revealed her approval. "Now tell me about Uncle Alfie. Is he still a darling?"

They spent the better part of two hours reminiscing, and the dark cloud that had hung over Maddie's head seemed less bleak by the time they finished lunch.

After she left the restaurant, Maddie checked her watch. Her meeting with John was scheduled for three-thirty at the water fountain in the center of Nelson Lord University. In exchange for the file, including her test paper, John would forget the entire incident and not report the break-in at his home to the police.

She thought of how long and often Brent had spoken of working in law enforcement. He loved his work, loved the challenge and the mental and physical demands. He would be a good police officer and touch many lives for the better. It helped to remember that as she biked toward the campus.

Her sacrifice was little compared to what she had to gain, she decided. John could accept the credit, she didn't care, as long as he stayed out of Brent's life and, for that matter, hers.

Maddie arrived on time and was left twiddling her thumbs and worrying. It was just like John to let her stew before he bothered to show. Fifteen minutes after their agreed time, she saw him walking toward her.

Perspective being what it was, Maddie took one look at him and wondered how she could have been attracted to such a man. At the time she'd thought of him as a modern-day Adonis. Now she could see he wasn't anywhere near as handsome.

"Hello, Maddie," he said when he joined her. He eyed her with undisguised approval. "You're looking good, real good."

"Sorry I can't say the same for you."

He laughed. "That's what I always liked about you. A smart-ass comment for everything."

"Let's get this over with," she suggested, eager to be on her way.

"Fine." He held out his hand, expecting her to surrender the file.

"Not so fast," she said, and snickered softly that he believed she'd be so naive. He'd taught her well in the area of mistrust, and she wasn't about to give him anything without a signed reassurance. "I'll need your signature to our agreement."

"You mean you don't trust me?" His hurt-little-boy look was almost laughable.

"Exactly."

He scowled. "All right, all right. What exactly do you want?"

"Other than your signature, I'd settle for a quart of your blood."

He laughed. "Damn, but I miss that wit of yours. You'll always be the same ol' Maddie, won't you?"

She didn't bother to answer. Knowing John had changed her forever. A part of her innocence had been forever destroyed. His treachery had tarnished a piece of her soul. It had taken her weeks to fight back, but she'd won that battle, thanks in part to Brent, whom she owed far more than she could ever repay.

From her backpack Maddie removed the agreement she'd written up. It was in an envelope, and she handed it to him to open and read. Since he refused to admit in writing that she'd been the one to solve the quadratic quandary, she'd listed some rather unsavory details about his personal life, and his signature gave her permission to use these facts against him if he made trouble for either Brent or her.

John set his briefcase on the cement rim of the fountain. He read and signed the agreement begrudgingly, then placed it back in the envelope and gave it to Maddie. In exchange she handed him the test file.

"I won't say it's been a pleasure," she said, reaching for her bike. "I hope I never see you again, John."

"Let me assure you the feeling's mutual," he said, and turned away.

Maddie climbed on her bike and rode off, eager to make her escape. She biked down the narrow cement pathway toward the parking lot. Only a few cars dotted the lot; when classes started up in a couple of weeks, it would be full again.

Not until she was close to the street did she spy Brent's car, or at least she thought it was. Her feet went slack on the pedals and she coasted several feet.

It *was* Brent's car, and he was sitting inside. When he glanced up and saw her, he climbed out.

"Brent," she asked, shocked to see him, "what are you doing here?"

"The library book, remember?" His words were charged with anger.

"Funny that we'd run into each other, isn't it?" He hadn't told her he was returning the book to the *college* library, and now she wondered how much he'd seen and how she could explain.

"You sold out, didn't you?" he demanded.

"Sold out?"

"You sold Theda that test file. Blackmailed him. How much did you get, Maddie? Forget justice, forget what's right. Forget anyone else he'll cheat and hurt in the future, right? I hope you made it worth your while."

The words to explain and defend herself stuck in her throat. "Matters aren't always what they seem."

"Yeah, right. I saw the exchange. He handed you an envelope and you gave him the file. I saw everything I needed to."

She considered showing Brent the contents of the envelope, but didn't, because then he'd know she'd surrendered the test file to protect him.

"I'm asking you to trust me, Brent," she said.

He stared at her for a long moment. "Show me the envelope."

Briefly she closed her eyes. "I...I can't."

His look hardened and she knew he was steeling himself against her. "That says it all, doesn't it?" He climbed back into the car. "I don't think it'd be a good idea if we saw each other again, Maddie."

"Brent—" She broke off before she could add "please."

"I knew something had happened when I saw you earlier at my place. Now it all makes sense. Goodbye, Maddie. I wish you well."

Chapter 6

"You told Brent, didn't you?" Gretchen asked. "You didn't let it end there. That would have been so unfair to you."

"I didn't have a choice," Maddie whispered. Even after fifteen years it still hurt to remember their confrontation that day. "I could never let Brent know what I'd done."

Gretchen, Carol and Maddie sat on the rim of the fountain, and Maddie realized they'd drawn closer to one another in the past couple of hours, both physically and emotionally. Fifteen years. Who would have believed time could evaporate that easily? Like an eraser wiping a blackboard clean, the years had faded away. Some things had changed and others had remained the same. Maddie wasn't the girl she'd been back then—the one desperately seeking to be noticed, no matter what the price. She'd paid dearly for those mistakes. The steepest price of all was the afternoon she'd lost Brent Holliday.

"You must have loved him very much to have sacrificed so much," Carol Furness said softly.

Yes, Maddie had loved him, heart and soul. "John taught me some valuable lessons, but Brent taught me even more."

"Can you tell us what happened after that day?" Carol asked, and placed her hand over Maddie's.

"I lost him," Maddie said. "I had a hard time accepting it in the beginning, but eventually I realized it was probably for the best. He'd come into my life like a knight in shining armor and then he was gone. I had no regrets."

"But you weren't any better off than before you met him," Gretchen said.

"Oh, but I was," Maddie hurried to explain. "Brent gave me a tremendous gift. He helped me find myself, taught me to take control. My level of self-esteem rose the moment I discovered that I could do something about the situation with John. In the end, allowing John to accept the credit was a small price to pay for what Brent had given me in return. He gave me back my soul.''

"Were you ever able to let him know that?"

Maddie shook her head sadly. "In the beginning I tried to fix matters between us, but soon realized Brent meant what he said.''

"That was pretty narrow-minded of him, wasn't it?'' Gretchen asked.

"I know now that he was as idealistic as I was. It's easy to look back and judge him from the perspective of time, but that would be wrong. Gradually the pain of losing him lessened. I refused to mourn when what he'd given me had been a tremendous gift. It was because of Brent that I made the smartest decision of my life.''

"Which was?'' Carol pressed.

Maddie smiled, knowing her friends would be amused. "I went back to school.''

"Nelson Lord?''

"Oh, no.'' Maddie shook her head. "I was paying my own expenses and I couldn't afford a private college. I started out working days and taking night courses. It took me nearly five years to earn my masters, but I did it, one course at a time.''

"In mathematics," Gretchen guessed.

"In mathematics," Maddie confirmed.

"Oh, my," Carol said, looking at her wrist. "Look at the time."

"Good grief!" Maddie cried, leaping to her feet. "We've got less than an hour before the dinner. I've got to shower and feed the kids and..." She paused, knowing her friends were equally rushed. "I'll see you there, right?"

"Of course," Gretchen promised. "And my husband. I'd like you to meet him."

"Me, too," Carol added. "With my husband. Let's find a table and sit together?"

Maddie and Gretchen both agreed.

Together the three rushed to the parking lot, chatting excitedly as they walked. Maddie smiled to herself. She was anxious for her friends to meet her husband, too. She'd almost given up on love when she met and married him a mere five years ago. That was when life had tossed her a second curve ball, only this time she'd stepped up to bat and been ready to swing.

Epilogue

Epilogue

Japanese lanterns swayed gently in the breeze, their lights flickering, telegraphing secretly coded messages around the lush garden patio. Gretchen stood in the doorway and looked about, then sighed when she saw him. So this was where her husband had taken off to.

The festive noise of the reunion faded as she stepped from the gaily lit hall to the peace and quiet of the flowering patio.

"I thought I'd find you out here," she said, moving to her husband's side.

Josh Morrow slipped his arm around her trim

waist and smiled down at her, his eyes filled with love. No matter how many years they'd been married, Gretchen had never tired of seeing Josh smile. Her heart was full to overflowing with the love they shared. They would celebrate their thirteenth wedding anniversary this year, and it seemed like yesterday when he'd roared up to her family home, his Harley spewing dust and fumes. Two years he'd kept her waiting. Two years, and he'd actually expected to find her home.

The irony was...she had been. She'd never been able to believe he wouldn't be back.

As long as she lived Gretchen would never forget the day he came for her. Defiant as ever, he'd parked the Harley, rung the doorbell and nearly given her mother heart failure.

Gretchen had been home visiting her parents. When she realized it was Josh at the door, she'd stepped outside. He'd looked at her and smiled and she'd smiled back.

"Do you still want to ride off into the sunset with me?" he'd asked.

"That depends." He'd kept her waiting all this time. She wasn't about to make it easy for him.

"Would a wedding band and life with a starving law student be inducement enough?"

"Plenty. Oh, Josh, what took you so long?" Simultaneously laughing and crying, she'd hurled herself into his arms. Josh had locked his arms around her waist and swung her around. By that time both her parents had been on the front porch, not knowing what to think. Josh had glanced at them, kissed her as if he'd dreamed of it every day for the two years they'd been apart, and then asked to speak privately with her father.

Gretchen had paced outside her family den until they were finished. When they appeared, she'd stepped to Josh's side and grabbed hold of his hand. Then her father had grinned and announced that he felt Josh would make her a fine husband.

He had. Thirteen years, and she hadn't regretted a single day. They had three children, a beautiful home, a good life. The children—a twelve-year-old boy and twin ten-year-old girls—and her charity work kept her more than busy. Josh needed her, too. Recently elected as a Supreme Court judge in Orange County, his position on the bench had almost been as demanding on her as it was him.

"Where'd you go this afternoon?" Josh asked, sipping his drink.

"To take a look at Nelson Lord."

"The fountain?"

How well he knew her. "I met up with some old friends."

"I don't suppose you ran into Roger Lockheart?"

"No." She pressed her head to his shoulder. "Don't tell me you're worried about my seeing Roger again."

"Well, you once loved him."

"Oh, Josh, be serious. Roger was a rat. You couldn't possibly believe I'd want anything to do with him." She ran her hand over Josh's back, never tiring of the special closeness they shared. "I will admit I'm curious about him. From what I understand, he's here."

"I saw him," Josh admitted.

"You saw him?" Gretchen couldn't believe he'd kept this information from her. "What's he look like?"

"Hah! So I was right!"

"Josh." She punched his arm playfully.

"He looks fine. He introduced me to his friend, and—"

"Friend? You mean he isn't married?"

"Three times, from what I understand."

"You're joking!"

Josh chuckled. "It's the truth, I swear. He apparently didn't join Daddy's law firm, either, because he's selling cars.''

"Roger is selling cars. I love it!''

Josh brought her into his arms, his eyes dark and serious. "I love you. I don't think I tell you that often enough. You're in my blood, Gretch, in my heart, and so much a part of me I couldn't make it one day without you." He held her close for a moment. "I tried to live without you all those years ago and couldn't. That was when I realized I had to make myself worthy of your faith in me. Every day of those two years we were apart I prayed you still loved me.''

"Not a minute went by that I didn't long for you.''

He kissed her softly. "It looks like they're ready to serve dinner.''

"Great." Gretchen slipped her arm around his waist. "Remember those old friends I mentioned? Well, I want you to meet them.''

Josh grumbled something about preferring to have his wife to himself, but followed her inside.

Carol was sitting in the hotel suite talking on the phone when her husband wandered out of the bedroom, unsuccessfully attempting to fasten the top button of his dress shirt.

Her husband was a fine figure of a man. She loved him more than she thought it possible to love another human being.

"Who are you talking to?" He asked, twisting his neck back and forth.

"Your mother," she whispered, covering the mouthpiece. "OK, Mom, yes, I'll wait." She looked back at her husband. "The kids are giving her problems. Timmy and Adam are fighting over the slide rule again. Erica refused to eat her vegetables, and Clark, Jr., has disappeared, but she thinks he's hiding in the library. Your father's searching for him now." Carol's mother-in-law came back on the line, and Carol nodded, relieved. "They found Junior."

Clark sank into a chair. "Does she want us to come home?"

"No, no. I asked her that myself and she insists we enjoy the reunion. She can always call Frieda if matters get out of hand." The nanny had her own quarters in the house, but was available any time Clark's parents felt they needed help.

Carol finished the conversation and hung up the phone. "It's a good thing we don't escape often."

Clark chuckled. "Every time we do manage to get away, you end up pregnant."

Carol climbed onto her husband's lap and brushed his hands away from his throat. "I'll do it," she promised, and quickly secured the button. "Four children isn't so many, is it?" she whispered, and nuzzled his neck, licking the skin with her tongue. She loved the taste and feel of him.

"Carol—" his voice was low and full of suspicion "—I know that tone of voice."

"You do?" she asked, playing dumb.

"You want another baby."

"Would it be so terrible?" she asked, her lips nibbling his ear.

Clark shivered with awareness, and if he'd intended to remove her from his lap, he changed his mind.

"I love being a mother and you love getting me pregnant," she reminded him. She'd always enjoyed children, and with Clark's software company so profitable, there wasn't any reason they couldn't have as many kids as they liked.

Clark sighed and rested his head against the back of the cushion. "I never could refuse you anything, you know that."

"That's not the way I remember it," she whispered, unbuttoning the very shirt she'd just spent time fastening. "You let me take off for Alaska without you."

"What brings that up?" he asked.

"I met a couple of women from my old sorority at the fountain this afternoon."

"And they thought you were married to Eddie Shapiro."

"At first, but I was quick to tell them I fell head over heels in love with you. We agreed to meet for dinner later—you don't mind, do you?" Gretchen and Maddie would be surprised and delighted when they saw she'd married Clark, after all.

"No...we can have dinner with whomever you want," he whispered, and closed his eyes as she continued to kiss the underside of his jaw.

"You were a big disappointment to my friends when I told them you let me leave for Alaska."

"But technically you didn't make it there."

"No, but that's beside the point." She eased the open shirt from his shoulders.

"I flew out to your parents instead."

He'd arrived Christmas Eve, and his timing couldn't have been better. "You were the best Christmas present I ever received."

"You could have married Eddie," Clark reminded her.

That was true. Two years into his pro career, Eddie Shapiro had torn a ligament in his knee that had ended his days on the football field. He'd called Carol from the hospital bed and asked her to marry him. It'd given her great delight to inform him that not only was she married to Clark Rusbach, but she was eight months pregnant with their first child.

"I wonder if he'll come to the reunion."

"I doubt it," Clark said, and reached for the zipper in the back of her dress.

"Clark," she teased, "we'll be late for the dinner."

"So?"

Carol couldn't think of a single reason it was so all-fired important that they be on time. She'd never been keen on eating her salad first, anyway. "I'd like a little boy this time," she said before directing her husband's mouth to hers.

Clark stood, lifting her with him and carrying her into the bedroom. "I'll do my best," he promised.

Maddie admitted to being nervous. Gretchen and Carol hadn't recognized her earlier at the fountain, and she doubted that anyone else at the reunion would, either.

Her husband placed his hand at the small of her back and steered her into the rented hall, festively decorated for the class reunion with banners and ribbons.

"I don't recognize anyone, do you?" she asked Brent.

"Not a soul." He glanced at her and chuckled. "You're actually nervous. I can't believe it. My wife, the woman who revolutionized the way mathematics is taught across the United States, is actually nervous."

"Brent, don't tease."

"The woman who's dined with the president."

"Brent!"

"And the queen of England."

"Brent, don't tell anyone about that, all right?"

"You'd rather I told them you wore falsies?"

"I did not." He always knew how to rile her.

"Yeah, but everyone would believe it."

Although she knew he was teasing, Maddie glared at her husband. "Sometimes I wonder why I married you."

"You loved me."

"For fifteen long years, I've loved you." But for ten of those years they'd had no contact with each other. Maddie moved from Seattle a few months after she'd graduated. For several years she worked at a day job while attending night school to obtain her masters degree. Her life was consumed with math. It was while she was working on her doctorate that she devised new methods of grasping basic mathematical concepts. Soon she was working with the Department of Education in Washington, D.C.

Out of the blue one afternoon she ran into Brent Holliday on the White House lawn. He'd come to Washington to receive a hero's award from the president, along with forty-nine other law-enforcement officers. She'd given him her phone number and really didn't expect him to call. But he had.

They met for dinner the next night, closed down the restaurant and then walked to the Lincoln Memorial. They'd talked there until the sun rose, and by then Maddie knew she'd never stopped loving Brent. He felt the same way about her.

They were married a month later, and she was pregnant almost immediately. Their second child was born the following year. Brent had recently become the assistant chief of police in Seattle. They were happy, exceptionally so, and very much in love.

Brent's hand reached for hers and their fingers entwined. "There's Gretchen now," Maddie said, waving to her friend. "She married Josh."

"Josh Morrow?"

"Do you remember him?"

"Sure do. The class troublemaker. Wow. So Gretchen Wise married him."

"Hey, troublemakers can be tamed. You should know."

"Indeed I do. Did you tell her about John Theda ending up in prison for fraud?"

"No." Maddie shook her head. "It's all rather sad, don't you think? I never wished him ill."

"But you were right—he ended up doing it to himself." John wasn't due to be released for another ten years.

"Come on," Maddie said, "I want you to meet my friends." She waved to Gretchen, who smiled and waved back.

Maddie stood on tiptoe and scanned the crowd for Carol. She wondered what could be keeping her.

* * * * *

Take 4 bestselling love stories FREE

Plus get a FREE surprise gift!

Special Limited-time Offer

Mail to Silhouette Reader Service™

3010 Walden Avenue
P.O. Box 1867
Buffalo, N.Y. 14240-1867

YES! Please send me 4 free Silhouette Special Edition® novels and my free surprise gift. Then send me 6 brand-new novels every month, which I will receive months before they appear in bookstores. Bill me at the low price of $3.34 each plus 25¢ delivery and applicable sales tax, if any.* That's the complete price and a savings of over 10% off the cover price—quite a bargain! I understand that accepting the books and gift places me under no obligation ever to buy any books. I can always return a shipment and cancel at any time. Even if I never buy another book from Silhouette, the 4 free books and the surprise gift are mine to keep forever.

236 BPA A3UV

Name	(PLEASE PRINT)	
Address	Apt. No.	
City	State	Zip

This offer is limited to one order per household and not valid to present Silhouette Special Edition® subscribers. *Terms and prices are subject to change without notice. Sales tax applicable in N.Y.

USPED-696

©1990 Harlequin Enterprises Limited

Welcome to the Towers!

In January
New York Times bestselling author

NORA ROBERTS

takes us to the fabulous Maine coast mansion
haunted by a generations-old secret and introduces
us to the fascinating family that lives there.

Mechanic Catherine "C.C." Calhoun and hotel magnate
Trenton St. James mix like axle grease and mineral
water—until they kiss. Efficient Amanda Calhoun finds
easygoing Sloan O'Riley insufferable—and irresistible.
And they all must race to solve the mystery
surrounding a priceless hidden emerald necklace.

Catherine and Amanda

THE Calhoun Women

**A special 2-in-1 edition containing
COURTING CATHERINE and A MAN FOR AMANDA.**

Look for the next installment of
THE CALHOUN WOMEN with Lilah and Suzanna's
stories, coming in March 1998.

Available at your favorite retail outlet.

Silhouette®

ELIZABETH AUGUST

Continues the twelve-book
series—36 HOURS—in
November 1997 with
Book Five

CINDERELLA STORY

Life was hardly a fairy tale for Nina Lindstrom. Out of work
and with an ailing child, the struggling single mom was
running low on hope. Then Alex Bennett solved her problems
with one convenient proposal: marriage. And though he had
made no promises beyond financial security, Nina couldn't
help but feel that with a little love, happily-ever-afters really
could come true!

For Alex and Nina and *all* the residents of Grand Springs,
Colorado, the storm-induced blackout was just the beginning
of 36 Hours that changed *everything*! You won't want to miss a
single book.

DEBBIE MACOMBER

invites you to the

HEART OF TEXAS

Join Debbie Macomber as she brings you the lives and loves of the folks in the ranching community of Promise, Texas.

If you loved Midnight Sons—don't miss Heart of Texas! A brand-new six-book series from Debbie Macomber.

Available in February 1998 at your favorite retail store.

Heart of Texas by Debbie Macomber

HARLEQUIN®

HPHRT1